OFF THE GRID

OFF THE GRID

You Can Hide, But You Can't Run

Blaine C. Readler

Full Arc
Press

OFF THE GRID
You Can Hide, But You Can't Run

Published by Full Arc Press

This is a work of fiction. Names, characters, places and incidents are either the product of the author's wild imagination or are used fictitiously. Any resemblance to actual events, locales, organizations, or persons, living, dead, or one foot in the grave, although inevitable and in a weird way complimentary to the author, since it shows he is not so insulated from reality that the products of his imagination are totally alien to the average mind, is nevertheless entirely coincidental and beyond the intent of either the author or the publisher.

Visit us at: http://www.readler.com

E-mail: blaine@readler.com

An acknowledgement and thanks to Lulu Enterprises, Inc. for making the publishing of this book possible.

You should use them to publish!   http://www.lulu.com

ISBN: 978-0-615-43578-7

Printed in the United States of America

First Edition: 2011

Dedicated to Ken Weidele: the standard upon which friendship is measured.

ACKNOWLEDGEMENTS

MTB—many late nights, many red pens, never a complaint.

As long as people believe in absurdities they will continue to commit atrocities.
—Voltaire

PART I

LILLY

Chapter 1

"**S**ee?" Carl yelled. "It just spits!"

The industrial-grade garden hose he held coughed like somebody realizing they'd swallowed piss instead of beer and splashed a spray of water across his face. "Shit!" he cried, wiping his sleeve across his face in an ineffectual attempt to remove the algae smell.

"It's spitting shit?" Defoe asked drolly, taking Carl by surprise as the grizzled old head suddenly appearing above the edge of the bank. His neighbor had been checking the inlet thirty feet below, and he must have started up the side of the ravine before Carl turned on the pump.

He felt another eruption coming, and he quickly tilted the hose away. When it belched the next spray, Defoe's balding forehead and thick, gray beard glistened with beads of water. His spare, rumpled friend didn't seem to care as he pulled himself over the bank and stood smiling.

Carl stared back, hesitating. He hated giving the old fart the satisfaction. Defoe just grinned, with his hands tucked in the pockets of his jeans. Carl knew his friend would stand there all afternoon if necessary, so he tossed down the hose and said, "What did I do wrong?"

Defoe nodded towards the hose, which jerked and coughed again. "*Horror Vacui.*"

Carl sighed.

"Nature abhors a vacuum," Defoe translated. "Aristotle's rebuttal of Leucippus' atomic theory."

Carl nodded and took a seat on a rock. It was going to be one of those explanations. "The ancient Greeks understood nuclear physics?"

He didn't mind playing along with Defoe now and then, usually coming away glad of the result if he was patient with the retired college professor. The incurable academic loved sharing what he automatically assumed was welcomed knowledge.

"Not the atomic theory that guides the design of nuclear weapons," Defoe explained, taking a rock seat for himself, "but not too far off the mark, either. The ancients couldn't, of course, glean the inner workings of atoms, but Leucippus's ideas represented a potentially important small step in the right direction. He posited that everything in the universe consists of either atoms—the smallest units of matter—or voids. Aristotle couldn't abide the concept of the voids, and so set physics back two thousand years."

"I thought you were a fan of Aristotle."

Defoe had been a professor of philosophy at UCSD until one day, without warning or explanation, he packed up his office and walked away to settle up here in the Cuyamaca Mountains east of San Diego.

"Oh, I am indeed a fan—a veritable disciple. Aristotle studied almost every subject available at the time, and made significant contributions to most of them. It has been said, and I agree, that he was likely the last person to know everything there was to be known in his own time. On the other hand, nobody's perfect, and along with his great achievements, he also pulled some real boners. He thought that the Earth was the center of the universe, that mathematics and physics were not related, and even that men had more teeth than women."

"They don't?"

Defoe ignored him. "But we digress."

Carl looked at him skeptically.

"I stand corrected," Defoe added. "It was I that digressed. What was the question?"

"You were going to somehow connect my busted pump with Aristotle's phobia for empty spaces."

The bright old eyes flashed with remembrance. "Indeed! We were talking about why your sprinkler system is not working. Your pump is not busted. It's just positioned at the wrong end."

"It's at the wrong end all right—the wrong end of a long line between here and San Diego."

Carl didn't talk like this around Fels. Although she resisted accepting it, the whole transplant away from the city had been her idea, and it upset her when he expressed regret at their extreme removal from civilization.

"Turds," Defoe disclaimed. "That suburban beehive of tourist frenzy and wireless techno-industry is no place for the likes of you and Felicity. Give it time, Carl. You'll learn that when it comes to genuine enrichment of life, there's nothing modern society can offer that the birds and flora don't offer up for free."

Defoe was the only person who called Fels by her given name, partly because he was the only person she didn't correct. "What about cold beer?" Carl countered.

"You know I brew my own."

"Yeah, but it's not cold."

"Wait until winter. Besides, beer was consumed warm for thousands of years before Americans decided they needed to appease the god of refrigeration that they foolishly freed from the depths of hell."

"That sounds like a contradiction: refrigeration and hell."

"Not if you contemplate the profundities of thermodynamics."

"Can we contemplate the profanities of my pump instead?"

"That was profundity, not profanity."

"I know, and I mean profanity, as in, 'Let's contemplate my goddamn pump.' "

The master of ancient and modern philosophy watched him a moment. Carl could almost see the mental gears turning. Defoe would be happy to protract the ambling conversation all afternoon. Human contact was the one thing his birds and trees couldn't offer up. But Carl wanted to find out if he needed any parts to get the sprinkler system working. It was over an hour to the nearest hardware store at Alpine in Defoe's old Toyota Tercel, and the first half of that was just navigating five miles of dirt track out to Route 79. Fels was due to return that evening, and he wanted to be back before she arrived. He had already missed two promised deadlines to have the sprinkler system working, and now it looked as though he was tripping on a third. The three days that she'd been gone, working with her client in San Diego, seemed to have flown by, even though he couldn't point to one useful thing he'd done for their household. Life happily filled itself if you didn't force your own agenda.

"Did you know," Defoe continued, leaning back into a more comfortable position against a tree, "that refrigeration was first demonstrated in Scotland in the 1740's, and commercially used in meat-packing plants by the time of the Civil War?"

"Bullshit," Carl replied.

He said it as a pronouncement, not an accusation. This was the penalty flag he used with Defoe to end the game.

The professor indulged in a dramatic sigh before pushing himself to his feet. "A pump can only pull water up to about thirty feet in vertical height," he explained, finally divulging the answer. "Above that, atmospheric pressure can't prevent a vacuum from developing in the pipe."

Carl kicked the dirt. He remembered something about that. That was why they put water pumps at the bottoms of deep wells. "I have to move the pump down to the reservoir, don't I?" he pondered.

The reservoir was a fifteen foot-wide pool he'd made to catch and store rain runoff.

"Only if you want your sprinkler system to do more than spit shit."

Carl nodded in resignation. At least he wouldn't need more parts.

Like their relocation to the mountain pine forests, the sprinkler system was Fels's brainchild. The water wasn't intended to feed landscaping, existing or otherwise. In fact, with any luck, the pump would never be activated other than for testing. Global warming had produced a series of dry winters with no end in sight. The open-ended drought was desiccating vegetation, transforming the southern half of the state into a tinderbox. Arrayed across the roof of their self-contained little cabin, snaking around the solar panels, was a network of PVC pipes and sprinkler heads. A thermostat turned on the pump when the temperature under the eves reached 140 degrees. Should the thermostat ever trip the pump, Carl hoped that he and Fels would be far away.

The sprinkler system was actually the second line of defense. When the crew of Mexican laborers built the three-room home, part of the deal with the contractor was to clear the Black Oak and Jeffrey Pines within a hundred-foot radius. It broke Carl's heart to see the beautiful old growth come down, but buffer zones were now pretty much mandated for fire safety.

To the busy contractor, though, "clear" meant "cut down." As a result, the squat stuccoed homestead hunkered in the middle of a small sea of felled trees. Carl had toiled many hours the last two months learning how not to cut off his fingers as he worked his new chainsaw clearing the mess. He'd managed to strip most of the downed limbs, and now they were piled in a wilting mountain at the western edge of their half-acre lot. "Ready for a Texas-sized bonfire," as Defoe had dryly observed. Carl wasn't sure what to do about the entangled mass. It was already home to a growing metropolis of forest rats. Eventually it would attract opossums, raccoons, and God knows what else. Fels, always a cooing softie when presented with something mammal and furry, had responded with, "Cool!" Carl, however, grew up in the San Diego suburbs where his mother had waged protracted battles with raccoons hell-bent on harvesting the gooey, aromatic treasures hidden away inside bungee-corded trashcans, and he had suffered torturous flea itches from the opossums that lived under the deck.

No, he'd decided, the massive pile of limbs had to go. But where? They were surrounded on three sides by National Forest land. It was tempting to just haul the debris down the hill, but he imagined Homeland Security helicopters suddenly hovering overhead in the middle of the night shouting federal commands through bullhorns.

"I stopped at the Kumeyaay memorial on the way here," Defoe said, breaking Carl's brooding ruminations.

He looked at the scraggly philosopher and laughed. "You're still nursing that idea?"

The Kumeyaay were the local natives that had lived along the coast and throughout the Peninsular Range Mountains of southern

California and Baja Mexico for thousands of years before the Europeans arrived. One November morning in 1775, a band of Kumeyaay, having had their fill of Spanish missionary forced conversion and slave labor, attacked the San Diego mission, killing the Padre. The Spanish soldiers quartered nearby grabbed their muskets and trotted off to exercise their trained skills, namely killing as many Indians as they could find, and then capturing many more to replace the unhappy slaves who had run off with the attackers. According to Defoe, the local chief Tekumewa led a dozen braves to hold off the guns, swords, and horses while the village women and children escaped. Tekumewa took four bullets before running his spear through the Spanish captain. Defoe insisted that he knew where the tribe had buried their hero leader.

"The Kumeyaay memorial is not an idea," Carl's neighbor replied. "An idea is a concept of pure reason not based on empirical experience. I can see and touch the Kumeyaay memorial, therefore it is not an idea."

"Yeah, yeah. Mumbo-jumbo. Your cairn may actually exist, but the idea that it's an Indian memorial is . . . well, just that—an idea."

"Touché. However, the Kumeyaay that told me about it was very real."

Carl looked at his friend with surprise. "That's where you got the idea that this rock formation was Tekumewa's burial site?"

"Not the idea—the information."

Defoe had talked about the supposed memorial perhaps a half dozen times without divulging this obviously key aspect. The old fart enjoyed his little jokes. Maybe he was just pulling his leg. "Why didn't you mention this before?"

"I promised the Kumeyaay I wouldn't."

"So, now all of a sudden you decide to break your vow?"

"No. Now all of a sudden the old Kumeyaay is dead."

"Oops. Sorry."

Carl was silent. Death always shut him up.

"You knew him," Defoe added.

"I did?"

"The Shell gas station at Old Pine."

In his mind, Carl saw the image of a brown and wrinkled face. "Sam?"

The old guy hung around the station, pumping gas for the ladies and occasionally cleaning a windshield or two. Carl was never sure if Sam worked there or was just tolerated. He seemed about as far removed from American Indians as Fels. His shiny new black pickup truck was plastered with American flags, and he had a distinctly southern drawl.

Carl shook his head. "Sam?" he said again. "No way was he an Indian."

"Way."

Carl blinked at the kid-talk. "How do you know?"

"He told me."

"And you believed him?"

Defoe shrugged. "Why shouldn't I? I believe the things *you* tell me."

"Why would he tell you about the burial site when he was trying to keep it a secret?"

"He gave me the information in trade."

"For what?"

"Whisky. He was visiting, as he did occasionally, and requested some libation. I told him that he'd have to tell me something I didn't already know. I was only making light, and was quite taken when he revealed it."

"You gave whisky to an Indian? Isn't that, like, illegal?"

Defoe just looked at him through critical eyes.

"Okay, that was pretty dumb. But, why didn't he want you to tell anybody?"

"Fair question. Either he wanted to avoid having the place desecrated by trampling tourists, or he was afraid I'd find out that he was lying."

"He took you there?"

"It was the middle of the night. He described it."

Carl squinted one eye at Defoe and shook his head. "Sounds awfully fishy. How did Sam even know?"

"His mother showed him. For a dozen generations, Kumeyaay mothers brought their sons to the site to pay respect. Sam was thirteen and visiting from Louisiana where he lived with his father.

It was forty years until he returned, but he said he could have found the burial site again with his eyes closed."

Defoe looked at him, and his eyes seemed to twinkle with anticipation. "Would you like to see it?"

Carl wanted nothing more than to traipse off with his friend in search of ancient Indian traces, but he had promised Fels about the sprinkler.

"It's not very far," Defoe urged. "The exercise will do you good."

Exercise was not something Carl lacked, living a self-sufficient life far from the helpful machines and infrastructure of civilization. And, he had promised Fels.

"Okay, but I have to be back in less than an hour."

That should be plenty of time.

It wasn't far, but lacking a path, the going was slow through the chaparral. After twenty minutes of tripping on roots and fending slapping branches, they broke out into a hilltop meadow. They were well into the National Forest, and this far from the marked trails, any others who might stumble upon it were probably lost and not contemplating the possibility of Indian burial sites. At the very summit, with unfettered views of the Cuyamaca peaks all around, was indeed a pile of rocks.

"This is it?" Carl asked.

Defoe stood with crossed arms, grinning as though one of the great wonders of world lay at their feet.

"It's . . . just a pile of rocks," Carl accused.

His cheek burned from the clawing scratch of a thorn. It stung when he touched it. He had worked hard to get here, and it was just . . . a pile of rocks.

"Rocks don't arrange themselves into piles," Defoe observed.

"Sure they do."

Don't they? he thought.

"Not at the top of a hill. Look," Defoe directed, pointing at the heap, "they were brought from different locations. This one is granite, this one sandstone, and this one, why, this one is flint. They wouldn't have left flint without a reason."

"But, but . . . it's just a pile of rocks!"

"You're not understanding Kumeyaay sensibilities. Our world consists of manufactured fabrications. For you meaning is in form and function. The Kumeyaay lived with the Earth, suckled by nature. For them, it was the *place* that held the meaning. The cairn is just a location marker."

"The cairn is just a pile of rocks."

Defoe sighed heavily. "You are a musician."

"Was, you mean. And, I'm not sure playing blues guitar qualifies."

Just saying the words "blues guitar" made his knees weak with a loss and regret. He hadn't even played any blues CDs since they'd moved into the clouds.

His friend waved off the detail. "When you follow the musical notation as you play your favorite piece, you surely don't *need* the notes; they're just a marker, a reminder. This pile of rocks is the musical notation for the Kumeyaay tribe."

Carl looked to see if Defoe was serious. "Have you ever seen a blues band play?"

The gray beard wagged. "Not my cup of tea."

"Most of the songs have exactly three chords. When I sat in with other bands, all I needed to know was the key.

Defoe absorbed this, clearly hearing new and astonishing information. How could anybody teach college and not know this?

"I get the point, though," Carl said. "I have to get back. Maybe I'll come again during a full moon and commune with Tekumewa, the brave Kumeyaay chief."

His neighbor studied him.

"What?" Carl asked, starting down the hill.

"Be careful of what you joke."

Carl stopped and turned. "You're not serious. Don't tell me you believe in ghosts."

Defoe laid his hand briefly on Carl's shoulder as he walked past him down the hill. "I reserve my beliefs for matters that involve me. But you don't need to wait for a full moon to hear Tekumewa's battle cry."

Carl watched Defoe make his way carefully down through the tufts of grass. "Oh, come on!" He called and trotted after him.

"You're telling me you've heard him? A dead Indian? An Indian that's been dead for over two hundred years?"

His neighbor glanced at him and shrugged. "Probably just a sick coyote."

"Now you're patronizing me."

Defoe laughed. "If you *want* to argue about something, let's pick a subject that can possibly have a conclusion. How about Voltair's oft mis-quoted pith, *I may disagree with what you say, but I'll defend to the death your right to say it* ?"

"How about we speed it up and hoof it back before I get in hot water with Fels."

"Your house doesn't have hot water."

"She'll boil it with the steam spurting out of her ears."

Defoe snorted.

After a few moments, Carl added, "Um, no need to tell her what I said about the steam spurting from her ears."

Chapter 2

Fels' pickup was already parked in front of the cabin when Carl and Defoe stumbled back into the log-cluttered clearing. They had gotten turned around and had followed the wrong dry streambed for awhile. "Perhaps I had better be going," Defoe said. "Marital debate is not my specialty."

"You mean the kind of debate that involves flying pots? Nothing to worry about; her aim is terrible."

Carl liked to pretend that Fels was a hard-nosed slave master, but the charade was obvious since she was anything but demanding. At least, with everybody but herself. She had always been an indefatigable go-getter, coming out on top in an engineering field dominated by men. Her energy sometimes bordered on manic, though, ever since her four year-old nephew's death eleven months ago. Little Tod was her sister's only child, and the he and Fels had been like brother and sister. After a neighborhood soccer-mom, fumbling with her cell phone, ran her giant SUV over him like so much road trash, Fels couldn't work for a week, but then earned a hefty bonus for eventually finishing two weeks ahead of schedule. Thinking that this total focus on work was just the ticket to pull her through, Carl was caught by surprise when she suddenly turned her back on the bustle of San Diego and set her sights on the solitude of the mountains.

"The forest seems to be getting crowded," Defoe observed, nodding toward the house as he climbed stiffly over a log.

A man was returning from the truck carrying a mesh case. He was about to enter the cabin when he glanced up and saw them. "Hey, Carl!" he called, waving with his free hand before continuing through the door.

"It's Rik!" Carl exclaimed.

What the devil was he doing here?

Henrik, known universally as Rik, was the founder of the company that Fels was working with under contract. GeneTrend did biotech research and had brought Fels in to configure and integrate a new database and quality tracking system. Rik was eloquent, erudite, and rumored to have gathered a pile of wealth from brilliant genetics patents—pretty much everything that Carl was not. He had also been Fels's fiancé back in their college days.

"A Brother?" Defoe asked next to him.

"Her boss."

"Seems rather young."

"That's just because you're so old," Carl replied, starting again for the cabin.

"Handsome devil. Are you sure she's safe with him?"

"They've already gotten that out of their system."

Defoe was silent for a moment. "I see," was all he finally said.

Carl stopped and laughed. "I didn't mean that they've had an affair. They were engaged a long time ago."

"It couldn't have been that long ago. You kids haven't been *alive* that long."

"What are you talking about? I'm older than most of my distant ancestors ever lived."

"That is true. Interesting perspective."

"You old goat! I got that from *you*!"

"Ah, yes. In that case, it is a *most* interesting perspective."

When they arrived at the cabin, Carl heard the familiar swooping guitar pulls of Buddy Guy, one of the last surviving second-generation bluesmen. Inside, he found Rik reading the backside of the CD case. Without a word, Carl strode over and hit the eject button of the player and replaced the Buddy Guy disc with that of a light jazz band. Rik looked at him in surprise when Carl handed him the disc to put back in the case.

"Carl doesn't listen to the blues anymore," Fels explained, coming over to give him a hug. Her slim waist always felt like a perfect fit in his arms, and her soft, auburn hair tickled his nose in a way that made him tingle with desire.

"Sour grapes," Rik declared, nodding slowly in understanding.

Carl had only met the genetics genius briefly a couple of times, but knew from Fels that the wonder-man didn't waste time with the usual social formalities, like basic manners.

"He's just broadening his horizons," Fels replied, going back to the stove.

"In that case," Rik said, eyeing Carl up and down, "I guess it's just a coincidence that he simultaneously decided to give up playing the genre?"

It annoyed Carl when people talked about him as though he wasn't there. He held up his left hand to demonstrate his crooked ring finger. "Not a decision, a consequence."

Unabashed, Rik leaned in to study the damage. "Looks nasty. I'm really sorry about that. Fels said you caught it in a truck or something."

And the thing was, Rik really did seem sorry. That's the way he was: dismissive one minute, and sympathetic the next.

"I was helping a friend move. I jumped from the back, and my wedding ring caught on a bolt. It broke the bone, and nearly tore the rest of the finger off."

"And that's the best they could do to fix you up?" Rik asked.

Carl took a moment to answer. The loss was still almost too much to bear. "Insurance," was all he managed.

"You don't have any?"

Carl couldn't respond. His vision was blurring from tears, and he turned to look out the window to hide them.

"We have insurance through an HMO," he heard Fels explain behind him. "The emergency room patched him up for the night, but told him he needed to see an orthopedic surgeon as soon as possible. As it turned out, 'as soon as possible' was over a week going through the HMO system. By then, the surgeon told him it was too late. The bone had already started to heal wrong."

"I don't believe they can't do anything about it. Christ, it looks like hell."

"Oh, they could make it look better," Carl said, turning back and wiping his sleeve across his eyes. "But they can't make it *work*."

Rik just looked at him, puzzled.

"To play guitar," Fels explained. "The ring finger is the most important one for blues. He'll never have the strength to pull the strings."

"I see. Shit, that's a real shame. You really screwed the pooch going with an HMO."

Silence filled the cabin. There was nothing to add.

Except by Defoe. Stepping in from the doorway, he said, "Fate rarely sets before us a straight path. If it weren't for calamities, our destinies would be limited by our meager imaginations."

"Fate?" Rik said, turning. "That's a load of horseshit. We might as well be talking about alchemy."

The corner of Defoe's mouth turned up a hair in anticipation of a worthy adversary. "Okay, let's. Newton was an ardent student."

Rik turned to Fels, obviously annoyed. "Who is this guy?"

"Uh, that's Defoe," she said, "our neighbor."

"At your service," their friend said, stepping forward to offer his hand. "I'm happy fate has allowed us to meet."

Rik shook Defoe's hand, but glanced back at Fels uncertainly.

"He's a philosopher," she explained, as though this would make everything clear.

At this, Rik laughed out loud. "A philosopher? How quaint. I'd have thought you'd all be dead by now."

Carl started searching for some way to come to his friend's defense, but saw that Defoe was smiling broadly.

"Philosophy may die when the last human is obliterated by our sun going nova, but that won't be for a very long time."

"Bah," Rik scoffed, releasing the handshake. "The subject is already dead. It was made obsolete by the only real method of understanding the universe."

"I presume you mean science."

"Of course. What else?"

"The human mind."

"That's nonsense. The human mind evolved within a specific niche in the environment. It's designed to interpret the subtleties of the African savannas, not the invisible world of molecules or the beginning of the Big Bang."

"Designed?"

"You know what I mean—call it 'structured for.' "

"The same African savanna mind invented science."

"Of course. But just because a system is created my man, doesn't mean that it can't surpass—"

"Rik, you take coffee, right?" Fels interrupted, placing a steaming cup in front of him.

She spoke pleasantly enough, but Carl knew that tone. She wanted to head off a potential argument. Fels was a peacemaker, a blanket thrown over any fire about to flare. It served her in her consulting, as people came to expect meetings to end productively when she was there.

"Uh," Rik replied, glancing from the cup to his host, "I think this is tea." He flicked at the paper tab hanging over the edge of the cup to demonstrate.

"No. It *is* coffee. We use dunking bags—no coffeemakers up here."

"Aha. No electricity out in the wild."

"We have electricity. We're off the grid, but we have solar panels and batteries. Not enough power for current hogs like coffeemakers, though."

"Or clothes dryers," Carl added. "Or toaster ovens, or refrigerators, or electric fans, or—"

"He gets the idea," Fels interrupted, playfully bumping him with her hip as she walked by.

Rik looked at the blue flame hissing steadily on top the stove and raised one eyebrow.

"Propane," Fels explained. "We refill the tanks in Alpine. We're not back-to-nature hippies, you know. We just wanted to get away from the crazy rat race of the city. This place is all we could afford."

Carl wasn't about to contradict her, but for the money it took to buy the land and build the tiny cabin, they could have picked up a small house in Alpine or Pine Valley. He didn't mind, though. The cozy three-room cottage was the first home they could call their own. They had a bedroom just slightly larger than their king-size bed, a small laundry room where Carl washed his clothes by hand in a tub, and the main area—what they called "The Great Hall"— which served as kitchen, dining area, living room, office, and library. Carl took showers outside under a sun-warmed bag he'd picked up at a marine store. Fels took her showers at her gym in San Diego. She also took her clothes to a dry-cleaner in the city.

At first, she had washed her own underwear in the tub, but reluctantly let Carl take over so they would have more time together when she was there . . . which wasn't very often. The original idea was that Fels would work from home, using a satellite Internet connection. It had seemed logical at the time, but unlike software coding, systems engineering consisted mostly of meetings, and despite the high-tech nature of Rik's company, teleconferencing was not yet a welcomed substitute for a communications channel consisting of ten feet of table-top.

"Self sufficient," Rik declared dramatically. His grin suggested that the very idea was indeed hippy-realm.

Fels didn't seem to catch the sarcasm. "Exactly! Off the grid. Independent of the fragile structure of modern civilization."

Rik nodded in mock-serious concurrence. "Except, of course, for propane."

She shrugged.

"And shampoo," Carl chimed in. "And food, and soap, and batteries—pretty much everything on the shelves of the market at Pine Valley."

Fels stuck her tongue out at him.

He heard a rustling in the corner. The mesh case that Rik had carried in was actually a cage, and Carl could see, lurking near the back, brown fur and a pink Mickey Mouse ear. "What is it?" he asked.

"A ferret," Fels replied, going to the cage and opening the door. She lifted the limp animal carefully out and hugged it to her cheek, comforting it with affectionate cooing. "Isn't she just the cutest thing you've ever seen, honeybun?"

Uh-oh. Whenever she called him "honeybun," it meant she wanted something. He'd never seen a live ferret before, and he knew the reason: they were illegal to own in California.

Fels held the animal out for Carl.

"You're just trying to get me attached to him," he accused, taking the warm bundle of fur.

"He's a she. Her name is Lilly."

The ferret's small eyes were dark and shiny, hiding the little soul within, but Carl had the distinct sense that the animal was studying him intently, as though gauging the degree of friendliness, or perhaps competence, of the hands now holding her.

"Lilly," he repeated, letting her settle into his lap. A pungent smell of musk assaulted his nose. "Whew! You sure don't smell like a flower."

"Her real name is Lilake" Fels explained. "She's not supposed to smell like a flower, she's supposed to smell like a ferret—and I happen to like the smell. It's the smell of natural life."

"So is a skunk, but you wouldn't ask me to hold one."

"That means she has active musk glands," Defoe observed. "It probably means she hasn't been spayed."

"How do you know about ferrets?" Fels asked.

"My father kept one when I was very young. He used it for hunting rabbits. He would put the ferret down one hole, and we grabbed the rabbits in nets as they fled out the other ones. It was quite effective."

Defoe watched the animal thoughtfully as Carl softly rubbed the top of its head with apparent satisfied effect. "Lilake," the old philosopher mused. "That sounds familiar somehow."

"So, Defoe," Rik challenged with an earnestness that surprised Carl, "how *does* a philosopher make a living these days?"

The old man looked up from his contemplation in surprise. "This one subsists on a professor's pension. How does a founder of GeneTrend make one?"

Rik slung one arm lazily over the back of his chair and sipped his coffee. "Bio-tech is lucrative. Pretty much any company with the word 'gene' in the name is guaranteed venture funding. We even have grants from the NSF."

Defoe absorbed this a moment. GeneTrend was pronounced JEN-a-trend, and Defoe had probably never seen it written. "Genetics research?"

"That's right," Rik confirmed.

"Like genetically altered corn?"

Rik snorted. "Not quite."

"They do brain research," Fels offered. She sounded proud; happy to be working in such an advanced field.

Defoe's eyebrows shot up. "Impressive. Can we look forward to improvements?"

Carl knew his friend was joking, but Rik's scowl made it clear that he didn't find the question humorous.

"They're working on brain disorders," Fels explained. "They're trying to find cures for Tay-Sachs disease and Alzheimer's."

"Cures," Rik interjected sharply, "are a long way off. We're still trying to nail down the genetic mechanisms involved."

"They recently hired Dr. Weinermach," Fels added brightly.

"A doctor who makes hot-dogs?" Carl quipped, realizing that the joke was falling flat. "Are we supposed to know who this was?

"The Nobel Prize winner for medicine?" Rik added a little impatiently.

"Indeed," Defoe said. "Something to do with bacteria that live in the stomach, as I recall."

Rik shook his head impatiently. "Brain research. He won the Nobel Prize for brain research."

"Ah. Well that would, I suppose, impress the Nobel selection committee a bit more than unicellular organisms that take up housekeeping in your gut. My hat's off to you, my friend," Defoe said, sweeping his hand dramatically across his forehead as though doffing an imaginary fedora. "You'll probably make a lot of money, but in the end, what matters the motivation when the result is vastly improved lives?"

Rik just stared at his coffee as he stirred it round and round.

Carl wondered why the entrepreneur didn't accept Defoe's olive branch. He decided to break the logjam. "So, what's up with Lilly? Ferrets aren't allowed in California, you know."

He caught Fels's eye with that, and she stuck her tongue out again.

"They're only banned as pets," Rik explained, seeming to come alive again. "Lilly was going to be used in the research."

" 'Was?' " Carl queried. "As in 'We changed our minds'?"

"That's right—technical reasons."

"Don't they usually use, like, guinea pigs?"

Rik shrugged. "Guinea pig brains are too simple."

"And a ferret's isn't?"

His guest stared at him impassively a moment. "Not at all. A predator is always smarter than the prey."

Carl laughed. "So what does that say about people?"

Again the impassive stare. After a couple of seconds, though, the corners of Rik's mouth turned up in a smile. "I guess it means that we're at the very top of the food chain."

"Not," Defoe offered, "if you happen to meet a polar bear in his own territory."

Rik's grin broadened. "Ah, perhaps the polar bear would weed out just those at the bottom of the top. The top of the top—the people who still carry useful survival genes—would end up eating the bear."

Defoe met Rik's grin with his own, relishing the sword-play with the worthy argument partner. "You would consider the ability to kill a polar bear still vital to survival? What about the ability to pick the right derivative investment? Or perhaps negotiating the best salary?"

"Nah," Rik countered, flicking his thumb as an umpire might do to send the batter back to the bench. "So what if you have a fancier car, or a bigger house? How does that help your survival? Maybe if you need to drive away very fast from the enraged husband of your mistress. Or maybe you have more rooms in your house to hide in when he comes after you."

"How about your children? They'll get a better education."

Rik laughed out loud. "No offense, professor, but I don't see how a Harvard degree assures that your genes will be better propagated. First of all, it's my experience that rich kids are more likely than the middle class to find an early grave from drugs and alcohol. Secondly, it doesn't take a college education to beget offspring. Statistically, it's the poor who are populating the Earth and diluting the gene pool."

Defoe sat back in shock. "Heavens! You sound like the Nazis. There's a word for what they were trying to do—"

"Eugenics, and that's *not* what I'm talking about. I said dilution, not trait selection. Dilution simply means that the gene pool is getting larger and larger, and without fitness selection, those genes favorable to survival are being spread more thinly."

The philosopher took a thoughtful breath and shrugged. "Then, what do you suppose *are* legitimate survival pressures in the modern world?"

The founder of GeneTrend raised both hands, palms up.

"You think there are none," Defoe concluded.

Rik raised one eyebrow.

"What about times of economic distress?" Defoe offered. "What if we were to have another Great Depression?"

His adversary chuckled. "Do you seriously think that the poor were pruned during the Depression? For every baby that starved, two more were born. In any case, FDR's bailout made sure the Depression didn't narrow the gene pool."

Defoe shook his head in amazement. "Well, bully for us then. We've managed to escape the bloody tooth and claw of nature."

Rik grinned in knowing victory. "On the contrary. This is the very root of the problem."

"What problem?"

"The extinction of humans."

Defoe continued to smile, but his brow was furrowed. "Extinction is quite an extreme condition. Do you know something we don't?"

"I know nothing more than any thinking man would—should—see. Evolutionary pruning has ceased in the human species, while population growth continues exponentially. Survival genes are spreading too thin to recover—too thin to manifest a viable compliment."

Defoe shook his head again. "I still don't see the problem. If there are no longer natural dangers to humans, why worry about survival genes?"

"Who said there would never be dangers?"

"What? Platoons of marauding polar bears invading from the Arctic?"

Rik shrugged again. "Perhaps an invasion of conquering space aliens."

Defoe's eye narrowed. "War," he stated. "There's your great pruner of mankind."

"Indeed," Rik agreed. "Unfortunately, modern wars affect only tiny proportions of the species."

"Un-*for*-tunately?"

Carl could see that Rik was blushing. It was an event to note.

The genetics entrepreneur looked at his watch and got quickly to his feet. "I should be going. It's a long drive back."

Carl looked from Rik to Fels. "You're going back already?" he asked her.

"No. Rik drove his own car. He left it back at the fire road."

"I didn't want to puncture my oil pan," Rik explained.

"You could have come all the way," Carl said. "The clearance is at least—"

"Not for a Lamborghini."

"Oh. I see."

Carl suspected that Rik also wouldn't want to get it dirty.

"I'll walk you back," Fels said. "It's only ten minutes."

Rik jingled his keys as he waited for Fels to grab her jacket. At the sound, Lilly's head jerked up in alarm. An instant later, she leaped from Carl's lap and scampered behind the kitchen cabinets.

"Damn!" Carl cried. "How are we going to get her out from behind there?"

Fels laughed. "Don't worry. She'll come out when she gets hungry. Boy, Rik, she really doesn't want to go back with you."

"Wait a second," Carl protested, catching on. "We're keeping Lilly?"

Could this have been the only reason for Rik's visit?

"Just for a while," Fels assured, still chuckling.

"Why? We should have talked about this."

"It's my fault," Rik explained. "I coerced Fels by letting her hold Lilly a moment."

"I still don't understand. Why is she staying here?"

"Oh, don't be such a poop," Fels reproved. "There's a GAO audit next week, and Lilly would be a pesky glitch."

"It's a technicality," Rik said. His tone indicated that the whole situation was too trivial to waste time on. "I don't want to screw around with the permit procedures."

Fels furrowed her brow. "I thought you didn't want the auditors to start digging into the research you were using Lilly for. In fact, I thought—"

"I don't care about that. It's a permit thing. Come on, Fels. Let's go; it's going to get dark."

"Wait a minute!" Carl cried. He felt like he was being bowled over. "It's not legal for her to be here—permit or no."

"Look, it's not a problem . . ." Rik started to say testily. He stopped and took a deep breath, as though gathering his patience. "It's the sort of law that's only enforced when somebody complains," he said calmly. "It's only for a while. In any event, GeneTrend will take care of any problems, including any fines in the exceedingly unlikely event there's trouble."

Fels gave Carl her puppy-look. Before he had a chance to protest further, Rik ushered Fels out the door. A second later the door opened and Rik's head reappeared. "Just to be on the safe side, though, don't tell anybody about Lilly," he said, and the door closed for the last time.

Carl listened to their footsteps and muffled conversation fade into the distance.

"It seems as though you are a daddy," Defoe said.

Carl heard a slight scuffle, and Lilly's head poked out from around the corner of the cabinet. She blinked once, and Carl could have sworn that the ferret nodded.

Chapter 3

"I wouldn't take Rik's views too seriously," Fels said as she rinsed another dish and handed it to Carl to dry and place on the shelf. "He used to talk like that all the time. 'What the human race needs,' he'd say, 'is another good plague.' He hasn't gone off in a long time. You have a talent for pulling the stuffing out of people, Defoe."

"Well if that's what they're full of," their friend replied, "then it should be pulled out."

He had stayed for dinner, and was playing with Lilly while his hosts cleaned up. "Lilake," he said, lifting the ferret's head with his knuckle under her chin so that he could look into her eyes. "That's quite an impressive name for such a little animal." The wrinkles of the time-worn face huddled in thought. "I know I've heard it somewhere before."

Lilly opened her little sharp-toothed mouth and let out a squeaky bark, as though encouraging the human to continue.

"It means trouble," Fels said.

"Really? In what language? Old Norse perhaps?"

"The language of a moody boss. I was waiting for Rik in his office and happened to see some of her paperwork with her real name sitting on his desk. He gave me a good lecture about sticking to my assigned tasks instead of snooping around. The guy may be a genius, but sometimes he acts like a brat on a tantrum."

Carl smiled to himself. That was exactly the sort of description he liked to hear about a former fiancée, particularly a handsome former fiancée who drove a Lamborghini.

Fels reached up to gently touch Carl's face. "Where did you get this?"

He flinched "Ow! Uh, I must have scratched myself on a branch."

She moved her hand and found another wound, then poked a finger through a rip in his shirt. "What were you doing? Wrestling a cougar?"

"No. We, er . . . Defoe, uh, took me up the ridge to show me a pile of rocks."

Fels just looked at him with one eyebrow cocked.

"It was really cool," he lied.

"Did you get the sprinkler system working?"

"Um, we found the problem. Actually, Defoe found it."

"So the answer is no," she confirmed calmly.

"Yes. Yes, the answer is no."

She didn't say anything, but instead put the leftovers in the plastic containers they would hang outside overnight where the cold mountain air provided refrigeration.

Sometimes he wished she'd get mad and yell at him. It wasn't like she was going to sulk. In five minutes she'd be over it and that would be that. But Carl still felt guilty, like he was always letting her down. She was so damn efficient . . . and ambitious. She didn't try to make him feel guilty, but he couldn't help it. *He* made him feel guilty.

"The rock pile was inspiring," he insisted. He knew that he was shoveling manure, but he wanted her to believe that he really did do something as important as the task he'd promised. "It's the burial site of an Indian warrior chief. It's, like, hundreds of years old."

Defoe just sat watching him with a wry smile. The old turd knew exactly where he was trying to go with this.

"Really?" she said, carrying the plastic containers to the door. "It does sound inspiring. You'll have to take me sometime."

"You don't have to patronize me, you know!" he yelled as the door shut behind her.

In fact, she probably hadn't been. He had a special knack for recognizing opportunities to kick himself in the gonads.

After a few seconds of hollow silence, Defoe remarked that Tekumewa wasn't a warrior chief.

"Eh?" Carl said, distracted by his own brain fog.

"Tekumewa's clan hadn't waged tribal war in generations. That's why his defiance was so heroic."

"No shit," Carl snapped.

He tried to tell himself that he hadn't wanted to make it sound so rude, but the the truth was that he had. "Sorry, Defoe."

"No, *I'm* sorry. It appears as though I've gotten you into trouble."

"Oh, it's not so bad—"

Fels opened the door and came back in. She walked up to Carl, put her arms around his neck, and gave him a big smooch.

"Does that mean I'm forgiven?" he asked.

"You were never in trouble," she replied. She then leaned down to give Defoe a kiss on the cheek. "Goodnight, our gallant philosopher neighbor. It's been a long day and I'm going to go and curl up in bed and read my Bible. You staying the night?"

"Thanks," Defoe said, "but these old bones will groan and moan all the long hours if they don't find their own bed. Besides, I might miss an opportunity to observe a pack of coyotes executing a nocturnal hunt."

"What if it's you they're hunting?"

"Coyotes are essentially cowards. I'll intimidate them with a rousing speech from General Patton."

"The days are getting shorter, you know. Are you sure you can find your way in the dark?"

"Set aside your fears, my dear. I could navigate these woods blindfolded . . . and drunk. Carl, shall we get drunk?"

"Okay," Fels said. "But you be careful."

Carl set a bottle of Jack Daniels on the table, and sat down. When she had closed the bedroom door, he said in a low voice, "We got lost a hundred yards from the cabin in broad daylight."

"Ah, but we lacked the advantage of being drunk. So let's get to it. What's with Fels and the Bible? Was she joking?"

"I'm afraid not. She's gotten onto a Catholic kick lately. She's all agog about saints and angels and being in a state of grace, whatever that is."

"A state of grace is when you've inched a bit closer to Christ and act as though he's in your heart and mind. I suppose the next step would be to speak in tongues. But I thought Fels was protestant. Fundamentalist, in fact."

"She was raised that way. They didn't even have a church. That would be too ostentatious. They met on Sundays in their living rooms—no minister; they each took turns leading the service. When I met Fels, she considered me gilded with earthly trappings, and my family is Lutheran, for Christ's sake."

"For Christ's sake indeed. Catholicism seems to lie at the far end of that metaphysical teeter-totter, though. How did she end up there? Purely academic interest?"

"I wish. Did you know her nephew was killed nearly a year ago?"

"She told me. She seemed heartbroken."

"Devastated would be more like it." Carl leaned in close so that he could talk just above a whisper. "Her father decided they needed to help little Tod into heaven, so they held an accounting session."

Defoe shook his head in bewilderment. "Something tells me this did not include balancing check books."

"It's an accounting of sins. The idea was that at three years old, Tod was too young to have experienced the encounter with God necessary for a born again conversion. They believe that's a fundamental requirement to get into heaven. So they had sort of a séance. I'm not sure I really understand this, but the idea was to confess his sins for him. Somehow by laying them out on the table for God to see, Tod could be forgiven for them."

Defoe's brow wrinkled skeptically. "God needs these sorts of things to be laid out for him?"

"It's not *my* religion; I'm certainly not going to try to defend it. Anyway, this sin accounting thing happened just days after Tod was killed. Fels was still reeling from the shock, and to sit and listen to her whole extended family go on and on about all the bad things the poor little guy did was too much. She stood up in the middle of the séance and just walked out. She hasn't talked to any of her family since."

He leaned in even closer and continued in a whisper. "I thought she was through with organized religion all together, but a few weeks ago she brought home the *The Passion of Christ* on DVD.

It was pretty intense, and a few days after that she stopped at the library while in town. Defoe, she has a stack of books on Catholicism sitting next to the bed in there."

His friend stroked his beard thoughtfully. "You're thinking it's somehow connected to her nephew?"

Carl shrugged. "I've asked her about her new Pope kick, but she just brushes it off. The truth is, she's always studying something or other, so it's not like it's unusual for her to bring books home."

"Hmm. You know Catholicism is replete with methods for maneuvering one's way into heaven both before and after one dies. By their doctrine, when you die, there's not an instantaneous reckoning about your heaven-worthiness. Even after you depart your earthly body, there's still a chance to navigate away from hell."

"The idea of Purgatory," Carl suggested.

"That and the funeral Mass itself. An important component is the prayers for the repose of the deceased. After all, why would you bother praying for their eternal tranquility at this point if the disposition had already been determined at the time of death?"

"So, you're suggesting that Fels may still be worried about Tod's soul?"

"Let's say that I don't think one can leave behind a lifetime of belief by simply standing up and walking out of a service, no matter how bizarre."

Carl sat looking at the bedroom door, behind which his wife of four years lay contemplating ideas as foreign to him as Defoe's occasional ramblings on Nietzsche's concept of Eternal Return. It was disconcerting. He'd thought he knew her so well, could almost predict what she was going to say sometimes. Now he imagined these new mental excursions carrying her farther afield than any business air travel. Suddenly, like a train engine latching securely to a line of cargo cars to form a new functional identity, Tod's death and the relocation to the Cuyamaca forest linked together in causal synergy. For Fels, the move into the wilderness was an escape. He heard in his mind's ear, as though the memory had been hiding, waiting for the right time to step forward, something she'd said about their apartment in San Diego a few weeks after her nephew's death: the rooms were "full of Tod."

"You okay?" Defoe asked.

Carl glanced at him, realizing he'd zoned out. "Yeah, sorry. I was thinking how the whole move out here was a flight from tragedy."

"Fels's or yours?"

"Mine?"

His friend pointed at Carl's ring finger.

He hadn't really gotten used to the crippled finger yet; the sight of it still shocked him. He sighed. "I was thinking that our little mountain cabin was Fels's refuge from memories of Tod, but you're right, it's also my own personal refuge."

"Also from memories?"

"From a future."

Defoe watched him with calm intent. "A future that was lost when that ring got caught inside the truck?"

He nodded. His eyes blurred from tears. He didn't want Defoe to see, so he got up and carried his cup to the sink.

"We all face an infinite number of futures every day," his friend observed, making a point to poke at a callus on his palm so that he wasn't looking at Carl.

"It's not just the playing I miss; it's the whole community. Some people have the idea that musicians are competitive. There's always at least one guy in every crowd with a jumbo-sized ego, but in general it's mostly . . . well, a community. At least for the blues and roots-rock crowd. If you're not playing, you go to watch others who are, and more often than not they ask you to sit in for a set. I'll tell you, sometimes I miss it . . ."

He stopped, knowing he'd start weeping otherwise. He kept his back to Defoe and used the washrag to clean out his cup for the third time.

"I know *exactly* what you mean, " Defoe said exuberantly. His enthusiasm contrasted the quiet contemplation of the minute before. "When I first moved out here, I desperately missed the interplay with my colleagues. The local squirrels are sufficiently argumentative, but they consistently fail to carry their logical structures to a satisfying end."

Carl knew that Defoe understood his embarrassment and was providing a diversion. The old philosopher was a good friend.

A slight thump from outside, followed by a scraping and rattling, interrupted his thoughts. He opened the kitchen door, and there, in the light cast from within, sat Lilly on her haunches looking up at him. Next to her was one of the plastic containers Fels had hung for the night. As though she'd been waiting for him, the ferret grabbed a corner of the container in its teeth and dragged it into the kitchen. A length of the string Fels had used to hang it trailed behind.

Carl glanced at Defoe, who watched in surprise, and when he looked back down, Lilly was working at the lid, prying the corner up with her sharp little teeth while holding the rest of the container in her front claws. The lid gave way, and she pulled it off, and then, instead of diving into the tasty contents, sat back on her haunches and peered up at him.

"I'll be damned," he said. "You're into mischief already."

Somehow it seemed more than that, though. The animal's behavior seemed so . . . confident, as though Lilly had just executed a well-rehearsed trick.

"She is apparently waiting for permission to proceed," Defoe observed.

Carl reached down and picked up the end of the string. Lilly had chewed it through. She must have gotten outside somehow and crawled up the porch post to where it hung from a beam.

"Well," Carl said, "you've worked hard enough; you might as well dive in."

Instantly she jammed her head in the container and the sounds of smacking and chewing emerged.

Carl glanced at Defoe.

"Fels's boss wasn't exaggerating," Defoe said.

He was referring to what Rik had told Fels before leaving. He'd explained that Lilly had been selected for her intelligence. "Don't be surprised," he'd said, "if she seems to be a step ahead of you sometimes."

"I was going to warn you," Defoe went on, "about letting her outside. My father's ferrets could get distracted and wander off, never to be seen again. It appears, though, that Lilly is too sharp to fall for that."

"Still," Carl said, watching as Lilly held the container in her paws as she licked the sides, "it won't hurt to keep her in the cage for now. She's obviously already found a way out of the house."

"And speaking of a way out," Defoe said, getting stiffly to his feet, "I had better be off. My pride will be severely battered if I don't find my way home before sunrise."

"What are you talking about? You're not even a half mile away."

"That's a half mile as the crow flies, or as the competent woodsman walks. It could be a distance measured in leagues after I get thoroughly lost along the way."

"What about navigating blindfolded?"

"Ah, I'm afraid it's your fault, Carl, my friend. I was expecting to get sufficiently drunk, but now I am burdened with a useless sober mind."

"Well give me a call when you get home. If I don't hear from you in an hour, I'll send Lilly out with a cask of whisky strapped to her neck."

Phone calls were a well-worn joke, as neither of them had service.

When Carl turned from saying his good-byes, he found that Lilly had disappeared, leaving the empty container lying on the floor. He wasn't sure what to do. Defoe thought that she was too smart to wander off and get lost, but on the other hand, his father's animals had apparently done just that. The safe thing would be to put her back in her cage, but he wasn't sure how to find her. She might already be outside, venturing off into the wild night.

"Lilly," he called softly.

He didn't want to yell too loudly in case Fels was already asleep. He carefully opened the bedroom door to check, and found that Fels had indeed nodded off with the Bible lying open across her chest. Next to her on the blanket lay Lilly.

"How the devil did you get in here?" he whispered as he reached over to pick her up. She seemed to give him a sullen look as he lifted her gently off, but she didn't resist.

Getting her into the cage was another matter. She obviously valued her freedom, as demonstrated by new scratches on his arms. Once inside, though, she accepted her temporary fate and lay watching him with what he imagined might be the look from a felon unjustly imprisoned.

Carl cleaned up the kitchen, slid a bowl of water in Lilly's cage, and fifteen minutes later slipped quietly into bed next to Fels. She stirred, moaned a little, and without waking, flopped one arm over him as she did every night. He smiled into the darkness, and lying motionless so as not to wake his wife, he too soon slipped off into a deep slumber.

Ж Ж Ж

Carl woke to Fels shaking him.

"Come on, hon!" she whispered ugently. "Wake up!"

He opened his eyes to darkness. "What's the matter?"

"Shhh!" she urged. "Do you hear it?"

He did. It sounded like a squeaky door continuously opening and closing, or maybe a baby's weak cry.

"What is it?" he asked.

"I don't know. It woke me up." Her grip on his arm tightened. "You went with Defoe to visit an Indian grave."

She said this as though in accusation.

No! It couldn't be. That was ridiculous. But he could well imagine the cry to be the pitiful wailing of a lost soul. Goosebumps crawled up his arms. At first he thought it was outside, but as he listened, it seemed to come from the Great Hall, just beyond the bedroom door. He rolled away from Fels and dropped his feet to the floor feeling for his slippers.

"What are you *doing?*" she whispered in a hiss.

"Going to see what it is."

He sure as hell didn't want to, but he was the man.

"You're staying right here," she said, grabbing his arm.

"What? We'll just lie here the rest of the night listening to it? It's probably just a . . . bobcat." That didn't sound good. "Or a raccoon. I heard they can cry like that at night."

"Well I'm going with you then."

He padded to the bedroom door and the sound suddenly stopped. Fels came up behind him and he could feel her breath on his arm. "Get back, behind the door," he ordered.

"No," she whispered.

He knew it was no use arguing. He turned the knob and slowly opened the door. Feeble light from the waning moon lit the Great Hall enough to show silhouettes of furniture. An animal could be crouching anywhere in the room and he wouldn't know until it sprang. He took a tentative step forward but froze at a rustling sound from the far window. A *sproing* of taught wire was followed by the same cry that had woken them, now distinct and imminent. "Oh Christ," he declared aloud, and flipped on the light.

"What is it?" Fels asked behind him.

He pointed at Lilly's cage where the ferret stood on her hind legs looking at them, her front paws clasping the wire of the cage.

"Ahh," Fels cooed, going to the cage and opening the door. "She's lonely."

Lilly stepped out into her waiting arms and she hugged the animal to her breast.

"If she had been sleeping," Carl said, "she wouldn't be lonely."

"She can't sleep. She's probably scared out here all by herself." She cuddled the ferret and rubbed her cheek across the soft fur. Lilly seemed content, having gotten exactly what she was whining for.

"I was the ones that was scared. I say we hang her cage outside in a tree and let her know what scared is really all about."

Fels gave him a dirty look. "Don't listen to daddy," she said into the ferret's fur. "He's gets grumpy when the world doesn't revolve around him."

" 'Daddy?' In the first place, Lilly is not a child, and in the second place, if I can't have the world revolve around me, then at least I can have a ferret revolve around me . . . by her tail."

"Don't listen to that bad man," she said, holding Lilly in one arm and picking up the cage with the other. "He's insane," she added as she returned to the bedroom.

Carl sighed and followed.

Fels placed the cage on the dresser, which meant that Lilly was about three feet from Carl's head when she cried out again ten minutes later. He had just fallen asleep, and he sat bolt upright at the sound. "*Damn* it!" he shouted. "What the hell's the matter with her now?"

"Oh, calm down already," Fels reprimanded, turning on the light. "You're going to scare her to death."

She opened the cage door and took the ferret in her arms again.

"I'm not going to scare her to death; I'm going to strangle her to death."

Fels turned out the light, and Carl felt the bed move as his wife got in. "She may not understand what you're saying," she said in the dark, "but she can sense your tone."

"Good."

He lay listening, but only heard the sound of Fels breathing. "I'm in bed with a ferret." he observed into the night.

"Go to sleep."

After a few minutes, he felt Fels jerk slightly, and then her breathing became deep and regular. He lay quietly, wondering why he couldn't sense the animal that must be there somewhere. After some minutes more, he finally felt a stirring, and then soft steps as Lilly picked her way carefully to the foot of the bed. The slightest thud, no more than a feather pillow dropping to the floor, was followed by the faint sound of the ferret moving about through the room. A dim sliver of vertical light indicated that she'd nosed the door open, and the faint scrabbling sounds faded into the Great Hall. Seconds later, he heard a distinct scraping and rattling. He knew that ferrets were world champions at navigating tight places, and he realized that Lilly was climbing out through the wood stove chimney that they'd installed, intending to someday buy a wood stove to go with it. This must have been how she'd gotten out earlier to retrieve her dinner.

If Lilly was lonely, it obviously wasn't for human company.

Chapter 4

"She loves it!" Fels cried, pointing to Lilly dancing around on the wood chips next to the cabin. "Look at her. She's lost her mind."

Lilly did indeed seem to have lost her senses. Carl had finally gotten the emergency sprinkler system working, and enthusiastic sprays of water were erupting along the peak of the roof, and under the eaves, soaking the sides of the cabin. The ferret pranced in the resulting shower raining down around their home. In fact, she didn't so much prance as hop drunkenly about as though showing off her best four-footed disco maneuvers.

"Maybe she's just trying to cool off," Carl offered. Rik had warned that ferrets don't do well in temperatures much above 80 degrees.

Fels laughed and clapped her hands at the show. "In that case, she's not doing a very good job. She must be building up quite a sweat—wow!"

Lilly had fallen over on her back in her excitement. Her legs waved in the air like a stranded turtle for a second before she flipped upright and bounded ten feet to the side.

"You know," Fels said, "Lilly looks just like Tod . . ."

She didn't finish, and he knew not to press her. Sometimes she seemed to forget about her nephew for days, and then out of the blue something would trigger a memory and she'd fall into another funk.

"Let's see how the little rascal does with the hose," Carl said. He twisted the nozzle to produce a narrow stream, and turned it on the ferret. Lilly squeaked at the sudden new shower and spun around to face him, chirping like a mad squirrel.

He wanted to distract Fels from her grief. He wasn't always successful, but today seemed to be one of the lucky ones. She laughed and took the hose. The ferret chirped and squeaked and danced back and forth, forcing Fels to wave the hose as she tried to follow the dodging animal. Lilly scampered to the left, then farther to the right, and finally she made a bee-line back to the left . . . behind Carl. An instant later he was doused as Fels tried to follow the ferret.

"Oh Honey!" she cried, quickly swinging the hose away from him. "I'm so sorry."

"It's okay," he said, laughing. "It feels good."

He was drenched. His shirt hung heavy and dripping from his shoulders. He wiped the water from his eyes. "The little devil did it on purpose."

"Did what?"

"Tricked you into turning the hose on me."

"Oh, come on. She's not *that* smart. It was my fault, and I take full responsibility."

"Meaning you'll wash these clothes?"

"Not that much responsibility. I'll give you a temple massage tonight for your emotional wounds."

"It's a deal. I have to change. I feel like I've just gone for a swim."

As he made for the back kitchen door, Lilly sat on her haunches watching him with what he took to be smug satisfaction.

After he changed and tossed the wet clothes into the laundry room, he saw through the window that Fels was busy playing catch with Lilly, so he sat down at the computer and checked their email. Before escaping civilization he had found email annoying, since he was a slow, two-finger typist. It had seemed silly to spend fifteen minutes laboriously tapping out a message that he could convey with a two-minute phone call. Now, though, thanks to the satellite Internet connection that they'd installed for Fels, he checked in on his messages with anticipation, even occasionally perusing the spam during dry periods. Fifteen minutes spent hunting out the letters needed to construct a paragraph now seemed a happy price to pay for a connection to the wide world beyond.

There were two messages: one for Fels from her sister, and one for him from his friend Kaj, a drummer he'd played with in different bands. There was something he wanted to check out, and now seemed like a good opportunity. Glancing again to confirm that Fels was still occupied with Lilly, he went to Google and typed "Kumeyaay," "spirit," and "myth." He hit the return key and sat back to wait. As always, nothing happened for few seconds, and then the screen suddenly filled with suggested links. Fels had explained that although the satellite connection hosted plenty of bandwidth, it also suffered from high latency. (Afterwards, he'd Googled "latency"). He scanned through the herd of uninteresting links, investigated one that took him to Wikipedia's article on Kumeyaay traditional narratives, backed up when he didn't find what he wanted, took a peek at a link sponsored by the Kumeyaay Two-Spirit society, and when he realized that "Two-Spirit" meant gay, backed up once more and continued through the list. Four pages down, he struck pay dirt. Deep down in the depths of a perky we-love-the-world-and-the-world-loves-us Disney family web page describing their home in the Laguna Mountains, he found a reference:

> *On moonlit nights, from the peaks to the west, the ghost of Tekumewa can be heard calling out in defiance against long dead Spanish soldiers.*

That was it. The rest of the page went on to describe how they were building a deck over the back slope.

He saved off the link and switched to the email window. He glanced through the message from Fels's older sister, Joan, and then moved on to Kaj's. His friend wanted him to call . . . to talk about a possible job. "I'm a Goddamned cripple, you idiot," he muttered.

He started to peck out a reply, typing M-y f-i-n-g-e-r h-a-s n-o-t m-i-r-a-c-u-l-o-u-s-l-y c-u-r-e-d i-t-s-e-l-f, but then sat back in the chair. He really, really missed playing gigs with the guys. The headset sat there on top of the monitor. They could make phone calls over the Internet connection, but because of that latency—the delay—the exercise required patience. Listening to Fels talk to her colleagues at GeneTrend reminded him of the dialogues between Houston and the Apollo astronauts on the moon. In fact, if the person on the other end—like, say, his grandmother—was not savvy, attempting a conversation could be downright dangerous. He'd given up trying to talk with her because he was never able to convince her that he wasn't just trying to annoy her by talking on top of her.

He grabbed the headset, jammed it on his head, and typed his city friend's number. After a half-dozen seconds, he heard a ring, and then Kaj say hello.

"Hey!" he called out. "This is Carl. Listen I'm talking on a—"

"Hello?"

The damnable delay. "Kaj, listen to me. I'm talking on a stupid Internet—"

"Hello. Is anybody there—uh, Carl?"

"Kaj, listen to me. Don't talk, just listen for a minute." He heard his friend talking, but he ploughed ahead. "I'm using Fels's Internet phone, and because of the stupid satellite connection there's this ridiculous delay. So the way this works is that we have to pretend like we're using walkie-talkies—we take turns. Okay? Wait, don't answer yet. I'm going to stop and wait for you, but then you have to stop and wait for me. Okay, here goes: your turn."

There was total silence. That was another thing he couldn't get used to. The Internet phone sounded dead when nobody was talking. Seconds ticked by. He fought to keep from saying something.

Finally, Kaj's voice said, "Got it. No problem. Hey, you skinny Daniel Boone bastard. How are you hangin'? Fightin' off all those wild Indians? I hope you're enjoying your little vacation up there in the woods with Fels-babe. I haven't seen her around. You must be keeping her busy. Yuk, yuk. Your turn—over."

Carl sighed. Kaj was a good guy, but you wouldn't guess it listening to him. Fels didn't care for him, not least because he called her Fels-babe, and it was a testament to her open mind that she'd gotten him a job at GeneTrend. He cleaned cages and drove around on errands, but insisted that he was a lab technician.

"We're doing fine," Carl replied. "The only Indians we have to fight off are ghosts. Hey, you dummy, you know I have a ruined finger. I can't play anymore. Over to you."

Endless seconds later, Kaj replied, "I know that. I may be a dummy, but I'm not stupid. You and Fels-babe can still come as my guests. You can play a few tunes and maybe discover that you're just milking that bruised finger for pity. Get this: we might be playing Croce's. Your turn."

Carl was impressed. Croce's was a club owned by Jim Croce's widow, and was one of the top spots in San Diego. "You had to wait until I was gone to hit the big time. Sounds exciting. I'll talk to Fels about it. I haven't been into town in a while. I could use a bit of civilization to make sure I remember how to eat with utensils. Yours."

Silence, then, "Bitchin', you little whacker. Hot times in S-D. To you, dude."

"I assume you're at work. I hope nobody's listening to you. Over"

. . . "Ah, screw 'em. So, what else is up, man?"

"Not much. I guess you heard that Lilly is staying with us for a while. Over."

. . . "No kidding? So that's what happened to her. They said that they'd de-commissioned her. That's their code for sending her to the big ferret cage in the sky. Glad to hear it. I was getting fond of the old girl, and that's dangerous in this line of business where a lab animal's life span is measured in the numbers of brain operations they survive. Yours dude—uh, actually, I'd better go. Der Fuerer, Herr Riktler just walked in."

"Got it. You don't want Rik to catch you goofing off. Let me know about the gig. Over and out."

Carl closed the Internet-phone window and sat staring at the screen. He realized that when Rik had said not to tell anybody about Lilly, he probably meant *everybody*—even the employees of GeneTrend. It seemed that he may have goofed. Oh well, it was them that were doing Rik the favor. And, it was just a ferret.

The back door opened and Fels came in holding a very wet Lilly. "Have you completed my project schedule for me?"

He chuckled. "If you want me to. Leave it up to me, and I'll have you finished in a week. I was just checking email. You have a message from Joan."

"She just doesn't give up. What verses does she quote this time?"

"I didn't really read it. I just wanted to make sure there wasn't some family emergency."

Joan had been trying to get Fels back into the family fold for months. The verses Fels was talking about were selected Bible quotes presumably intended to trigger deep automatic responses of guilt and family duty. Instead, they only seemed to push Fels further away. Frankly, this was fine with Carl. Her Bible-thumping family made him nervous.

"Ha!" Fels snorted, rubbing Lilly down with the kitchen hand towel. "A family emergency would be if she was planning a vacation trip to visit us."

Carl smiled, but held his tongue. He went outside to pee, and when he came in, Fels was sitting at the computer reading Joan's message. Suddenly she stood up, sliding the chair back with a rattle, and strode off to the kitchen, where she started yanking bags of vegetables from the half-size refrigerator and tossing them on the counter in preparation for making dinner. The change of mood was not unexpected. Joan's communications rarely pleased her. She took a package of sausages out, but just stood staring at them. With one quick motion she slammed them on the counter and stormed out the back door. Carl caught a glimpse of tears.

Uh oh. That was not normal. Fels often got mad at Joan, but he'd never seen her cry. He went back to the computer, sat down, and read the message. Joan started by updating mundane family news, finally getting around to the poke. This time, she hit below the belt:

> *Pappa held another vigil prayer last night, beseeching Christ for mercy on your mortal soul. Here's the scripture that he chose.*
>> *"He has put my family far from me, and my acquaintances are wholly estranged from me. My relatives and my close friends have failed me."*
>> *Job 19:13*
>> *" 'Sirs, what must I do to be saved?' They answered, 'Put your trust in the Lord Jesus, and you will be saved, you and your household.' "*

> *Acts 16:30*
> *"A church leader must be able to manage his own family well and make his children obey him with all respect."*
> *1 Timothy 3:4*
> *Fels, Satan's powers are to be feared. A mortal consort can be a door for drawing down other souls. His guile is irresistible without surrender to our Lord's grace. I pray for your strength in finding your way back to Christ, and know that we will forgive you. I pray that our Lord will also find forgiveness for losses beyond reconciling, no matter how terrible.*

Carl sat back and whistled. "What a bitch," he muttered. Fels's fundamentalist family members were masters at passive-aggressive language. And like so many self-righteous driving their evangelical campaigns, they could arrange scripture quotes to say anything they liked. It reminded him of cutting out words from newspapers to create anonymous messages. He'd gotten used to it, though, and had become adept at deciphering encoded meanings. Joan had basically said:

1) by leaving the family, you're making Papa (church leader) look like he's not doing his job in God's eyes;

2) in doing so, you're jeopardizing the salvation of the entire family;

3) in fact, you've gone to bed with the devil (not sure what that implied about him), and thus had allowed old Beelzebub to snatch Tod down to hell.

The last part was the meaning behind *a door for drawing down other souls*, and *find forgiveness for losses beyond reconciling*. He was sure of it.

Fels could weather warnings about her own loss of salvation, and even howls that she was damning her parents and siblings, but to imply, to even hint, that Fels had damned little Tod to hell, well that was something beyond even God's forgiveness.

No question; Joan was one bitch.

He went outside, and heard Fels crying. It was coming from around the west side of the cabin where they'd set a bench against the wall to watch the sunsets. As he came around the corner, she lifted her head, and he saw that her eyes were red.

"Leave me alone," she yelled and buried her head again in her arms.

He hesitated only a moment before retreating. His heart cried out to her, and his impulse was to run and comfort his wife, but he knew from experience that she wanted to be alone for a good cry. He suspected that she might simply be embarrassed, but he never had the nerve to ask.

Back inside, he reread Joan's message and fantasized about the different methods he might use to strangle her. Then with a sigh, he went to the laundry room to fold some shirts he'd hung there to dry the day before. The bench outside was next to the window, and he worked quietly, listening. He heard a few sniffs and the brattle of Fels blowing her nose, and then he heard her call out a snuffled hello.

Wondering if he'd heard correctly, he went out to the Great Hall to find Defoe coming to the door. Behind him was a young teenage boy shuffling along with his hands jammed deep into baggy pants.

"Let me guess," Carl said, opening the door for his tousled friend. "You never made it past our property line last night."

"It was a close call," Defoe replied, "and a most tempting alternative to a trek towards home quarters, but I persevered and slept soundly in my own bed."

Carl held out his arm to usher them in, and the boy gave him a quick glance through coal-dark eyes as he loped past. Longish hair, shiny in its absolute blackness, coordinated with a dark complexion to divulge a long ancestry of sun dwellers.

Defoe introduced his companion as Toby, Sam's grandson from Louisiana.

Carl stared blankly, trying to guess who he meant until it finally came to him that he meant Sam from the gas station—the Indian.

"Sure! Sam talked about you," he said to Toby. "He told us you were coming out to visit . . . and here you are!"

Carl refrained from explaining that old Sam had claimed this so often that everyone assumed it was one of those personal dreams that are repeated in the hope that it might someday come true.

"Toby and his mother are here on vacation," Defoe explained. "She's driven down to Mexico for a day or two. She had heard that Sam and I were friends."

Meaning, Carl thought, that Defoe had become a babysitter for the interim.

Fels came in, forcing a passable smile. Her eyes were still red and puffy, but Defoe pretended that nothing was amiss. After introductions, Lilly ambled out from the bedroom looking sleepy, and soon she and Toby were playing a spirited game of hide-and-seek.

"Showing him around all the wide lands his ancestors *used* to own?" Carl asked as the three adults sat down to tea. He glanced quickly at the boy who seemed not to have heard, realizing it was probably an insensitive remark.

Defoe nodded, "That; and visiting Tekumewa."

"You showed him the site?"

"Sam made me promise. I never thought it would ever happen. Normally Toby's mother would have shown him, but Sam's relocation to Louisiana broke the long mother-son tradition."

"You make a fine surrogate Indian mom," Fels offered, seeming to finally come alive again.

Defoe gave a little bow. "We invoked a Temesaa ritual."

"Let me guess," Carl said. "You tried to raise Tekumewa from the dead."

He was only kidding, but Toby looked up quickly, and Defoe just grinned.

"You can't be serious," Carl objected, looking to Fels for confirmation that their neighbor had cashed in his sanity chips. She just shrugged, though, as if to suggest they should listen to what he had to say.

"Bringing the dead back to life," Defoe explained, "is, of course, not possible. We simply asked that his spirit visit us so that we could honor him. The Kumeyaay believe that by doing this, you can avoid the dead haunting you."

"I didn't realize that this would be a problem after two hundred years."

"I said that this was a Kumeyaay belief, not necessarily mine."

"So why the ritual, then?"

"I mean," Defoe elaborated, "that I don't necessarily subscribe to the haunting part. It's just too tempting to blame difficult problems on the dead who aren't there to defend themselves. In any case, I don't see how harassing the living serves the dead."

"Wait a second, you don't believe that the dead come back to haunt us, but you do believe that they can be brought back by this ritual?"

"It's not quite as easy as you make it sound. The ritual has to be performed by a blood descendant, and the dead person is not brought back, just their spirit."

"So, you do believe it."

"Belief is not required. It happened."

Chapter 5

"You *saw* Tekumewa?" Carl squeaked.

Defoe smiled like a parent might when asked if a sawhorse is made from a real horse. "If spiritual regeneration were that obvious, there wouldn't be debate about the subject."

Toby had tired of playing with Lilly and had quietly taken the fourth seat at the table. The boy's shyness was almost uncomfortable for others, as though any attempt to converse would bring pain.

"Toby," Defoe continued, "how did your august ancestor manifest himself?"

Sam's grandson shrugged, studied his hand a moment, and then without looking up, said, "A coyote."

It was the first words Toby had uttered, and Carl was struck by the softness of his voice. He was about to make a joke about Wiley Coyote and roadrunners, but held his tongue in respect for the boy's potentially fragile personality. Instead he asked, "What did he do . . . the coyote, I mean?"

Toby shrugged again. The gesture seemed an introduction to each response. "He spoke."

"With words?" Carl asked, unable to hide his incredulity. "In English?"

"Of course not," Defoe cut in. "A coyote can't form words. This fellow advanced from the trees and spoke to us in coyote."

"Coyotes have a language?"

"Naturally. Yips, whines, barks—you've heard them plenty of times."

"I have. And I think that's exactly the point."

"You're not thinking. This coyote *approached* us, and besides, they're never out and about making a ruckus during the day."

"I've heard them."

"Rarely."

Like, once a week, Carl thought, but he didn't want to argue about it. "How close did this possessed coyote come to you?"

Toby and Defoe answered at the same time. Toby said, "A hundred yards," and Defoe said, "A hundred feet."

Carl grinned as Defoe waved it off and defended with, "The point is that coyotes normally avoid people."

"Maybe this one was rabid," Carl offered. "You should have run away."

Defoe sighed dramatically and looked knowingly at Toby while flicking his thumb at Carl. "Some people hide inside skeptical boxes and caulk them with logic." The old man winked at Toby and said to Carl and Fels, "Kumeyaay tradition requires that the family of the deceased cut their hair short as a sign of grieving. Toby refused, however."

"Defoe!" Fels admonished. "You didn't try to cut Toby's hair!"

"I only suggested."

"He also wanted me to eat a poisonous plant," Toby added, grinning. He was obviously happy in the middle of the repartee.

"Jimsonweed," Defoe explained with exaggerated dignity. "The Kumeyaay call it tolvaach, and the kuseyaay—the shaman—reserves exclusive use for spiritual insight. However, boys participating in the coming of age ceremony are allowed one experience in order to choose their life's path."

Fels's brow was scrunched in dismay. "Defoe! Shame on you! That could have been dangerous, giving Toby a hallucinogenic drug."

Defoe grinned and held up his hand to fend off her attack. "I didn't give the plant to the boy, and yes, it is extremely dangerous. The difference in dosage between a proper hallucination and death from overdose is too small to challenge, lacking a full-blown death wish."

Fels nodded knowingly, guessing that he'd just been playing with her. "Did the coyote walk upright like a man?"

"Ah!" Defoe exclaimed, as though expecting just this remark. "You are referring to a common Indian belief that returning spirits manifest in just such a manner. The animal did indeed lift himself on his hind legs and was about to walk when a . . . small disturbance interrupted the delicate multi-dimensional balance."

"Mr. Defoe got excited and fell down," Toby explained. "He scared the coyote away."

"Toby," Defoe said sternly, "I am nobody's master."

"I . . . I . . ." the boy stammered. He appeared crestfallen at the sudden turn.

"Don't worry." Carl reassured. "The old goat is just teasing you. He means he doesn't want to be called 'Mister.' He's just trying to steer the conversation away from his clumsy fall."

Turning to Defoe, he said, "So, Master Defoe, what about it?"

His friend lifted his chin high and replied, "Advancing age and accompanying loss of balance may be an easy target for the young and nimble, but time waits for no man, and the day will come when you too will have your turn at the whipping post."

"Boohoo. Somebody hand me a handkerchief. You seem to muster up enough balance to stumble your way here once a day for tea and cake."

"Which only demonstrates the superb quality of dear Felicity's cake."

She laughed. "The cake that I take off the grocery shelf, you mean." She studied Toby a moment, and then asked, "Do you believe in ghosts?"

He shrugged. "I don't know. Maybe."

Carl guessed that Fels was trying to draw him out again. Toby, on the other hand, was hedging his bet, waiting to see what the adults around him thought about the subject.

She nodded knowingly. "I saw one once—at least I thought I did."

"Really?" Toby said. "Out there?" He waved vaguely towards the window. "In the woods?"

"Oh no. This was years ago when I was even younger than you. A friend loaned me a book about ghosts. One story was about a little girl, just like me, who kept seeing a ghost in her bedroom, but nobody else ever saw it. She finally figured out that the ghost could only be seen by, and therefore haunt, people who believed in it. So she made herself not believe in it, and it went away. I couldn't understand that part. I could buy a ghost, but I couldn't swallow that she'd be able to just stop believing *after* she'd seen it."

"What about yours?"

"My ghost? Oh, I did just the opposite. The girl in the story got rid of hers by not believing; I kept thinking that maybe there are ghosts all around us, but we only see them when we believe in them. This scared me and I tried to stop thinking about it, but of course that only made me think about it more—all the time, in fact. I'd lie awake in bed at night wondering if they were right there in the room with me until one night I finally saw one."

Carl had been watching Toby. At first, the boy had kept his guard up, but now he watched Fels with rapt attention. "What'd it look like?" Toby asked.

"A man. No colors—all gray and white. He just stood there motionless, watching me."

"What did you do?"

"I screamed."

"And then he went away?"

It seemed to Carl that Toby wanted this to be the case, that you could make a ghost go away.

"Sort of. It woke up my father, and he got mad at me. He explained that the ghost that I thought I saw was just my imagination, that I had made it up in my mind. In a way, his anger saved me."

"He was mad because you woke him up?"

"Not so much that . . . my family is very religious. To my father, the idea of ghosts is blasphemous. When I showed him the book, he burned it."

"But, it wasn't even yours!"

"Oh, that didn't matter. In his mind, he was helping save my friend from Satan."

Toby nodded slowly, thinking about this. "Did it ever come back? The ghost?"

Carl noted that he didn't ask if she'd seen it again, but whether it had come back.

"No. My father's anger was much stronger than any ghost."

Carl noticed that Toby had been rocking from side to side in his chair, as though the cabin was actually a boat riding a rough sea.

He looked down and saw that Lilly was trying to play. She batted Toby's shoelaces as he moved his feet around, idly keeping her occupied. The ferret suddenly sprang back a couple of feet, arched her back as though on the verge of a seizure, and then began hopping back and forth like some kind of cartoon character. This was the same behavior she'd exhibited under the hose earlier. Carl wondered if there was something wrong with the animal's brain. Maybe Rik had broken something, poking around in there. Kaj had said that the test animal's lives were measured by the number of brain operations they survived—perhaps Lilly had lost the game of Russian roulette after all.

"What's wrong with it?" Toby asked in a whisper.

"I'm not sure," Carl replied. "Maybe it just—"

Without warning, Lilly shot off and dove under the sofa. A second later her head popped out the other side, and she shot across the room again, this time disappearing behind the kitchen counter.

"It's called a war dance," Defoe explained. "Ferrets can get themselves excited to the point of nonsensical behavior. They appear drunk, and in a way they are—with joy."

"Well—" Carl started to say, but saw the look on Fels's face. It was a look both of recognition and apprehension. "What's up, hon?"

She shook her head as though clearing it. "That dance. Something about it looked just like what Tod used to do . . ."

Silence filled the Great Hall for a few seconds until Toby asked, "Who's Tod?"

Carl was afraid that he'd have to provide an answer, but Fels finally replied, "Tod was my little nephew. He was killed . . . he was run over by a car."

Toby's smile evaporated. "I, uh—" he glanced quickly at Defoe for guidance, but the philosopher just raised one eyebrow. This was one of those hurdles he would have to learn to negotiate by himself. "I'm sorry," the boy finally said.

Defoe nodded. Sometimes a sorry is all there is.

Fels stared into the distance, concentrating, or maybe just remembering. "It was a game we'd play when I would baby-sit," she said without looking at them. "I'd set his mom's exercise

50

trampoline next to the sofa, and then I'd hold his hand as he jumped back and forth between them just like Lilly was doing . . . until he fell one day and hit his head. He was sad that we had to quit after that. He said, 'Aunt Fels, it was the most happiest thing I ever done.' Ever since then I've wondered . . ."

They looked down at their hands as she wiped her eyes.

"I always protected him," she went on, crying as she talked. "Sometimes," she said, smiling and crying at the same time, "he ran to me instead of his own mom when he was hurt or in trouble."

She took a deep breath, as though determined to get through this. "At first—after we stopped doing the bouncy-game—I felt guilty, since it was his happiest thing ever, but now . . ."

She choked down a sob and struggled to continue against the rending memory. "Now I wonder if his fall somehow dulled his reflexes and . . . and—oh, excuse me!" she cried and ran into the bedroom, slamming the door behind her as though this might barricade against a reality impossible to accept.

Defoe appeared to be pained at her grief, and Toby just looked shocked at an adult exhibiting such emotion. Carl didn't know what to say. Most of her confession was new to him.

"And then there are ghosts," Defoe said, "that haunt us within our own skulls. No father's anger can rid *their* burden."

"What did she mean about his reflexes?" Toby asked in a hushed voice, as though she might be listening at the bedroom door.

"I think," Carl explained, "that she means that she's worried that Tod's fall may have somehow damaged his brain so that he . . . I guess she's worried that he might have gotten out of the way of the car if he hadn't fallen."

He didn't finish to the conclusion, which was that her nephew's death, in that case, would be substantially her fault.

"I'm sure it's not true," Carl continued. "She's still coping, and well, sort of not thinking clearly."

He didn't know if he was trying to reassure Toby or himself. He was confident, though, that Tod's fall had not contributed to his death. As he understood it, Tod didn't have a chance once he found himself in the path of the hurtling mass of metal.

Silence hung in the Great Hall, waiting to be displaced. Carl resorted to the first conversation subject ever invented. "They say that the weather in southern California will be extra dry this year."

"Toby," Defoe said, "as a recent inductee to junior high school, can you tell us what was wrong with that statement?"

The boy blushed and shrugged.

"The subject lacks an antecedent," Defoe declared.

Toby seemed even more flustered.

"I think," Carl said, "that Mr. College Professor may be trying to say that I didn't explain who the 'they' are that made the weather prediction. It's painful for him to come right out and ask it in plain English."

Defoe lifted his chin. "I challenge you to express it in fewer words."

"Okay, 'Who are they?' How's that?"

His friend pursed his lips and nodded slowly. "Touché. And the answer is . . . ?"

Carl rolled his eyes. "NPR. There, are you happy? 'They' said it's not clear yet if we're headed for a La Niña condition."

"Well, there's no better 'they' than NPR."

"Was that supposed to be sarcastic?"

"Not at all. I trust the folks in public broadcasting as much as I trust anybody who's paid to present news. But this means, of course, that Felicity is going to be even more resolved that you to finish clearing the fire buffer zone."

"It's pretty much done."

"Really? What about that mountain of dried limbs? Or the fact that your house sits in the middle of a field of logs? You are essentially a marshmallow suspended in the center of a giant's campfire just waiting for the match to be struck."

"Those logs wouldn't burn. The wood's still green."

"Then why did you cut them down in the first place?"

"Look, whose side are you on?"

"I am always on the side of grace, charm, and beauty."

"What do you think, Toby? Is he describing me?"

Sam's grandson had recovered from the adult curve balls and was smiling again at the sparring. "Maybe if he leaves out the beauty part."

"Which still leaves grace and charm. I'll fold my card hand and walk away with those winnings."

"And speaking of walking," Defoe declared, getting to his feet, "we should be going. I promised Toby that we'd drive down to town and catch a BBC mini-series version of *Crime and Punishment* playing tonight only at the North Park Theatre."

"You said we were going to Sea World!" Toby cried in dismay.

"Did I? How foolish of me. What can we possibly learn from dolphins and whales held in captivity and forced to perform tricks for their sustenance?"

"Don't worry, Toby," Carl said, seeing them out. "Old Goat is teasing you again."

Turning to face him at the door, Defoe placed his hand on his chest. "Sir, you have not only forsworn your beauty, you have now also forfeited grace and charm."

Carl nodded agreeably. "It's worth it to be free of you, you mental sadist."

He closed the door and stood a moment, then sighed and walked to the bedroom.

ж ж ж

The next morning Carl woke to the click and clatter of Fels typing a storm on the computer. She had spent the previous afternoon working away, and had then gone to bed right after dinner. They hadn't talked much after Defoe and Toby left. He'd mostly just held her close until she was done crying. He suspected that the concentrated work was an escape from her grief and guilt, but since she billed by the hour, her torment translated into increased family revenue. Yin and Yang. Balance of the universe. Economic gain in exchange for personal devastation.

They were supposed to have gone off the grid to escape that wheel.

He avoided disturbing her when she was working, and so, after a breakfast of coffee and a power-bar, he went outside. The late June sun was already hot, and surveying the expanse of giant pick-up stick logs, he decided that the chainsaw would make too much noise anyway. Instead, he worked on the solar panels. The array was mounted on the southern half of the roof, and consisted of twenty panels, each delivering an average of about fifty Watts. In the summer, the panels delivered over eight kilowatt-hours to the batteries each day. This was plenty to power the computer, lights, and small refrigerator, with enough left over for blasting the stereo when Fels was away. They had to forego other appliances with motors and/or heating elements: dishwasher, clothes dryer, toaster-oven, bathroom fan. They'd considered a small microwave oven, but finally decided against it, more on principle than power draw. Had he still played, his guitar tube amp would probably have been contraband.

He climbed the ladder attached to the roof. It wasn't really necessary to adjust the angles of the panels since they already supplied more power than they used and they had no means to store extra. He loved fiddling with the panels, though. He'd become enamored with the whole idea of capturing sun-juice to fuel their simplified lives—for free! Well, sort of. They'd calculated that the solar power system would pay for itself in about ten years of use, based on current electricity fees from the utilities. Carl checked the rates every month, hoping they'd continue to go up along with the price of oil. In this way, their system would reach zero-balance sooner.

When he climbed down, he saw Fels through the window. She was sitting on the sofa. He went inside and found her holding Lilly in her lap. She was talking softly to the pliant ferret. She looked up at him, and Carl knew immediately that something was up. Her eyes were bright with some enchantment. She looked just like she did when they used to get high together.

"Lilly's an angel," she said, cupping the ferret reverently in her two palms.

Carl nodded slowly, wondering where she was going with this. "Sure . . . when she's not being a devil."

He was thinking of the morning before when he'd found her with a baby rabbit in her mouth. He hadn't told Fels about that one yet.

She scrunched her brow in annoyance. "No. I mean she's really an angel." She tilted the ferret's head up and gazed into its eyes.

"An angel," he repeated. "For real."

She nodded without looking up.

"How did you figure that out?"

She finally looked at him, and her eyes were now serious. "She was sent by Tod."

Carl's heart stopped. The implication and what it suggested about her mind, was terrifying.

After a few seconds of frozen time, she turned her attention back to Lilly.

"Where's her wings?" he asked, walking slowly to the sofa. He didn't mean to sound sarcastic. He just didn't know what to say.

"I didn't expect you to believe," Fels replied. She had that tone where he wasn't sure if she was angry with him or hurt. "All you have to do, though, is open your eyes."

He sat down next to her, and Lilly squirmed away from Fels to smell his hands. "I want to understand, hon, but you have to help me. Tell me why you think that Lilly is an angel . . . sent by Tod."

"Can't you feel it? The energy? She just radiates peace and harmony."

He didn't remind her that she'd just admonished him to open his eyes, presumably to see, not feel. "Fels. Honestly, all I feel from Lilly is ferret energy. She just wants to eat, sleep, and snoop around and get into trouble."

"But don't you see?" she insisted, twisting around to face him. "You're describing Tod!"

"Uh, you think Lilly . . . *is* Tod?"

He felt a hard, heavy lump in his stomach at the idea that Fels believed this.

"No! Of course not. Do you think I'm crazy?"

Carl bit his tongue.

"She's just a messenger," she went on. "An angel sent by God to reassure me that Tod is in heaven."

"Um, I thought that Tod sent her."

"Don't make fun of me. You know what I mean."

He was afraid that he did. "Has Lilly . . . talked to you?"

"Carl Mason, just stop it! I won't sit here and let you make fun of me!"

He held up his hands as if to ward off a physical attack. "Sorry! Fels, honey, I'm really, really trying to understand. Please help me."

She studied him a moment and then sighed and took his hand in hers. "I'm sorry, honey. I know this must sound nutty. You are a sweetheart for trying to understand. I just know for sure that Lilly is an angel from God. I started to understand yesterday—"

"The war dance!"

He remembered that it had reminded her of Tod.

"That's what Defoe called it, but he didn't know Tod. You did, though. Don't you see him in Lilly?"

Carl looked at the Ferret. The beady eyes peered at him, and the nose sniffed for some telltale clue of food. "Sure, hon. I know what you mean."

"You do see Tod in Lilly?"

The line of truth was thin and precarious. "I, uh, understand what you're saying."

She sighed, placed Lilly on his lap, and got to her feet. "I have to get back to work."

She went to the desk and jiggled the mouse to bring the computer out of sleep mode. "I know for a fact that it's Tod communicating with me," she added as she sat down.

For a fact, he thought. Facts seemed to come easily. Just believe.

Chapter 6

"Fantasies can be coping mechanisms!" Defoe yelled above the idling chainsaw as he kicked aside the next in an endless series of foot-thick slabs Carl was slicing off. "They allow our conscious minds to temporarily step away from reality in order to give our subconscious a chance to get a grip."

This was only the second log that day, and at this rate, Carl thought, it would be months before he got through the killing field of massacred pine trees. The conversation slowed down progress, but at the moment he didn't mind, as his arm ached from holding the gas-powered saw. He turned off the beast, and the silence rang in his ears. "What if the subconscious can't get a grip?"

He lay down the saw and helped Defoe roll the pine slab farther out of the way. It was surprising how heavy the wood cheese wheels were—hard to believe for something that floats.

Ignoring the fresh sap, his friend sat on the new makeshift stool and mopped his brow. "In that case," he replied, "I guess that's called insanity. But I'm sure this is not the case with Felicity."

"You're sure, eh? Would that be a belief, or a fact?"

The philosopher sighed. "You're right. I was feigning authority for your benefit. Let me re-phrase that and say that I am confident in Felicity's sanity. I have never heard of a pathologically delusional state reaching such a sustained mode so quickly, but I am no psychiatrist."

"You talk like one."

"That's because they also like to use big words. Give her a chance, Carl. Let her rest inside her waking dream a bit. Perhaps this is what she needs to heal from this grief."

"It scares me, Defoe. What if every minute she hides inside this delusion, it's taking her farther down a dark path? What if she goes down this path so far that she can't find her way back? I'm telling you, it scares the shit out of me."

His friend sighed again, this time in resignation. "I believe that you are wrong, but I respect your wish. I'll have a talk with her."

Carl placed his hand on his friend's shoulder. "Thanks. I know she has a lot of respect for you."

It came to him how much respect he also had for the old goat. It would be difficult finding someone with greater intelligence and integrity.

A sudden, excited yip drew their attention. It came from below the hill, north of them. Lilly bounded into view, and hard on her tail was a scraggly and determined coyote. Just when the predator seemed about to snatch the ferret up in its jaws, Lilly leaped onto the trunk of a tree at the edge of the clearing and scampered up to safety. The frustrated coyote growled and leaped about, while Lilly watched calmly from the lowest branch. She then looked up, straight at the two men standing a hundred feet away.

"Hey!" Carl yelled running towards the tree and waving his arms. "Get out of here!"

As if noticing the humans for the first time, the coyote backed away, snarling, then turned and slunk away. Lilly watched it for a minute until it was out of sight before stepping down into Carl's waiting hands.

"That was a close one, girl," he said. "Fels will kill me if I let you get eaten. I may have to keep you in the house."

He doubted that was actually possible.

Defoe arrived, breathing heavily.

"The damn coyotes are getting bold," Carl observed. "They're not even bothered by the sound of the chainsaw."

"At least this one," Defoe added. "Perhaps Tekumewa is hungry."

Carl glanced at his friend. "You're kidding, right?"

"When am I not?"

Carl snorted. "The goal of philosophers is to answer a question by never actually answering the question."

"You're catching on. In this way one's answer is never wrong. So why do you think Lilly waited to climb a tree?"

"Huh?" He hadn't thought about it, but she came into view some seconds after they'd heard the coyote's yip—plenty of time for her to climb a closer tree. "Maybe she was caught by surprise, and didn't have time to—"

He remembered the look she'd given him after she was safely on the limb. "I know why. She wanted to make sure we saw her. She wanted us to chase the coyote away!"

Defoe considered this doubtfully. "That attributes quite a degree of intelligence."

His friend was right. It was tempting to assume human thinking in animals.

"On the other hand," Defoe mulled, "Lilly's behavior could be explained if she really were an angel."

"Ha! If she were an angel, I don't think she would have been running from a coyote."

"What should she have done? Miraculously sprouted wings and flown away? The Catholic Church recognizes quite a complicated menagerie of angel classes: a nine-tiered hierarchy, in fact. It is commonly believed that an angel manifesting on Earth takes on the form of the mission to be fulfilled. In Lilly's case, why should we expect her to have physical powers beyond that of the animal that—"

"Hey!" Carl shouted.

Defoe looked at him in surprise. "What's wrong?"

"You're doing it."

"Doing what?"

"Don't give me that innocent look. I promised myself that I was going to cut up four logs today, and I'm not going to let your intellectual masturbation get in the way."

He took Lilly inside, came back, and picked up the chainsaw.

"A lesser man would be wounded by such raw imagery," Defoe objected, pouting.

"A lesser man might also be more enthusiastic about working."

Carl yanked the cord on the saw and it roared to life. A moment later he stopped it again. "Besides," he added, "there's no such thing as angels."

He yanked the cord again without waiting for a response and lay the blade down against the log, letting loose a blizzard of sawdust.

Ж Ж Ж

Carl didn't make his four logs by the time Fels arrived home from San Diego. After the third log, he and Defoe had taken a short tea break that had escalated into a long discussion about why voters always split very nearly fifty-fifty for presidential elections, and from there had combusted into a full-blown argument about whether the Republican Party had squandered the patriotic loyalties of Americans and broken the back of military morale. When he finally closed the debate down and got back to work, he was amazed that he'd been defending the Republicans. That's the way it was with Defoe. The man could maneuver you into arguing that the only way to cure your headache was with a lobotomy.

At least they were outside, working, when Fels pulled up. She didn't even ask how much progress he'd made, and so he chalked up the day's work as successful. He started putting together a dinner of turkey hotdogs and fried potatoes while she made tea and sat down at the table with Defoe. Lilly lolled on her lap, and Fels included the animal in the conversation, as though the ferret understood perfectly but maybe had a bad case of laryngitis.

Defoe leaned back in the chair and clasped his hands behind his head. "Carl tells me that Lilly's an angel," he said, one eyebrow raised.

Fels shot Carl an expectant look as he covered the pan to let the hotdogs and potatoes simmer for a few more minutes. "You believe it?" she asked him instead of responding directly to Defoe.

"No!" Carl exclaimed.

He wondered why Defoe would say that. The old fart leaned forward and sat looking at him with his elbows resting on the table, the fingers of each hand touching the other, forming a teepee. Carl realized that his friend was probably setting the stage.

"Oh, excuse me," Defoe said to Fels. "I guess it is your belief that Lilly is an angel."

"It's not a belief; it's a fact," she replied, adamantly.

"A fact," Defoe repeated, nodding with interest. "You probably have some evidence?"

Carl realized that Defoe had placed Fels in a defensive position with that little twist of fabricated miscommunication without coming across as adversarial.

"Enough," she replied.

"Such as?"

Fels looked flustered. "Lilly is not a normal ferret."

Defoe nodded again, encouraging her to go on.

"Lilly's . . ." She looked down at the ferret in her lap. "Lilly's clearly special."

"I agree," Defoe said. "But how does that make her an angel?"

She met the old philosopher's gaze a minute. "Lilly's way too smart for a normal animal," she finally offered.

"Lilly is indeed very intelligent."

He just looked at her.

Fels glanced from Defoe to Carl. "You set this up, didn't you?"

Shit! "You have to admit. It sounds crazy!"

"Sounding crazy doesn't make it crazy. They thought Galileo was crazy too, you know."

Yeah, Carl thought, *and crazy is, as crazy does.*

"Carl Mason," she accused, "you have been conspiring against me. You've betrayed my trust. Excuse me, Defoe, but I'm sure you know what I mean."

Their friend nodded sheepishly. He even blushed.

"Fels," Carl pleaded, wiping his hands and coming to the table, "I'm sorry. But, you have to look at it from my perspective."

"You do think I'm crazy, don't you?"

The truth? Not now. "Honey, I think that you've had a lot on your mind lately, and maybe you just need to slow down and not jump to conclusions."

She didn't answer. Instead, she placed Lilly on the floor, got up, went to the stove, and dished out portions onto a plate. Balancing the plate on one hand, she went to the refrigerator, took out a soda, and then headed for the door.

"Where are you going?" he asked.

Without looking back, she replied, "I'm going out to enjoy the evening air. Come on, Lilly."

She struggled to open the door with the soda in her hand, and then almost tripped as the ferret scampered out ahead of her. She closed the door behind her with her elbow and it slammed shut just loudly enough to make her point: he and Defoe were not welcome.

"That wasn't exactly successful," Defoe observed.

"What do you mean? We got rid of her, didn't we? Now maybe we can eat in peace."

"Is that what you really think?"

Carl sighed. "Hell no. I feel like ripping my intestines out and hanging myself with them."

His friend nodded approvingly. "Excellent imagery."

ж ж ж

Carl pecked out Rik's number on the cell phone and held it to his ear. He gazed idly at the community bulletin board on the front wall of the market. In an age of monster.com and craigslist, the announcements, neatly printed out on index cards, seemed quaint: fill dirt for sale; woman seeking a carpool to El Cajon; lost pet named Coydog. Barely a forty-five minute drive from San Diego, the market building nestled peacefully among the Oaks, apparently oblivious to the universe of cyberspace. Of course, that's why they had relocated up here.

It had taken over an hour and a half to walk here, but he wasn't going to trust this call to the unwieldy Internet phone service. He'd found adequate reception a quarter-mile back, but he'd decided to come all the way and have a soda while he thought about how much to explain.

"Hello," he heard Rik say. "Fels?"

"Uh, no. This is Carl." Fels sometimes called her boss on the phone, and her name was probably in his contact list.

The barest pause, then, "Carl! What's up? Is Lilly okay?"

"Oh yeah, she loves it up here. She likes to tease the coyotes."

"What? You let her outside?"

He sounded alarmed, maybe even angry.

"Not much," Carl lied. "Only when we're there to supervise her."

He didn't mention that she came and went as she pleased, and there probably wasn't a thing he could do about it anyway.

"Well, what's up, then? I have a meeting in a few minutes."

"Right. Uh, it's hard to explain, but I was . . . well I was wondering if you could sort of talk to Fels."

"What about?"

This was tough. He didn't want to jeopardize her position there, but he didn't know where else to turn. They'd promised Rik that they wouldn't tell anybody about Lilly, and he was afraid that if Fels didn't come to her senses soon, she'd be spending her days in a sanitarium, and in that case she wouldn't be working anyway.

"She's been having a difficult time with the loss of her nephew," he finally said.

"That was a while ago—last year."

"Yes, but they were close. She's still struggling with it."

"Okay. What can I do to help?"

He seemed impatient, anxious to get off to his meeting. The tone implied he doubted there was anything he *could* do to help.

"It, uh, involves Lilly."

"Lilly? How so?"

That got his attention.

"This is going to sound a little nutty, but you have to understand that Fels grew up in a very religious family."

"I know that; I've met her parents. So what? Look, what's up with Lilly? Are you sure she's okay?"

"Lilly's fine; it's Fels who's in trouble."

Crap. He'd wanted to downplay the problem. He wanted Rik to think Fels was one hundred percent on the job.

"Okay—what do you want from me?"

To hell with it; cut to the chase. "Here it is: Fels thinks that Lilly is . . . well, an angel."

"An angel—what the devil are you talking about?"

If Carl wasn't so nervous, he would have made some joke about throwing the devil in with an angel. "Fels thinks that an angel has manifested in Lilly. She believes that it's come to comfort her and let her know that her nephew is in heaven."

"Christ!"

Rik was angry. Was it because he was worried that she wouldn't be able to do her job? Or, did he just not want to be bothered?

"Look," the genetics engineer went on tersely, "Fels is working from home tomorrow. I'll come up after noon."

Carl didn't know what to say. He'd figured that Rik would sit Fels down in his office for ten minutes, not take a whole afternoon to deal with this. The phone made a beep. "Rik? Hello?"

His last hope to help Fels had hung up. Carl slowly folded the cell phone and started his six-mile hike back home.

Ж Ж Ж

Carl wasn't sure at first what to tell Fels the next day. If she was sane, then she would understand his concern and actions, and if she wasn't, well in that case the truth wasn't necessarily relevant. He decided that, nuts or not, she trusted him, and he wasn't going to lie to her. So he told her the truth.

Nuts or not, she did not understand and she went ballistic. After ten minutes of verbal lashings, including accusations that he knew she would later claim were merely hyperboles, she yanked her jacket and hat off the rack and declared that she was "going for a walk to decide if I can live in the same house with you." When she picked up Lilly, he started to explain that it wouldn't look good if Rik arrived and the ferret wasn't safely inside, but stopped in mid-sentence when she threw him a look that nearly singed his eyelashes.

So much for Fels getting in some billable hours at home. He knew he should go out and attack a couple of logs, but it was chilly out there and he had the whole day. Besides, it would be better to be out there working after Fels got back. He felt guilty about that thought, but not enough to drive him outside.

He sat down at the computer and checked in on the news, and then, on a whim, Googled "ferret," and "war dance." Sure enough, a multitude of sites featured articles on the animal, all of them including inspired descriptions of the war dance, or "happy dance." This was apparently a universal phenomenon of this particular member of the weasel family.

Defoe was right. Lilly was just doing what ferret's do. On one hand it was a relief to have confirmation that the world was what he'd always thought it to be and not breached by the unpredictable meddlings of supernatural beings. On the other hand, though, the information was a new row of nails in the coffin of Fels's fantasy.

With both Fels and Lilly gone, the cabin was quiet as only a homestead miles from other humans can be. He reached down and pulled up on the lever under the high-tech executive chair so that he could recline back, lifting his feet onto the edge of the desk. Yes indeedee. Life in the woods. This was how it was meant to be.

He woke to the sound of voices approaching outside. He heard Fels's voice, and then recognized Rik's. They were talking about work. Fels must have happened upon her boss out on the road.

His feet suddenly slipped off the desk, and he almost fell out of the chair as he scrambled to gain his composure. He felt like he'd been caught by the teacher. The computer monitor still displayed an article about ferrets. He fumbled with the mouse to return to the main Google page just as the door opened and Fels walked in, followed by Rik. He looked at them, and Fels just shook her head as she walked to the kitchen. "Have a nice comfy nap?" she asked.

"How did you . . . I was . . . okay, I did. I had a great nap. Hi, Rik."

He realized that the back of the chair was still almost horizontal. Good clue, there.

Rik nodded a hello and sat at the table.

Well, this was uncomfortable. How to start?

He didn't have to.

"I'm sorry Carl made you come all the way up here for nothing," Fels said to Rik.

"Wait a second!" Carl cried. "It was his idea—"

"It's okay," Rik assured. "I wanted to check to see how Lilly was doing anyway. Where'd she go?"

Fels had been carrying the ferret when she came in, but Lilly had already disappeared.

"She'll come out eventually," Fels replied. "She's probably just not used to you anymore."

Carl looked at Fels in surprise. She was talking about Lilly as though the ferret was nothing more than a ferret. Fels gave him a quick, hard look. *Don't blow this*, it said.

Rik studied Fels a few seconds, and then glanced at Carl before saying to her, "So, what's this about Lilly being an angel?"

She shook her head in annoyance. "Carl is overreacting."

Rik eyed her some more. "So you don't think she's an angel, then?"

Her brow wrinkled in consternation and she glanced around as though afraid that Lilly would hear what she was about to say. "Not like Carl probably told you."

"What do you think then?"

Fels's mouth tightened into a thin line. She idly fingered a washcloth that lay on the counter before replying. "My religious beliefs are my business and I shouldn't have to be interrogated about them, but I know that Lilly is a ferret, an animal."

Carl noted that she also hadn't specifically said that Lilly was *not* an angel.

If Rik had caught this dodge, he didn't let on. "You understand that Lilly is not an ordinary lab specimen, either. She was selected for her intelligence."

Fels's defenses remained at full alert. She nodded grudgingly. Carl could tell that she knew that she was being handled.

"We develop certain expectations about how animals should behave," Rik continued. "Even a moderate degree of intelligence above the norm may come across as extraordinary. We have an innate tendency to anthropomorphize, so when we encounter an exceptionally smart specimen we often view the exceptional actions as human-like . . . or perhaps angelic."

"Look," Fels asserted, "I understand that Lilly is a smart animal." She was impatient with the coddling.

Rik nodded, and then went on as though there had been no interruption. "Lilly is smart, but still within the ninety-seven percentile for ferrets. You understand that, don't you?"

"I *told* you I did. What do I have to do? Sign an affidavit?"

Carl wished Rik would talk about more than just Lilly's intelligence, but he saw the logic in convincing Fels that the ferret was just a normal animal. At least Rik was credible. In fact, he went at it with a passion, as though the only hope for Fels lay in accepting Lilly's normalcy.

Carl didn't mention the incident with the coyote and the tree, or how she had tricked Fels into turning the hose on him. These did seem extraordinary, even for a ninety-seven percentile ferret. This was one of those times, though, when the truth just muddied the waters, and he held his tongue.

Instead, he decided that it might be time to lighten things up a bit. "And Rik should know since he's seen Lilly's brain."

The genetics engineer gave him a hard look.

"Er," he stumbled on, "you've operated on Lilly, so you would have, uh, you know, seen her brain."

The hard look turned angry. "What the hell are you talking about?"

He remembered now that Rik had told them that Lilly hadn't been used in the research, for "technical reasons." But hadn't Kaj told him that Lilly . . .?

"Where did you hear that?" Rik barked.

Carl just looked at him, dumfounded at the unexpected reaction.

GeneTrend's founder turned an accusatory glare onto Fels and demanded, "It was Kaj, wasn't it?"

Fels shrugged. She also seemed flustered by Rik's anger.

"My mistake," Carl explained, quickly. "I misunderstood what he said."

Rik's eyes flared. "You *told* him that Lilly was *here?*"

Carl leaned back from the blast. "I . . . he . . . I thought he would have already known!"

Carl suddenly found his own anger. "He's *your* employee, after all. Why should we take shit over your little secrets?"

He realized what he'd done, and looked aghast at Fels. This was her boss he was creaming.

Rik didn't seem to take offense at all, though. In fact, after a moment he smiled and held up his hands as though calling a truce. "I'm sorry. You're right. I'm sure there's no harm done. It's just that I'm, well, fond of Lilly and want to make sure she's safe."

Carl wouldn't have guessed that this genius harbored fondness enough for any living thing to get that angry, but maybe there was more to the man than he knew.

Rik glanced at his watch and excused himself, explaining that he had to get back to the office.

Carl's anger didn't dissipate so easily. As they saw their guest to the door, he consoled himself with the thought, *What a dummy for coming all this way to talk to Fels for just five minutes.* They waved as he climbed into the SUV that he'd driven up instead of the Lamborghini, and Carl consoled himself with another vindictive thought: *If he's so in love with Lilly, why did he leave without even trying to say goodbye?*

After they'd closed the door, Carl turned to Fels. "I'm so sorry honey for getting mad at your boss."

She wrapped her arms around him. "The jerk deserved every word," she said into his chest.

He savored her embrace for a while, and then asked, "So, you think Lilly is just an animal and not an angel?"

"Shut up," her muffled voice came from below, and then she lifted her head and said, "Just kiss me."

He did.

PART II

KAJ

Chapter 7

"A woman knows pregnant, and she's pregnant," Fels insisted, placing her hand gently on Lilly's upturned belly as the ferret lay sprawled in her lap. Lilly, in turn, placed her front paws on Fels's hand as though saying, *be careful, there's valuable cargo in there.*

June had eased into July almost unnoticed, as one unmarked day after another slipped past Carl. It seemed to him that he had performed a Herculean effort slicing away at the log sea, but other than a widened band of sawdust-covered ground immediately surrounding the cabin, the jumbled field of denuded trees remained, a log jam frozen in place. Next to the aging mountain of dry limbs at the clearing's edge, another mountain of wooden slabs was growing, oozing sap that glistened under the summer furnace sun: two problems too visible to ignore. The owner of the market had laughed when he'd asked about selling firewood, explaining that pine is considered junk wood, suitable for kindling only.

"You told Rik?" he asked, reaching over to feel the sack of nascent pups, but Lilly flipped around upright and jumped to the ground. He was used to this preferential treatment towards Fels.

"He shrugged it off. He guessed that someone must have slipped up and left her unattended with the male. Actually, I think he was pleased. He hates letting people know when he's happy, like it's some kind of weakness."

"There were two ferrets? What happened to the other one?"

What he really wanted to ask was, "Why are you so tuned in that you know when he's happy?"

"I asked him about that. I thought it would be fun to bring the father up to see his kids. But Rik said they sent the male back to the company they'd bought them from—a company that sells lab animals for research."

"Somehow I doubt a ferret father would even recognize his offspring. But why did Rik send the father back and not Lilly?"

She shrugged. "I guess he just likes Lilly."

Carl thought that Rik acted more like an inattentive uncle, which was just fine by him. The geneticist hadn't made the trip up from San Diego to visit them since the angel disaster, and Carl was glad to let the whole thing fade away. Fels hadn't admitted that she no longer believed that Lilly was an angel, but whatever her beliefs, she now kept them to herself. Carl suspected that this might not be the healthiest situation, but it was a lot easier living with a wife who at least acted sane.

He went off to the laundry room to finish the clothes he'd started to wash, but Fels poked her head around the doorsill a few minutes later. "Kaj sent an email—he wants you to call him."

"Okay," he replied, lifting a pair of soapy jeans from the tub. "Thanks."

"He wants you to call him right away. He says it's an emergency."

He looked up. Fels rolled her eyes and disappeared back into the Great Hall. Emergencies tended to be a staple of the drummer's life.

He dried his hands, placed the headset on, and typed in Kaj's number.

After some seconds he heard his friend say, "El-oh, Kaj-pizzazz here . . . hello? Is anybody there?"

"Kaj, it's me. Listen I'm on the Internet phone so—"

"Carlaroo! Uh, wait—we have to do the walkie-talkie thing, don't we?"

"Yeah, sorry—"

"Over."

Carl closed his eyes and took a breath. "Kaj, you wanted me to call. What's the emergency? Your turn."

Silence, then, "Yeah. We got the gig—the one at Croce's. To you, dude."

"That's the emergency? Your turn."

Fels was right: Kaj was missing a few key bolts.

"Hey, emergencies are important and require attention. What could be more important than a gig at the top nightspot in San Diego? Come *on*, dude. Over."

"Yeah, well someday, Kaj, you'll cry wolf and nobody will come running. Yours."

Lilly had trotted over when he'd first mentioned Kaj's name, and now at the second mention, she hopped up on his lap and sniffed at the mouthpiece.

"Hey!" He cried. "Get out of here!" Her whiskers tickled his nose.

"Listen buddy, when the wolves come howling—what was that?"

"Sorry. It was Lilly. She seems to want to talk to you. Yours."

. . . "Lilly-baby! How's my little girl doing? I've been thinking about her. Volley back to you."

"Your little girl is a mommy. Yours."

Fels looked up from her work and gave him a surprised, disapproving look.

Carl winced. Of course. Rik wouldn't want him to talk about it. This intrigue stuff just wasn't his bag, as his mother might say.

"Lilly's pregnant? Very excellent! The pitter-patter of a herd of Lillyettes will soon be filling your mansion-in-the-woods. Ball's in your court."

"And since they've sent the father back where he came from, you can come out and be their surrogate daddy. Listen, Kaj, I don't think I was supposed to tell you about this. So, don't mention it to anybody. Yours."

. . . "Ha! Back where the father came from, like dust-to-dust? Birdie to you."

"What are you talking about? Uh, over."

. . . "You didn't know? They off'd the male ferret. You know, bestowed everlasting peace. That's why I was worried about old Lilly-girl. To you."

"But, Rik—" He decided he had better not say any more. "I should let Fels have the computer back. We'll try to make it to the gig. Yours."

. . . "*Try?* Dude! Be there. I'll be watching for you in the crowd of screaming fans. Over-the-river-and-through-the-woods and out to you."

"Goodbye, Kaj."

Fels was watching him as he took off the headset. "Well, thank God you called him," she said. "Who knows how the horrible emergency might have otherwise turned out."

He grinned but sat staring at the monitor.

"What's up?" she asked.

"Didn't Rik tell us that they gave the male ferret back to the lab animal supply company?"

She nodded, brow wrinkled.

"Kaj says they killed the father."

"He probably hallucinated it," she scoffed.

Carl shrugged. He knew a bit about the effects of recreational hallucinations. They were sensory in nature, and involved armies of bugs parading up and down your arms, or maybe the checkout clerk turning into Big Bird. He'd never heard of anybody fabricating such an elaborate alternate reality.

Then again, medical science probably couldn't keep up with Kaj in cataloging the combination effects of mixing drugs.

"He invited us to their show at Croce's."

"Okay," she said, turning her attention back to her work. "As long as we can go shopping at Horten Plaza."

The downtown mall was only a couple of blocks from the nightclub. Carl figured he could drag her that far if he had to.

ж ж ж

Four days and six hours later, it was Fels who was dragging *him* from a store. Carl had perused the bookshop while she was shopping for clothes, and he'd gathered together a pile of eighteen candidates, ranging on subjects from the history of the English language (Bill Bryson), to anthropology (Jared Diamond). When she returned with just one small bag, she suggested he whittle the collection down to an even dozen. That had sounded reasonable, but he struggled, deciding which ones to put back on the shelves. He'd never been a big reader, preferring to spend his money and time on music, but lately he'd become drawn to the wide horizons that opened between the covers. He blamed Defoe. His friend made the human world so damn interesting. He couldn't resist delving deeper, and Google and Wikipedia took him only so far.

"If you can't decide," she suggested, "then go ahead and buy them all."

He scanned across the collection. "We're talking, like, two hundred dollars."

"More like three hundred. Don't worry about it. I'll put in extra hours. Besides, we can deduct some as a business expense."

He held up a copy of Huckleberry Finn and looked at her.

"An IRS agent wouldn't know Mark Twain from an engineering reference. If we don't get going, though, we're going to miss the first set altogether.

They gathered up the books and ferried the whole mass to the checkout counter as the lights blinked, indicating the store was about to close. He looked forward to excuses to come into town; the hustle and bustle that was once an irritation now seemed exciting and alive. It occurred to him now, though, that he was not particularly looking forward to seeing his friends play. He hadn't been to any gigs since his accident, and it was time to face the music in a literal way.

They dumped the spoils in the car and wound their way through the Saturday night crowd of the Gaslamp District. This was the hip, rejuvenated downtown that once catered to the rough tastes of sailors on leave, but now glowed with upscale restaurants, dance clubs, and hotels. At Croce's they discovered that there was an hour wait for a table, and the trim model-pretty hostess smiled thinly and shook her head when he explained that he had been invited by the band. They found one empty stool at the bar, so Fels sat down, and he stood behind her, jostled by a continuous stream of people coming and going who-knew-where. On the small stage in the front window, his friends finished up a slinky version of the old Classics IV hit *Spooky* and announced their break. Fels had been right: they'd missed the first set.

He hadn't been able to catch Kaj's eye, and the place was so crowded, his friend got up from behind the drum set, came off the stage, and disappeared before Carl could get his attention. He knew where Kaj was going—through the kitchen and out the back door for a joint. He was tempted to join him, but decided it wouldn't be fair to leave Fels alone, and he knew that she wouldn't have anything to do with pot. Instead, Pete, the bass player, saw them when he came to the bar, and the three of them chatted, or rather, yelled at each other until Pete glanced at his watch, grabbed his beer, and excused himself.

Out of nowhere Kaj suddenly appeared. His eyes were red, and a nonsensical grin hinted that this had probably not been the first joint of the evening. He called out to the bartender for two shots of whisky, wrapped a heartfelt hug around an unenthusiastic Fels, and then followed with another for Carl. That was the clincher: Kaj only hugged his guy friends when he was stoned. "How'd you like the first set?" he asked.

"Fels was shopping and made us late," Carl joked. She gave her head a disgusted shake—she didn't much care what Kaj thought anyway. "But the last half of the last song smoked."

"Yeah," his drummer friend agreed, grinning even wider at some inner thought, "that was the best half song of the set. We have a whole pile more of bitchin' half-songs coming up." His eyes suddenly went wide at another random thought. "Hey! Listen. There's something I have to tell you." He glanced around the crowded bar as though he might find somebody aiming a gun at him.

Just then, Pete stepped up to a microphone and asked if there happened to be a drummer in the house, since they had apparently lost theirs.

Kaj didn't seem to be listening, but was leaning in close to talk directly into Carl's ear.

"Didn't you hear Pete?" Carl interrupted. "They're ready to start."

Kaj gave Pete an annoyed look, which wasn't easy considering he was still grinning ear-to-ear. He grabbed the two shot glasses from the bar and leaned in towards Carl. "Lilly is Marty Feldman's pet," he confided, giving Carl a knowing look while slopping whisky on his leg. His dissolute friend then turned and elbowed his way through the crowd towards the stage.

"What did he say?" Fels asked.

Carl looked at her, mystified. "Lilly. He said she's Marty Feldman's *pet*. What do you think he means?"

She snorted. "I think it means that he's high. He looked high, didn't he?"

Carl shrugged and smiled to himself. To a random middle-aged stranger Fels would come across as suave and hip as any other young cosmopolitan. If the subject happened to land on drug abuse or fringe sexuality, though, her exuberant naiveté unmasked her protected religious upbringing. Carl found it endearing, a precious innocence in an age of ubiquitous and continuous television exposition.

Carl tried to keep an open mind during the next set, but all he could think about was how *he* would play the guitar parts. He'd heard about the new guitarist, but had never seen him play. His replacement was older, a Washington DC transplant in his forties, and to Carl's unobjective ear the solos were too precise, a little too programmed. This was the blues; you were supposed to play from the heart. Mistakes should trickle forth in your rush of passion. That's why they were called blue notes.

Actually, he didn't know that for sure, but it sounded right.

As the second set came to a close, Fels suggested they take off. It was a long drive home and they weren't used to staying up late anymore. He nodded and lay money on the bar for their drinks. He'd had enough anyway. He was developing dark and criminal thoughts about the new guitarist.

The crowd seemed to have gotten thicker, if that was even possible. By the time they'd made their way to the door, the band had finished, and he managed a goodbye wave to Kaj before stepping out into the shockingly cool and clean night air. He'd imagined that the Gaslamp streets would now be empty since everyone had evidently already squeezed themselves into Croce's, but reinforcements continually poured in, and the perfumed, gooped, cologned, primped, and dolled crowd spilled into the street, where cars edged along slowly through the festive crowd, which flowed around them like river foam. He heard his name called, and he grabbed Fels's sleeve, holding her against the current, and turned. A hand waved above the heads and Kaj appeared, pushing through the masses.

"Where are you going?" he asked, eyes wide with alarm.

"Home, Kaj. We have a home, and it's an hour and a half drive away."

"I have to tell you something!" He grabbed Carl's shoulder, demonstrating the urgency, and then leaned in. "It's about Lilly," he whispered hoarsely. The smell of whisky was sweet on his breath.

"I know!" Carl practically had to shout above the crowd streaming by. "She's Marty Feldman's pet!"

The alarmed look grew to near panic. "Keep it down! Do you want everybody to hear?"

He pulled Carl, with Fels in tow, away from the street to the relative safety of a dark entranceway.

"Kaj," Carl said, "you're drunk."

His friend waved off the accusation. Off course he was drunk. "I realized something during the last set."

"That drummers can't play while sober?"

Kaj shook his head, annoyed. "You have to kill the babies."

"What are you talking about?"

"Lilly's babies. You have to kill them. They're monsters."

"What the hell are you talking—"

It came to him what Kaj had meant about Marty Feldman. The British comedian had played the part of the hunchbacked assistant in Mel Brooks' *Young Frankenstein*. "What kind of monsters?"

Kaj glanced around dramatically, looking for eavesdroppers. "I heard rumors that there was secret research and that Lilly was somehow involved—something about probability enhancement. At first I thought he'd only made Lilly better, but then I saw something in his notebook—"

"Who?"

"Lilly!" Kaj cried impatiently.

"No. You said he'd made Lilly better—who's the 'he' you're talking about?"

"Rik!" he yelled, then shrank down as though avoiding a bullet.

"What about the notebook?" Carl asked.

Kaj waved downward, urging them to be quieter. "What about it?"

Carl sighed. "You saw something that made you think it was more than just Lilly that was involved."

"Yeah! I did! He wrote about her progeny—that means kids, right?"

Carl shrugged and nodded.

Kaj pulled him in so that he was talking directly into his ear. "Lilly's babies are going to be half-human."

Carl jerked up straight. "What the hell . . . you're nuts!"

Fels snorted. She was getting impatient with all this inebriated nonsense about Lilly and monsters.

"No!" Kaj pleaded. "I saw it in the notebook. He wrote that he was going to combine ferrets and men. Their genes were going to collide together." As he said this, he twisted his hands together, demonstrating the merging process. "This will create a new master race that will rule the whole galaxy!"

His friend stepped back and looked at Carl expectantly, waiting for him to wring his hands and cry out in despair over the devastating news. Instead, he put his finger to his head and cocked his thumb, indicating that it might be best if Kaj just ended his misery.

"Come on," Fels urged, tugging at his sleeve. "It's getting late." She'd clearly had enough.

Carl had as well. He put his hand on his friend's shoulder. "We have to go. Listen, will you do me a favor? Promise you won't drink any more tonight. You need to sober up enough to drive home."

Kaj shook his head in dismay. "It's true! I saw it! You have to kill Lilly's babies!"

Carl could tell that Fels was getting mad as she walked off.

"Sorry bud," he said as he waved and trotted off to catch up with her. He turned for one last look. "Break a leg in there! AND NO MORE DRINKS!"

Kaj's distressed face disappeared among the party crowd and a minute later Carl was walking next to Fels. "He's a good guy," he encouraged, feeling protective of his friend. "He has an active imagination is all."

"He has a brain that's been fried by too much drugs, you mean."

Carl knew that the topic of Kaj would be a minefield for the rest of the evening, so they walked through the cool San Diego night in silence.

Chapter 8

That night Carl was pulled from the netherworld of sleep by the sound of a demon in the night. As full wakefulness cleared the echoes of secret imaginations from his mind, he lay in bed, his heart pounding, and listened to the howling anthem of hell itself. It's just some animal, he assured himself. Probably mating. The howling twisted into a yip, and then a growling bark. A coyote. He knew they hunted at night. He'd heard packs of them in the darkness, platoons of banshees whose malevolent cries of doom he imagined could bring down prey by sheer terror alone.

Tonight was different, though. There was just one. Carl listened, waiting for others to join in, but he heard only the battle cry of one lone coyote. A final yip, and then dreadful silence. The hunter had apparently vanquished his prey, and a stillness born of reverence and relief filled the night woods.

Later, he woke again, this time with a dream projected in his head like an afterimage that glows sharply for an instant, but quickly blurs and fades. He'd dreamt that he had walked into the Great Room to find Lilly nursing hellish little creatures with human faces, but ferret ears and bodies. Following the illogic of dreams, the beasts were suddenly man-size, and although now appearing completely human, the dream maintained the dreaded certainty that they were still unholy monsters. He suddenly realized that they all looked like Rik. He found this reassuring in its familiarity, but also somehow even more horrific. They were talking to him, and they seemed angry. "You let Mommy out!" they cried in despair. He saw that there was a miniature door built into the bottom of the kitchen door, and it stood open.

Fels didn't say anything when he told her about the dream over breakfast. He knew what that meant. If she just didn't want to talk about it she would say so. When she was silent, it meant that she had a lot to say on the subject, but for the sake of peace in the marriage she was refraining. It meant that if he had a brain in his head he would drop the whole thing like a potato fresh from the microwave.

He apparently left his brain on the bedroom dresser because he said, "Do you think there's anything to what Kaj told us?"

Still his beautiful wife said nothing. Instead, she stood up and took her cereal bowl to the sink. Suddenly she spun around. "That man is the best example I know of why drugs are ruining this country. Not only is he destroying his own life, but now he's endangering others as well."

Carl didn't have time to recover completely from the sudden dam burst. "What are you talking about? Who's he endangering? Rik?"

She picked up the wet wash rag and threw it at him, but missed so that it flopped to the floor behind him. "You're as much an imbecile as him! No wonder you two are friends!"

It suddenly came to him why she was mad, and he realized that he was indeed an imbecile for not seeing it coming. "Lilly!"

"Of course, Lilly! Carl, what if somebody believes his insane delusions? What if somebody doesn't even necessarily believe them, but just wants to play it safe? That's the standard American approach, you know: if in doubt, eliminate the source of possible trouble, no matter how unlikely. Towns tear out playgrounds because one kid fell and hurt himself."

"Oh, come on. You're overreacting."

But he knew she wasn't. By law they shouldn't even have Lilly—she was an illegal alien. He could see that the authorities would indeed play it safe and destroy the animal at the slightest hint of trouble.

"Okay," he conceded. "You win. I'll talk to Kaj. We don't want to draw attention to our little Mommy."

Hearing himself say that word invoked the image of the dream, and he shuddered.

She nodded, pouting.

She was a sweetie. Her devotion to the vulnerable little creatures of the world was endearing, and he loved her for it.

"Now that the can of Kaj worms is open," he went on, "what about that secret research Kaj talked about? Have you heard anything about this?"

She gave him one last hard look, then shrugged and sat down at the table. "Kaj is probably just confused. There's tremendous competition in biotech. Everything GeneTrend does with its own funding is secret. Kaj has been working on the NSF project, which by definition can't be secret, so he's mostly kept out of the in-house labs. He hears rumors from the other techs, and you know how rumors grow, especially among the semi-educated."

"Semi-educated?"

"You know what I mean: no college."

"I never went to college."

"You can't compare yourself to Kaj. You're . . . different. You could have gone to college. You could still go any time you want; just say the word."

College was a continual bone of contention. She'd been gently nudging him ever since they'd met.

"I'd rather hang out with the likes of Kaj," he replied, "if Herr Rik Fuehrer is the college type."

"Now you're the one that's exaggerating. You can't use Rik as a typical example of anything. Besides, he didn't go to college in California. He went to MIT."

"Right. And I keep forgetting to prostrate myself in front of him."

"See? There's a good example. I'll bet Kaj wouldn't know what prostrate means. He'd think it has something to do with the doctor sticking his finger up his butt."

And leaving that image for him to contemplate, she left to get ready for her drive down to GeneTrend.

ж ж ж

Carl dallied longer than he'd intended before stepping out into the hot summer sun to take up the day's toil: segmenting dismembered trees. As he yanked the chainsaw cord, he imagined himself shackled to other inmates. A pot-bellied, shotgun toting, southern-drawling deputy kept a watchful eye on the gang, delivering a gun butt to the head of anyone who seemed to slack off. "We can take him, boys," Carl urged to himself. "Some of us will fall under the bastard's gun, but the rest will be free."

He had to entertain himself since he couldn't hear his MP3 player above the roar of the saw.

Motion caught his eye. Lilly slunk along at the edge of the clearing. It looked like she'd just come from the pile of branches. The ferret stopped and looked at him, and then sat back on her haunches licking her paws, as though this was exactly what she had intended to do when she came out from the cabin.

He'd seen this sort of behavior before when he would catch his younger brother in his bedroom. The little twerp pretended that he just happened to arrive there innocently and randomly, when in fact the evidence of his crime was spread around him in the form of scattered and grievously bent baseball cards.

Carl turned off the chainsaw and walked to the mountain of branches. Lilly paused in her grooming and watched him. He got down on all fours and saw a tunnel that had been formed, leading into the dark depths of the jumble of twigs and sticks. The butt of a large limb covered the entrance like an awning, making it invisible from above.

He smiled. "You don't trust us with your babies."

He turned and jumped, astonished to find Lilly right behind him, eyeing him with what Carl took to be a baleful glare.

"Don't worry, girl, this will remain our little secret."

He noticed a nasty scratch on her forehead and another smaller one on her nose. "My God!" he exclaimed, making the connection with the disturbance the night before. "It was *you!*"

He reached out to take her, to get a closer look and see if she needed patching up, but the ferret suddenly turned and trotted away towards the cabin. Carl watched her, amazed, wondering how she had escaped the coyote. She'd obviously been lucky. "You'd better be more careful!" he called after her. "You have a family to think about now!"

An hour—half of a log—later, Carl had the uncanny sense that somebody was spying on him. He looked up and there, not fifty feet away, was the coyote watching him intently. Surprised, the animal shuffled backwards, and then in one smooth, surrealistic motion lifted up onto its hind legs. It stood there for several heartbeats eyeing him curiously, its front paws held out for balance, and then with one quick motion, turned and galloped away on four legs, becoming, once again, an everyday animal.

He stood transfixed until it disappeared into the trees. It dawned on him that it had run off in the direction of Tekumewa's burial site.

Still dazed by the sight of a coyote walking like a man—or at least standing like one—he killed the chainsaw and lay it down. He looked back at the cabin, but Lilly was nowhere to be seen. He turned his face to the sky, and small, fluffy clouds floated, marking the tops of updrafts shoved heavenward by the mountains. He wiped his hands on his jeans and set off into the woods.

He was afraid—afraid of a coyote that was itself fearless of the roar of a chainsaw, a roar more powerful than any natural predator. It was, in fact, Carl's fear that drove him through the Cuyamaca pines towards the pile of stones marking the grave of a centuries-dead Indian. He didn't believe in ghosts. He demanded of himself that he didn't believe in ghosts, and so his fear angered him. He understood that sometimes fear can be de-clawed by turning to face it, and so set off to see for himself that Tekumewa's memorial was just a pile of stones.

He paused now and then to listen, but heard only the sound of squirrels and chickadees skittering around in the branches above, anxious about his intrusion. When he came to the final slope, it felt as though a new type of gravity pulled at him so that each step required an effort beyond the purely physical. He'd only been here the one time with Defoe and wasn't completely sure he even had the right hill, and so was almost surprised when he emerged from the pines to find the grassy expanse before him.

An instant later he froze, and his heart seemed to stop mid-beat. There, at the top of the hill next to the pile of stones, stood Tekumewa, silhouetted against the bright cumulus clouds clustered densely above the distant horizon. Next to the Indian chief was the coyote . . . which was wearing a baseball cap. Tekumewa turned his head, and Carl saw that he sported a bushy beard, just like . . . no, it *was* Defoe. The coyote stood up from its squatting position, and he saw that this was actually Toby.

His heart resumed its thumping and he shook his head at his own capacity for self-delusion. "Yo!" he called out, and Defoe jerked in surprise, then turned and waved to him.

"Welcome to the Keruk," Defoe said when Carl topped the hill.

"Sorry," Carl replied, breathing hard. "I don't do karaoke."

He smelled arresting wafts of cologne, and saw that the two had laid a cornucopia of personal effects—gloves, comics, CDs, paperback books—on the ground in a pile next to the rocks. "What's with the Old Spice?"

"It's Brut, and that's 'Keruk,' not 'karaoke,' " Defoe informed. "We're performing a Kumeyaay anniversary ritual of the dead, not a Japanese ritual of the better-off-dead. We heard your chainsaw; we discussed coming to offer you help after the ritual."

Toby grinned at this.

"What's Defoe plotting now?" Carl asked the teenager.

"He said we should come back to visit you some other time, since today you'd want us to help. He said he wasn't born to be a lumberjack, and you always hogged all the fun using the chainsaw anyway."

"That's not accurate," Defoe declared, crossing his arms across his chest. "I explained that I obviously lack a lumberjack gene, and in any case, deciding not to come today is still 'discussing coming to offer you help.' "

"What about the hogging part? Did you say I hog the chainsaw?"

"Do you claim not to?"

"It's mine. That's not hogging; that's owning."

Defoe tsk'd. "Semantics."

Toby stood by, smiling at the sparring. Carl had the sense that the boy may have been inhibited from free expression as a young child. He realized that humorous repartee with adults was probably opening horizons for him. If Defoe was good for anything, it was expanding horizons.

"What brings you to Tekumewa's grave?" Defoe asked.

Carl explained the encounter with the coyote, feeling a little foolish as he explained the fear that drove him here.

Defoe didn't seem to find it foolish, though. Just the opposite, in fact. "Our little Keruk may be more timely than we guessed."

"What do you mean?"

"The Keruk is a ritual that the Kumeyaay traditionally performed on the one-year anniversary of a death. By burning possessions that might be useful in the afterlife, the idea is that the deceased person's spirit would be content and not return."

Carl nodded, and then remembered. "Wait a second. A few weeks ago, you performed that Temesaa ritual. Wasn't that specifically supposed to *bring* the old warrior back?"

Defoe sighed. "Indeed. One can't always predict which actions are noble and which are folly."

Carl surveyed the pile next to the rocks and pointed with his toe at a small plastic box. "Tekumewa will be content to have a Game Boy in the afterlife?"

"Who's to say that the afterlife hasn't gone high tech?" To Toby, the tutoring philosopher urged, "Go ahead and light the offering." He then winked and gestured for Carl to step back with him as they watched the boy pour lighter fluid over the stash of loot.

"I want to engage the lad in his heritage," Defoe explained in a low voice. "Besides a ritual to keep the dead spirits away, the Keruk was also a means of redistributing wealth among the tribe. A key to the Kumeyaay's long history of peaceful coexistence was abstinence from acquisition of wealth beyond one's actual needs. The Keruk was one way to effect this. Some of the family's possessions were distributed throughout the tribe, but others were burned. I thought it would be good for Toby to give up things of value."

"Brut?"

"What could be more valuable to a teenage boy than smelling like a man? Unfortunately I dropped the bottle and it broke on the rocks."

Defoe went on to explain that Toby would be staying with him the rest of the summer, as his mother had taken a job driving trucks cross-country, and for the time being had no permanent home.

"As long as you're taking in adolescent boarders," Carl added, "I have a friend who could use some chaperoning."

He related Kaj's wild ravings of the previous evening, the drummer's insistence that they kill Lilly's kits when they were born.

When he explained why—that Kaj claimed that Rik had somehow combined human and ferret genes—his friend raised one eyebrow.

"They've cloned sheep, genetically modified bacteria to produce human growth hormone, and are preparing to grow new organs from stem cells," Defoe recited. "What sounds too fantastic to be true today becomes tomorrow's miracles of science. In this case basic ethical considerations, though, would seem to warrant further investigation."

Carl nodded glumly. He'd promised Fels that he'd try to get Kaj to clam up about Lilly, and now Defoe was urging him to get the drummer to open up. This was going to be an interesting conversation, one he wasn't particularly looking forward to.

The breeze shifted and acrid smoke from burning plastic drove them down the hill. Carl paused, though, and looked back. "Hey!" he called to the retreating philosopher, "Do you realize that you've broken the law by starting an open fire in the park?"

His friend stopped short and trotted back. "Goodness! You're right! Do you think they'll make an exception for a sacred Indian ritual?"

"This, coming from a man of Irish and Italian ancestry? I would make sure it doesn't spread before it goes out, and then hope you can get away before the rangers follow the black plume here. But if you do end up under a bright lamp with a detective interrogating you, don't mention this stuff about Lilly. It's supposed to be secret."

Carl continued down the hill, leaving his friend watching the roiling billows.

Back at the cabin, he sat down at the computer to call Kaj, and noticed that an email had come in from Pete. He was writing to tell Carl about Kaj. Halfway through the message Carl's brain froze and he sat motionless as the world shifted on its axis. Kaj had overdosed. His irreverent friend, a drummer who played with a joy and passion that wrapped the band around him into a single musical voice, was dead.

Chapter 9

It was the longest drive Carl had ever taken to Pacific Beach. Kaj had lived there all his life, and the funeral was to be held at the Methodist church he'd attended with his parents as a kid. Carl felt numb, and Fels had given up on her attempts to make conversation.

She hadn't really been friends with Kaj; in fact, she probably wouldn't have given him the time of day under other circumstances. She respected Carl's grief even though didn't share his devastation. As they were getting ready, she had remarked that maybe an overdose was inevitable. From her limited exposure, she had the idea that any musician who took drugs eventually ended up, as she put it, "among the ranks of those fallen under the needle." He hadn't tried to explain that only a small percentage of druggies actually use needles, and that in any case it wasn't possible to die from an overdose of pot.

Kaj had always freely admitted that drugs held a special place in his heart, but he'd also adamantly insisted that he wasn't stupid enough to dabble in the dangerous varieties. And Carl had believed him. So now he found that on top of his grief was guilt at losing touch to the point that he wasn't even aware that his friend had apparently crossed over to the darker fringes. The reason he'd lost touch, of course, was because Fels had dragged him away to live in isolation from those he cared about.

He knew these thoughts weren't fair. He'd had plenty of opportunities to weigh in against the move, and he knew that Fels wouldn't have pressured him. Still, he'd gone along with the whole idea mainly because he thought it might help her with her own struggles over Tod's death.

Christ. It seemed like his life was one long juggling act of guilt and grief.

The funeral home parking lot was full, but Carl found a spot on the street. He felt constrained and itchy as he walked along the sidewalk in his only suit. As he had anticipated, he found the memorial service almost unbearable. Kaj's mother sat alone, weeping and moaning softly, while most everyone else, although trying to appear sad and respectful, couldn't resist falling into barely audible conversations about the upcoming Chargers season or the Padres chances at the Series. Only Kaj's band mates, it seemed, felt sincere loss, and he huddled with them along with Fels who was now sobered, faced with the formality of the man's end.

Kaj's mom had asked him and other band members to be pallbearers. They carried Kaj to the grave at the small cemetery near the foot of Mount Soledad, and Carl's eyes blurred with tears as the minister spoke a few final words before the small crowd dispersed with relief back to their various lives.

Through the tears, he noticed Rik among the gathering, seeming somehow out of place. Kaj had worked under him, so of course it wouldn't be considered unusual for him to attend the services. Still, it seemed like a panther taking time to pay respects to a dead beetle it found lying along the path. Carl noticed Rik eyeing him, and sure enough, as soon as the minister was through, the GeneTrend executive worked his way against the stream of people departing the cemetery to get to him.

"My condolences," Rik offered, shaking his hand. "Fels told me you were friends—you played in a band with him."

"He was the best drummer in San Diego."

This wasn't really true, but it felt good to say it.

Rik nodded, accepting it without question. "You must have kept in touch, even after you moved away."

Carl shrugged. "Sure. Not as much as I should have. I guess that's what you always think after it's . . . too late."

Rik nodded again. Carl had the impression that the geneticist would have nodded agreeably at anything he said. People develop a tender touch at funerals.

"You talked with him about Lilly," Rik said in the same careful funeral tone.

Carl blinked. Was it a simple statement, or a question? Rik knew that he'd told Kaj about Lilly. In fact, Rik had gotten upset about it. He must mean recently. Carl had pretty much forgotten about Kaj's ravings at Croce's, but now it came back. The drug induced fantasies seemed all the more endearing in their naiveté and over-dramatization.

"Kaj talked about Lilly the night he died," Carl related. He smiled at the memory. "He thought you had somehow cloned human genes with Lilly."

Rik's brow furrowed in consternation. He shook his head, perplexed. "Where the hell did he get that idea?"

Carl lifted his palms, begging ignorance. "He was stoned. Who knows what twisted ideas bubbled up from his subconscious."

He took a breath. No use hiding from the truth. "Whatever he took," he went on, "it was enough to kill him. It's no wonder he was beginning to hallucinate."

Rik nodded sagely. "Drugs can make you believe almost anything, I suppose."

Carl figured this was enough obligatory funeral socializing and was going to excuse himself to go find Fels, but Rik went on. "Of course, he may have gotten confused about some things he heard."

Carl just looked at him. The genetics engineer was not one to initiate idle conversation.

"I mean," Rik continued, "Kaj may have heard about human gene mappings that we've been correlating to the mappings from the animal brain findings. He probably thought that we were somehow splicing between humans and ferrets."

Carl nodded, only half listening. He just wanted to get Fels and go home.

"Which is impossible, of course."

"Of course," Carl agreed.

"So, that's all Kaj said?"

Carl looked at him. What the hell. "He said that Lilly's babies are going to be monsters, and that we should kill them."

Rik's eyes widened in alarm. "He . . . why, that's ridiculous! I wouldn't—"

"Oh, don't worry," Carl reassured, "I know it was just the drugs talking."

He wasn't sure why he'd even mentioned this. Probably just to see Rik's reaction. And now that he had seen it, he didn't know what to make of it.

Somebody tapped him lightly on the shoulder. Kaj's mother was behind him, looking tiny and frail. Her face seemed inanimate, like washed leather, and her eyes were red from crying.

"Thank you, Carl," she said, her voice on the verge of breaking. "I know Kaj thought a lot of you."

His vision blurred again. His friend was really gone, forever.

She took a breath, as though just being alive was physically taxing. "I tried to get him to stop with the drugs. You know how he was, though. He didn't listen to nobody, let alone his own mother."

"I know," Carl said, nearly choking on his words. "He was a free spirit." It was cliché, but he didn't give a damn. "He was happy, though. You have to give him that."

She nodded vigorously, as though a welcomed substitute for talking.

The three of them stood there. He didn't want to be the one to break away, and he wished that Rik would do the deed.

"I got the coroner's report this morning," she added dully, as she might if she were remarking on unremarkable weather. "It was jimsonweed."

He wasn't sure if he'd heard her correctly. He thought it might be just his imagination—it would be too much of a coincidence. He'd told Kaj about the hallucinogenic plant just a couple of weeks ago. Carl had become curious after Defoe had joked about it, and he'd told Kaj what he'd found, thinking his friend would find it interesting as well . . . and apparently he had.

"Did you say jimsonweed?" Carl asked.

She nodded. "Yeah. It grows wild. Dangerous stuff. Nothin' to be messin' with."

Carl's head felt as though it was filling quickly with air. He'd killed his friend. He should have known. Telling Kaj about a new drug was as good as handing him a loaded gun and daring him to play Russian Roulette.

"Yes," Rik said. "In fact, I heard him talking about it at work. What a shame."

"It was me," Carl heard himself say.

"What do you mean?" Kaj's mother asked.

He seemed to wake up where he was standing, and he looked at her. He wanted to get down on his knees and beg her forgiveness. "I told him about it. I told him about jimsonweed. I *told* him how dangerous it was. I never thought for a minute that he'd . . ."

She shook her head. "It's not your fault, Carl. He had his own mind. If he hadn't heard about it from you, it would've been someone else."

He was thankful for her words, but he looked to Rik for additional support. The dapper man's face was screwed up in alarm. "*You* told him about it?" he asked almost incredulously.

Carl closed his eyes against the assault. "I didn't . . . I had no idea he would . . ."

He felt a gentle hand on his arm. He opened his eyes to find Kaj's mother looking him gently in the face. "It's not your fault, Carl. You listen to me. You were his best friend and would have done anything for him. He knew that. He would've done anything for you too. It's just one of those things. We gotta' go on. You understand?"

He nodded, barely able to see through the welling tears.

An elderly man standing next to an old Buick called to her and she waved to him and said, "I have to go. Now you stay in touch, you hear?"

"Sure," he replied, wiping his sleeve across his eyes and sucking the phlegm back into his nose as she turned and shuffled away. Rik held a tissue out to him and be blew a bleating rattle into it.

Kaj's boss had regained his composure. His face once more relaxed into calm indifference. "She's right, you know," he said. "It was inevitable. He would have done himself in sooner or later. The lottery is a tax on the ignorant, and drugs are the pruning shears."

Carl wished the smug executive would just disappear along with his snide remarks. He remembered, though, the conversation weeks ago in the cabin when Rik had also talked about pruning. "Sure," Carl chided. "Evolution in action."

He'd meant it to be sarcastic, but his stuffed up nose muffled the effect.

Rik cracked a small smile. "Precisely."

Carl snorted in disgust, but only managed to blow more snot out onto his shirt. "I was the one who told him about the jimsonweed."

"Still, it was his own choice to experiment with it." The GeneTrend executive studied him a moment. "Besides, you couldn't have known," he stated with confidence, as though reciting a simple fact. "Still, it is a shame . . ."

Carl looked at him, and the man met his stare with a steady gaze that finished the sentence: *what a shame that you killed your friend.*

Before Carl could react, he heard Fels call his name. Rik glanced quickly at his watch and hurried off towards his Lamborghini without even a goodbye.

A moment later his beautiful wife was by his side asking him if he was okay. How could he tell her? How could he explain that he wasn't okay at all, but that he could at least carry on as long as she was there with him.

"I think I may hate Rik," he declared instead.

She looked deep into his eyes, checking for damage. "You're allowed to hate him today," she said. "Tomorrow we'll talk about it and see if perhaps you just detest him."

She slipped her arm under his and they walked to their car.

He stopped and looked back. Kaj's coffin sat all alone now under the canopy. The cemetery workers stood to the side waiting to finish their job.

He took Fels's hand in his and they left.

PART III

THE BROOD

Chapter 10

Of all the months, it seemed to Carl that August most differentiated his boyhood home of El Cajon, just east of the city, from his new home in the Peninsular Range Mountains. Granted, February had seen snow, something experienced in El Cajon only when old refrigerators were defrosted, but the winter blanket had melted after a couple of days and seemed more a lovely, if ethereal, visitor than a climate. For the most part, winter days in the mountains were just cooler versions of the clear, dry days of the city.

August, though, lifted the cabin into the clouds. And what clouds they were. Ocean air, warmed as it was carried eastward by the strong onshore breezes, was lifted up and over the Range Mountains, the moisture condensing out as miles-high towers of billowing clouds, towers that paled the grandest structures of man to insignificance. When viewed from the beaches fifty miles to the west, these cumulonimbus monsters loomed over the distant mountains like doom-shaped Hiroshima clouds, as though Russia had been just faking it for twenty years, and the nuclear mini-suns were finally marching westward across the continent.

The cabin hunkered among these roiling heavenly behemoths like a fragile cocoon hidden in the grass among prancing Kumeyaay braves in the throes of the Temesaa ritual dance. Thunder grumbled against nearby peaks, and then, enraged by the obstruction, cracked and roared down the canyons and back up the ridges, searching for some sacrificial dweller of the impetuous Earth to crush flat. To Carl, sitting at the kitchen table watching the startling flashes of lightning flicker among the pans above the stove, it seemed that if the cumulus sky-beasts, powered by updrafts and writhing amidst tearing sheer winds, should decide to reach down a stormy hand to touch him, the walls would explode in splinters and he would find himself sailing away, high above the pine trees. Occasionally a storm did find them, but despite the threatening booms of the ripping thunder and the lightning's intimation of jolting electrocution, the storms merely pattered the roof comfortingly with welcomed rain and rattled a window here and there with a playful gust, like Defoe tapping to be let in for a cup of tea.

It was soon after one of these summer storms, as the sun returned to manifest in a thousand miniature replications among the drops still clinging to the tips of the pine needles, that Lilly finally decided it was time to introduce one of her children. Her tummy had grown and bulged until one day she had disappeared, leaving the cat food Fels had spooned into her dish to turn brown and crusty overnight. Later the following day she had returned, looking distracted, disheveled, and startlingly leaner, but had stayed only long enough to eat a few bites before disappearing again. For two weeks they had caught only fleeting glimpses of her on her way to and from her food dish, but now here she was with a pinkish brown bundle covered in thin fuzz dangling from her mouth. Under other circumstances Carl would have guessed that the ferret had found a rat's nest and carried home a meal of rat veal.

Lilly placed the ferret kit gently on the floor, and Fels clapped her hands against each cheek, exclaiming, "Oh my God, how cute!"

Carl thought the baby ferret looked unfinished and maybe should have stayed in the oven a while longer, but he held his tongue, the same way he did when presented with human newborns. He'd decided early on that finding beauty in babies was a talent exclusive to females that he didn't particularly envy.

"What do you think Lilly's up to?" he asked. "Maybe this one is the troublemaker of the litter and she's offering it up for adoption."

"She's showing it off," Fels countered, getting down on her hands and knees and leaning forward to peer at the tiny bundle of fuzzy pink skin. "She's proud of the little guy."

"How do you know it's a guy?"

Fels gave him the look that warned him he had better pretend to be joking. "Ferrets have sex organs too, you know."

If there was a ferret penis present, it was far too small for Carl to discern. This was another of those unique female senses: they knew the sex of any baby—human or otherwise—with one glance at a hundred feet. It was an instinct as foreign to a man as a dog's insatiable urge to sniff other dogs' butts . . . not that he was comparing baby appraisal with butt sniffing.

Shaking with the effort, the kit managed to push itself up with its front legs and peer blearily around at them. Carl guessed that they must be unfocused blobs to the infant ferret. In fact, it looked as though it may have just opened its eyes for the first time that very day. Carl sat down on the floor next to Fels, and Lilly picked the kit up and sat it down right in front of him.

"What does she want me to do?" he asked, looking nervously at Fels.

"Tell her how adorable her son is, of course."

"Sure." Turning back to Lilly, he said, "Your kid's an adorable mass of pink skin, and only looks a little like something a space alien might have accidentally left behind."

"Carl!" Fels cried, slapping him backhand across his arm.

"Hey! She can't understand what I'm saying."

"I can, and I don't like it."

Lilly must have decided that the visit was over, for she picked up the kit delicately with her teeth and trotted away.

"Well, that made my day," Fels proclaimed, getting up and walking back to the computer.

Carl watched the mommy ferret exit through the little hanging door he'd made for her. "I'm not sure if she was showing her spud off, or introducing it to us."

As soon as Lilly was through the swinging ferret exit, Carl jumped to his feet, ran to the door, and looked out the window, but she had disappeared. Shortly after he had found her entrance into the pile of branches the morning after her coyote encounter, she'd abandoned it, even going so far as closing up the hole. He was curious were she had moved her den to, but could never catch sight of her long enough to guess. It would seem that she didn't want him to know.

Ж Ж Ж

Over the course of the next week Lilly brought other kits to show them, or as Carl suspected, to introduce her children to the humans. She made four trips altogether, and although Carl couldn't tell one kit from another (Fels claimed she could), he assumed this meant that she had this many children.

It was soon after this that food began to disappear from the kitchen. Carl blamed Lilly, but Fels pointed out that ferrets were strictly meat-eaters, while the missing food was mostly fats and carbohydrates: almonds, dried apples and apricots, and even individual portion bags of pasta shells. She decided that it must be a rat, and by the way, what did he intend to do about it? After some thought he concluded that, morphologically, a ferret was not much different from a very large rat. Further, ferrets tended to be more inquisitive, and of the two, would be the more inclined to probe and poke. Consequently, whatever means he set out to trap the rat would likely catch Lilly first. Since she was a blooming mom with critical responsibilities, he hated to traumatize her by catching her in a trap, no matter how humane the operation.

Fels agreed and they left it at that.

And the food continued to disappear.

ж ж ж

The library books about angels also disappeared, but a steady stream of others continued to sprawl on the table next to the bed. The subjects varied depending on her interest of the week, but Carl noticed that a common thread developed around Eastern religions, focusing in on Hinduism, and finally sliding sideways and settling on Jainism. Still gun-shy from the Angel Wars, he didn't ask about it, even when he caught her talking quietly to Lilly a couple of times when she thought he was outside.

Lilly, meanwhile, continued to bring the kits around, always one at a time, and they seemed to grow visibly with each visit. The fuzz filled and thickened into fur, and Carl began to think of Lilly's offspring as young ferrets instead of her latest hunting catch. They, in turn, grew confident that their legs were meant for transportation, and an era of exploration began. Carl had read that ferrets were instinctively attracted to holes, closed spaces, and essentially anything that resembled a tunnel—a remnant of their weasel ancestry hunting ground-dwelling prey—and Lilly spent most of the time during the visits keeping them from disappearing into the cabin's many cavities.

At least for the most part. One time, when Fels was off at GeneTrend, Carl went outside to tackle a log or two, but realized that he hadn't put a CD into his portable player and went back inside. As he came through the kitchen door, he heard claws scratching and slipping on the linoleum floor, followed by an anxious-looking Lilly scampering into the living room from around the other side of the small island. She stopped, glanced quickly at him, and then sat back on her haunches nonchalantly, just as she'd done when he'd found her entrance into the pile of branches.

"Okay, toots," he demanded. "What's up?"

She just licked her paw, ignoring him.

He heard rustling somewhere in the kitchen. Walking softly and listening, he guessed that it was coming from one of the lower cabinets. He grasped the handle, and bracing himself to greet the big rat that had been stealing food, jerked the door open. There, staring at him in surprise, was a kit. A moment later, Lilly nosed her way past him, and the kit followed her out the little swinging door.

"You can't digest carbohydrates!" he called after their little retreating butts, but the ferret door swung to a stop, and the house was empty and quiet.

Ж Ж Ж

They decided to call the kits The Four Stooges. Each ferret offspring developed its own distinctive features. The dark fur between Moe's ears, contrasting with the white bands around his eyes, looked like Moe Howard's bowl-cut flop of hair. Curly's face was broader, and when he got excited, Carl imagined his right eyebrow rose slightly, just like that of his vaudeville namesake. The smallest ferret was clearly a Larry, for he was obviously the underdog whom the others constantly batted around. Shemp became Shemp by default, and it was simply fortuitous that, of all the various Three Stooges members, the real Shemp most resembled a ferret anyway. The fact that *their* Shemp was actually female was a point they doubted the original Shemp Howard would have minded.

The Stooges kits had grown quickly until they were now nearly as large as their mother, and Carl thought of them more as teenagers than youngsters. Lilly no longer chaperoned them, and the ferret gang came and went on their own, often playing together for an hour or more in the cabin before their mother arrived to shoo them back outside, as though she was concerned that they might wear out their welcome.

Carl still hadn't figured out where Lilly kept her den. He had thought he would find it for sure once the teens struck out on their own, but she must have taught them well, for try as he might, he wasn't able to follow them once they left the cabin. As soon as they exited the ferret door, they scampered around the side of the building away from him and then disappeared into the forest. And they didn't even head off into a consistent direction into the woods. It was uncanny the way they protected the location of their home, and although he tried to chalk it off as innate genetic programming, he couldn't help feeling slighted, as though he couldn't be trusted.

One evening the whole family—he, Fels, and the five ferrets—happened to be all together in the Great Hall when the problem he dreaded resurfaced. Lilly was playing boot camp sergeant, putting her platoon of ferret cadets through the paces by lightly pawing at them, one at a time, and then sprinting away so that they followed in pursuit. In the excitement, Larry forgot his turn and took off next to Moe. The larger ferret wasn't about to be usurped, and with motion almost too fast to discern, sprang at his brother, sending him tumbling before taking off again after his mother. As though driving home the lesson, Curly and Shemp ran to Larry and continued the punishment by batting at him as though he were some prey to be subdued. Their little brother, meanwhile, seemed clueless to the fact that he'd done anything wrong and became all the more excited with the attention. He welcomed the play—at least what he thought was play—and hopped about joyfully. As Curly and Shemp persisted with their assault, Larry's hops developed into loping sideways leaps, until he was executing a bona fide war dance.

Carl heard Fels cry out, and she leaped up and ran to the fray, pushing the haranguing brothers away with her bare foot while picking up Larry and hugging the young ferret to her breast. She sat back down next to Carl and held Larry's head between her hands so that she could look him directly in the eyes. "You shouldn't let them bully you like that," she admonished. She then hugged the ferret to her chest again. "Don't worry; Auntie Fels will take care of you. She'll be more careful this time."

Auntie Fels? More careful *this* time?

Carl felt his stomach drop away, replaced by a hollow nausea.

Later, as they were cleaning up the kitchen and the ferrets had departed to their hidden home, he commented, as casually as he could manage, "I see that you've been reading about Jainism."

"Uh huh," she agreed, giving him one cautious glance.

"Jainism believes in reincarnation, doesn't it?"

Fels continued wiping the counter as though she hadn't heard him. "Jainism," she finally replied, "is a religious philosophy. It can't 'believe' anything."

She was on the defense. He'd have to tread carefully. "You know what I mean."

The next instant she wrapped her arms around him and buried her head in his neck. He hugged her with one arm and held the washrag out with the other so that it wouldn't get her back wet.

"Honey," she said to his chest, her hair tickling his nose. "I can't stand it when you think I'm crazy."

"Are you?" he asked over the top of her head.

She pulled back and looked at him. "No! At least, I don't think so." She suddenly looked concerned. "They say that if you're crazy you probably don't know it. Do *you* think I'm crazy?"

Instead of answering her question, he said, "I think that if you're worried about it, that's also supposed to mean you're *not* crazy."

She sighed and lifted herself up from behind so that she was sitting on the counter. She stared off into the distance a minute, lost in thought, and then looked him in the eye. "This is definitely going to sound crazy, but I think that maybe Tod has been reincarnated in Larry."

"Because of the war dance?"

"Not just that. His eyes, his behavior; he's different from the others."

"More playful."

"Yeah. More . . . joyful."

She was right about that. Moe, Curly, and Shemp had their playful moods, but they could also stalk like serious predators, which, Carl noted, they were in their own smaller-scale world. Just the day before, he had watched out the window as Shemp and Moe sneaked up on a small ground squirrel. Their actions, evidently instinctual, uncannily resembled a carefully developed plan. Once they'd made their way through the scattered logs to within twenty feet of the squirrel, one on each side, Shemp jumped up—not *at* the squirrel, but just up—so that their prey flew off towards the waiting Moe. The rodent escaped with its life only because Larry chose that moment to come bounding over to play and the squirrel dove under a log instead.

It was then Larry's turn to flee from his angry brother and sister. While his siblings were practicing to be small predators, Larry seemed to want nothing more out of life than to play.

"What about Lilly?" Carl asked.

"What about her?"

"Do you still think that she's . . . you know—"

"An angel?"

"Yeah."

She shrugged. "I don't know."

He smiled.

"What?" she asked.

"You're really mixing up the religions here."

She pushed herself off the counter and, taking both his hands in hers, looked him in the eyes. "Who says that any one religion has all the answers? You know, my love, maybe it's okay if you and I don't share all the same beliefs. Can you accept that I might believe some things that you don't?"

"Well, sure," he replied.

With the exception, he thought, *that Larry is actually Tod, reincarnated.*

She hugged him. "Thanks. You're the best."

"Sure," he said, returning the hug tentatively.

He would have felt more like the best if he could shake the nagging doubt about her sanity.

Chapter 11

"I don't think a man like Rik exaggerates for effect," Defoe said as he squatted on the floor and held out a piece of his ham sandwich to entice Moe to come closer. "He's too proud of his precise scientific mind to unfocus his thinking that way."

Carl sat on the sofa and watched his friend. Fels was on-site at GeneTrend, and he was supposed to be out liberating slabs of pine. Defoe had come to "help."

"I remember Rik talking about how human genes were becoming weak," Carl replied, "but I just can't swallow the idea of cloning people with ferrets."

His friend cocked an eyebrow at him. "I don't think a gene can become 'weak.' Rik described it as dilution of the human gene pool. And cloning is an exact replication of one organism; this would be . . . I don't know, maybe gene splicing."

Carl snorted. "Do you even know what gene splicing is?"

"Not really. But that's not the point."

"Then what is the point?"

"Kaj's warning."

"You really think that Rik has been somehow combining humans with ferrets, like in the movie *The Island of Dr. Moreau*?"

"That un-credible movie was based on a story H. G. Wells wrote around the turn of the last century before they even knew the structure of atoms, let alone DNA."

"You didn't answer the question."

Defoe wasn't able to tease Moe into coming closer, but Larry came up from behind and sniffed at the piece of sandwich.

"You're right, I didn't," his friend agreed. "I can't have an opinion about what Rik has been doing since I have no direct evidence." He took Larry into his arms and fed him the food. "I can hold cautious suspicions, though."

Carl heard the beep of an incoming email on the computer. Thinking it might be Fels, he walked over to look. It was from GeneTrend, but not Fels. Rather, somebody named Weiner; at least that was the first part of the return email address. Below, in the email preview window, he saw that the sender was asking about Lilly.

That's unusual, Carl thought. Nobody was supposed to know she was here. Also, the name Weiner was familiar somehow.

Unable to resist, even though it had been addressed to Fels, he opened the message. He immediately saw why the name had seemed familiar: "Weiner" was just a shortened version, as people sometimes used in email addresses. The man's full name was Weinermach, and Carl recognized it as the Nobel Prize winner that Rik had hired earlier that year. The scientist was asking how Lilly was doing. Specifically, he was wondering whether the ferret's behavior was reduced.

Reduced? Carl thought. What an odd thing to ask.

He turned to Defoe and found him inspecting Larry's paws closely. "Trying to see if you can glean fingers in there?" Carl asked.

The philosopher looked up, blushing. "If I tell you the truth, you will never let me forget it, so I will take refuge in the Fifth Amendment of the Constitution."

Carl told him about Weindermach's message, that he was asking if Lilly's behavior was reducing. "Reduction in chemistry," Defoe explained, "is the opposite of oxidation. Perhaps the Nobel Prize winner is asking if our ferret mother is freeing her mind of rust."

"In other words, you don't know either."

"I prefer my other words, but yes, the query seems inexplicable. By the way," he added, putting Larry down and getting to his feet, "Speaking of inexplicable, let's go for a walk and stretch our legs. I have something to show you."

"What about the logs?"

"There's plenty of time in the day for that. Come on, let's go."

Carl sighed. Unlike Defoe, he technically wasn't retired, and he was supposed to be holding up his end of the home maintenance. On the other hand, there was still plenty of time.

Defoe headed off in a familiar direction.

"I think I've had enough of Tekumewa if that's where you're taking me."

"No you haven't," was Defoe's response.

As soon as they emerged into the hilltop clearing, Carl could see that something had changed. The pile of rocks was still huddled in a tight mass, a humble tribute to a native leader centuries dead, but beside it lay something brown and scattered. As they climbed the hill, he saw that it was dirt. Somebody had been digging around the base of the pile. In fact, when they arrived at the Kumeyaay memorial, Carl could see that an animal had dug a deep hole under the pile, throwing the dirt back over the grass. Scattered about were incongruent droppings of civilization, the charred remnants of Defoe's Temesaa offering, and Carl still caught fleeting whiffs of Brut. He bent over to peer into the hole, but the interior was lost in darkness.

"Toby told me about it," Defoe explained. "It was the coyote."

Carl stood up. "How does he know?"

"He caught it digging when he came to visit yesterday."

Defoe looked at him expectantly.

"What?" Carl asked.

"The coyote greeted Toby."

Carl eyed his friend cautiously. "What do you mean?"

Defoe grinned conspiratorially. "The creature stood up on its hind legs and waved hello."

"Sure," Carl agreed cynically, peering again into the inscrutable blackness of the hole, "and then it probably tipped its hat and asked Toby to join him for a biscuit and a nice cup of tea."

He remembered, though, how the coyote had reared up when they'd confronted each other in the log patch. He pushed the memory away, putting his mental foot down. He wasn't going to fall into that pit, where shadows and hints fed the superstition fire.

"What do you think the coyote was after?" Carl asked.

"Perhaps what we all seek."

"Money?"

"Besides the empty promise of fool's gold."

"Sex?"

"Perhaps it would save time if I just told you."

"Perhaps."

"Freedom."

"It was looking for freedom in a hole?"

"Perhaps it wasn't trying to hide, but rather letting something *out*."

Carl shot a quick glance at the hole, feeling the hairs prickle on the back of his neck. *Ghosts*, he thought. *Bah! Humbug!*

Primal fear urged him to get away from there, and so he forced himself to look again into the black cavity. He remembered that he had a pocketknife with an LED light built in—a Christmas present from Defoe, who had bought a dozen and then declared his yearly shopping complete. The tiny beam was invisible under the bright sunshine, but when he lay flat on his stomach and bent his arm over his forehead, blocking the daylight, the little twinkle of light was sufficient to reveal barely discernable details within. The hole angled down for perhaps eighteen inches, and to Carl's great relief ended—no opening into a subterranean tomb, no flicker of hellish underworld fires.

He was pulling himself back and away when something besides dirt caught his eye. At first he took it to be the smooth surface of a stone, but there was a pattern too regular to be natural. Two dark bands, one wider than the other, ran parallel across the two inches of exposed surface.

"What the devil?" he muttered.

"What do you see?" Defoe asked from above.

"I'm not sure."

Bracing himself for the cold grasp of a skeleton's hand on his wrist, he reached in and felt the surface. It was cool and smooth. He dug away some more dirt with his fingers, and could tell that the surface was actually concave, bending away more to the sides than vertically.

He pulled back and sat up, staring thoughtfully into the again-impenetrable hole.

"Are you trying to torture me?" Defoe asked.

Carl looked up. "Sorry. I just don't know what to make of it."

As Carl described what he'd found, Defoe nodded, grinning broadly even before he'd finished. "It's Tekumewa's burial urn," his friend confidently declared.

Defoe explained that the Kumeyaay often cremated their dead and buried the ashes and remaining bones in a clay vase.

"My God!" Carl exclaimed. Even as only a supposition, the idea that an ancient Indian chief was buried here had been discomfiting; now that he'd felt concrete evidence with his own fingers, it was downright unnerving.

"Any germs would have expired centuries ago, you know," Defoe assured.

Carl realized that he'd been unconsciously wiping his hands on his pants. It was a grave, after all. "What do you think we should do? Take it to the Balboa Park museum?"

Defoe frowned his disapproval. "Why, for heaven's sake? Would you want your great-grandfather's casket dug up and placed on display?"

"We're just going to . . . leave it?"

"Why not? Tekumewa has lain here peacefully for two and a half centuries. What right do we have to defy the wishes of his tribesmen?"

Carl knew that his motives were self-serving. He'd have peace of his own should the mighty warrior who had been killed by Carl's own race depart the mountain.

"What about the hole?" Carl wondered. "Do we just leave it?"

The philosopher stroked his chin. "Yes, that is something of a dilemma."

Carl shrugged. "Why don't we just fill it back up?"

Defoe looked at him, still contemplating. "Interfere?"

"Interfere with what? A wild coyote looking for a rabbit's lair?" He liked saying this, describing the coyote in very normal terms.

"Who are we to judge the ways of the universe?" Defoe replied.

"It's the same as always," Carl accused, shaking his head sadly. "When I want an answer, all I get is another question."

In the end Defoe agreed that they should fill in the hole. "They," of course, being Carl using a flat rock as a shovel.

On the way back to the cabin, Carl thought that he caught movement off in the trees. He wasn't sure if it was just a trick of his imagination, but he seemed to catch glimpses of brown fur pacing them, following along behind and to the side, just out of sight.

Bah! he thought. Next he'd believe that Larry was indeed Tod reincarnated.

Ж Ж Ж

Fels stayed over in San Diego that night, and so Carl got up late the next morning. Normally he would have taken the opportunity to blast some music, but he listened instead to coverage of a wildfire in the San Bernardino Mountains on the radio, and this was why he caught the coyote by surprise when he opened the kitchen door. The animal was nosing around the branch pile and froze, staring at him. Carl decided to wait out the critter, and stared back. After a few seconds his adversary whined and wagged its snout back and forth as though protesting Carl's rudeness.

"You're not going to intimidate me," Carl warned, stepping slowly through the doorway and onto the gravel they'd scattered just outside. He could feel his heart pumping with an intensity appropriate if the animal were a mountain lion, rather than a small-game hunter barely a quarter his weight.

The coyote watched him intently, frozen, as though sculpted from stone.

Carl took one small step forward, and then another. He walked slowly onward, but still the coyote stood watching him. When he was halfway, he stopped and put his hands on his hips. "This is my property, and you are trespassing," he declared.

He realized that he was talking to the animal as though it really did harbor Tekumewa's spirit.

The coyote whined again and sat back on its haunches.

Carl advanced another step, but this seemed to take the coyote by surprise, for it scrambled to its feet and backed away. Carl held out his hands, as though demonstrating that he harbored no weapons, and in response, the coyote, this animal that had been hovering at the periphery of his life, rose gracefully up on its hind legs and spread out its front paws as though mimicking him. For three eternal heartbeats, man and animal gazed in each other's eyes as equals. Then with a little yip of broken resolve, or perhaps victory, the coyote twisted and sprang away as though fleeing a rain of bullets.

Carl watched it disappear into the pines. "I'll be damned," he muttered, turning and stopping short. Crouching behind him, were Moe, Shemp, and Curly, watching intently. Carl laughed. "Well, deputies, it looks like we scared away that varmint but good."

Larry came bounding from the house, only to turn and, like the coyote, flee when his brothers and sister bounded after him.

ж ж ж

That night, after Carl had related the strange encounter, Fels suggested that maybe he was misinterpreting a natural coyote behavior. He looked at her a moment and then said, "In other words, you think I'm imagining the whole thing."

"That's not what I said at all. I was simply offering that sometimes we . . . well, we sometimes—in our minds—exaggerate the meaning of things."

As soon as she said this she threw him a quick glance and furrowed her brow.

He just smiled.

"I know," she added, "you think that *I'm* the one imagining things."

"That's not what I said at all," he replied, imitating her. "However, the pot should definitely be careful about calling the kettle black."

She didn't say anything as she turned on the computer. "You can't deny that Larry is different, you know," she finally declared.

He couldn't deny that. If anything, Larry and his siblings continued to diverge; the odd brother wasn't actually smaller than the rest, but compared to his playful abandon, their no-nonsense demeanor suggested a degree of physical power. It was as though the other three had a serious plan, while Larry was trying to have a party.

"That kettle remark is racist, by the way," she added.

He was still processing this, wondering why he had never before considered that a pot's remarks about a kettle's blackness would be derogatory, when Fels followed with a "Huh!"

"What's up?" he asked, walking over.

"I got a message from Weinermach. He's asking if Lilly's behavior is reduced. What a strange question."

"Yeah, it's weird, isn't it?"

She looked at him curiously.

"I, uh, opened it accidentally." He sighed. "That's a lie. I couldn't control my curiosity."

"No," she remarked absently, reading through the scientist's message again, "you were right the first time; pretty much everything you do is an accident—nobody's supposed to know that Lilly is here! How am I supposed to respond to this?"

"Hmm, maybe you should ask Rik?"

She immediately began typing, and he watched over her shoulder as the message unfolded, asking her boss how she should respond, and finishing up by asking whether he could explain why the Nobel Prize winner would inquire whether Lilly's behavior was reduced.

"Defoe thinks Weinermach is asking whether Lilly is cleaning the rust from her brain. Maybe the guy just wants to know if the easy mountain life is making her lazy."

"Weinermach is Swiss. He talks with a thick German accent, and he often has trouble remembering English words. My guess is that he meant something else, something similar to reduced."

"Maybe he really meant discount, like whether Lilly spends all her time looking for them. He's wondering if Lilly has found the equivalent of a ferret Wal-Mart. That way they'll be able to measure her intelligence by how much ferret junk she accumulates."

She rolled her eyes. "A better way to measure her intelligence would be to drop the two of you on a deserted island and see who survives. Actually, that would be predictable. They could still measure her intelligence, though, by how long she manages to keep you alive."

"That's not a very loving thing to say."

"Do you want love, or truth?"

"Let me think about it."

"By the way," she added, scanning through a Wikipedia entry," I was wrong about the kettle and pot remark being racist. The idiom goes all the way back to the seventeenth century—before slavery in America was even an issue."

"I knew that," he lied. "I just didn't want to hurt your ego."

Later that night they paused the movie they were watching for a pee break, and when he returned, he found Fels at the computer. Her face was screwed up in thought, so he went over to see what she was looking at. It was an email message from Rik in response to hers:

> *will talk to Weinermach. no need to respond. probably time to visit the kids. i'll be up tomorrow.*

"Great," he uttered over her shoulder. "Tomorrow" was Saturday. "We don't get any days off. Why doesn't anybody use capital letters anymore?"

" 'We' don't get any days off?" Fels queried. "He's my boss."

"Yeah, but I won't be able to run around in my underwear. It's just like being at work."

Fels did as instructed, and Weinermach's email sat on the computer unresponded. Early the next morning she received another message from the Nobel Prize winner. He apologized for the bother and asked her to disregard his earlier message.

"Sounds like Rik did indeed talk to him," Fels observed.

"I hope the poor man was able to make it to an urgent care facility afterwards," Carl remarked.

She smiled thinly and nodded.

Humor fails if you cut too close to the truth.

Chapter 12

R ik arrived late the next morning amid a cloud of dust and the growling whine of a high-powered engine exercising its muscles. Instead of either the SUV or the Lamborghini, he now piloted a Hummer, which barely fit between the boulders lining their road. Carl wondered if the genetics genius had bought the monstrosity just for his infrequent trips here.

Rik climbed down from the faux military vehicle grinning broadly, obviously exhilarated by the adventure.

"Hit any land mines?" Carl called.

"It felt like it there a couple of times," Rik replied with uncharacteristic glee.

When they went inside, they found that Fels already had water boiling.

"Mountain people drink a lot of tea," their guest observed, reverting to familiar sarcastic Rik-mode. "Where's my little girl?"

Carl pointed towards her cage where a most unhappy ferret lay curled, moping. The night before, Carl had been a most unhappy man laying in his bed thinking about this. From the beginning they had led Rik to believe that Lilly essentially lived in the house, only going outside under close supervision. The truth, of course, was that the mother ferret rarely even came inside once the kits were weaned. When she did, it was usually just to eat, and then she'd immediately disappear again. Carl had waited since sunrise, and was relieved when she ambled in for her breakfast, unaware that she was about to be kidnapped.

The kits were a problem he hadn't been able to solve. Once he'd corralled their mother, they seemed to sense something was up, and he'd seen neither hide nor fur of them since. He was hoping that Rik considered the offspring an accidental and insignificant byproduct.

In fact, Rik hardly glanced at Lilly before asking about the kits.

Carl looked to Fels but she seemed equally at a loss. He realized that it was pretty dumb not to have talked this over before Rik arrived. "They, uh . . . we sort of thought that Lilly was your main concern—"

"What are you trying to say?" Rik demanded, suddenly earnest. "Are the kits okay?"

"Look," Fels interrupted with a quick glance at Carl, "we can't hide this any longer—"

"What the hell is going on!" Rik cried, throwing his hands up. "Where's my kits!"

"If you'll let me explain," Fels continued, trying to control herself, "it's impossible to keep Lilly inside the cabin." She walked over and pulled aside the laundry basket they'd placed in front of the ferret-door. "Get the idea?"

Rik looked from the little swinging door to Lilly's cage, where the ferret seemed to watch him with suspicion.

"We put Lilly in the cage just before you came," Fels went on. "She hasn't been in there in months."

Her boss raised one eyebrow and then smiled.

An instant later his brow furrowed again. "But what about the kits?"

"They're fine. They come and go as they please. They're just not around right now."

Rik nodded, seeming to take stock of the situation. "Anything we can do to get them to show themselves?"

Fels shrugged. "They come around pretty often. If we wait, we'll probably see them eventually. I'm not sure how they'll react to a new face, though."

"Indeed," Rik agreed, nodding. "Indeed."

Carl and Rick took lawn chairs out back and placed cans of open cat food on the sawdust while Fels put together an early lunch. Carl sat down to wait, but Rik took a small bottle from his pocket and squeezed a few clear drops from the eyedropper into each open can, explaining that these were vitamins. He handed Carl the bottle with instructions to do the same each day. "Be careful not to get any on you," he added. "If you do, wash it off with soap and water."

Carl looked at the brown, unmarked bottle. "I didn't know vitamins could be dangerous."

"The vitamins aren't," Rik explained, "but there's also enzymes to help absorption. You don't want these to be on your skin very long."

Carl slipped the bottle into his pocket. It seemed strange: vitamins that you didn't want on your skin, but he wasn't a doctor.

Hell, he didn't even know what an enzyme was.

"How do they seem?" Rik asked, sitting down and stretching his feet out, enjoying the warm sunshine.

"The kits?" Carl asked.

"Yes. Do they seem well adjusted?"

Carl assumed he didn't mean emotionally. "They seem healthy. To tell you the truth, we don't even know where they live."

"You mean you don't know where Lilly has made the den?"

"Right. It almost seems like they go out of their way to keep it a secret."

Carl glanced over and saw that Rik was smiling.

The genetics engineer shrugged. "That seems natural enough. You'd keep your home hidden from adversaries as well."

"They think we're adversaries?"

Rik shook his head, almost annoyed. "No. I meant in general. An animal is instinctively going to keep its lair hidden from other species larger than itself."

Dogs and cats routinely give birth in their owners' coat closets, but Carl decided not to toss monkey wrenches around the finely machined gears of the scientist's mind. "Sometimes I think I should hide my house from *them*."

Rik gave him a curious look. "Why do you say that?"

"They're stealing our food."

Carl could tell that their guest was trying to hide a smile. "It's true!" Carl insisted. "We've caught them!"

This wasn't strictly true, but close enough.

Rik shrugged, smiling openly now. "Ferrets hoard things—it's their nature."

"Yeah, but it's supposed to be shiny doodads, like jewelry, not dried fruit and bags of pasta. They can't even digest carbs—according to Fels."

Rik studied him a moment. "I wouldn't worry about it."

"Worry about what?" Fels asked, coming out with a tray of sandwiches.

"Ferret food thieves," Carl explained.

"They took your last chocolate bar overnight," she announced.

"My chocolate! Wait a second, now that's going too far. If they think they can—"

Fels nudged him and pointed. Curly had suddenly appeared from behind a log off to the left. She pointed again, and he saw Moe off to the right, and then Shemp in the middle.

"See them?" Carl asked.

"Yes!" Rik whispered excitedly as though he was witnessing the appearance of Bigfoot's clan.

Shemp took a few tentative steps forward, staring at Rik and sniffing the air.

"That's the female," Fels narrated quietly. "She's the boss of the gang."

Carl realized that she was right. Lately Shemp was the first to show her snout and the last to wave her long, pointy tail goodbye.

"Well, what do you know?" Rik said without taking his eyes off of Shemp. "And here I thought ferrets and weasels were strictly solitary carnivores."

It was difficult to tell from the whisper, but it seemed to Carl that Rik was being sarcastic, as though he expected this all along.

"Isn't there a fourth one?" Rik asked.

"That's Larry," Fels replied. "He's different."

Rik looked at her. "Different how?"

She gave Carl a quick glance that warned, *don't say a word!* "He's nicer."

"Nicer?"

"Not so . . . competitive," Fels said, flustered. "Not so rough."

Carl chuckled. "Sounds like Larry isn't the different one."

He hadn't thought about it before, but Larry acted like Lilly had when she first arrived, before she became the responsible mom.

Rik was looking at him with interest. "What do you mean?"

Carl shrugged. "Larry likes to just sleep and play. That's what ferrets are supposed to do."

"Says who?"

"Wikipedia."

Rik snorted. "Now *there's* a reliable source."

Carl didn't say anything. He wasn't going to argue with somebody with Rik's credentials, but he'd come to trust the communal web-based encyclopedia. It seemed to him exactly the sort of resource the original Internet pioneers had in mind.

Suddenly a flash of brown fur shot between their chairs from behind, did a quick U-turn, and the next instant Larry came to rest on Fels's lap, sniffing her chin, as though checking out what she'd had for lunch.

"Here's my little buddy!" Fels cooed, wrapping her arms around the wriggling ball of fur.

Carl distinctly remembered that she had always called Tod her little buddy as well.

Rik glanced at Larry but seemed mostly interested in the other three, as though waiting to see their reaction. The three siblings— what Carl had come to think of as The Hood—came slowly forward, until they converged twenty feet in front of them.

"You my buddy, aren't you?" Fels was saying to Larry in baby-talk, rubbing the young ferret so that the fur stood up at odd angles, like he'd just crawled out of ferret-bed.

Larry's head swiveled suddenly around, and he seemed to see his brothers and sister for the first time. An instant later he squirmed free of Fels's grasp and jumped to the ground to greet his brothers and sister.

The Hood's reaction was immediate. Shemp stepped carefully forward to meet her brother, while Moe and Curly slunk around to each side. Not for the first time, Carl wondered why Larry kept walking into the line of fire. The teen ferret was either admirably optimistic, or dumb as a turnip. As if on cue, all three of The Hood sprang on their prey. To a casual observer, and certainly to Larry, the attack might have seemed like so much ferret-play. Carl had watched the three of them gang up on Larry enough, though, to see that, of the four, only he considered it great fun. If The Hood were merely adolescent carnivore kits using rough play to develop their hunting skills, the graduation ceremony should have been held weeks before. They attacked Larry—grabbing, growling, and biting—with a fervor that made Carl flinch.

He glanced at Rik who followed the action with rapt wonderment. Fels, on the other hand, looked mad as hell, and he knew she was about to come to her "Buddy's" rescue.

Another flash of fur streaked in from the left, though, and Lilly broke up the rumble. Although now hardly bigger than her children, she was still Mom, and for a time yet held final authority.

The Hood slunk away, seeming to dissolve among the logs, and Larry got to his feet and shook himself off, like a man might after falling down a flight of stairs. His mother glanced once at the humans sitting in their chairs, as though indignant that they had used her children as entertainment, and ambled away with as much dignity as an elongated, cartoon-shaped animal could manage.

"Did you see that?" Rik exclaimed gleefully.

"Amazing," Carl agreed. "Mothers keep the peace across the entire animal kingdom."

"No, I mean the coordination."

"The three kits, you mean?"

"Of course! They attacked the weak one as though operating off the same plan."

"Seems to me like just a bunch of bullies."

"No! It's a paradigm of aggressive cognitive empathy."

"You mean they cooperate?"

Carl couldn't help himself.

Rik waved off the poke, peering around, trying to get one last look at one of the Hood. "Have you seen any unusual aggression in their behavior?" he asked.

"I don't know," Carl replied. "That seemed unusually aggressive right there."

"I mean towards you."

"Not really. To tell you the truth, we don't have a whole lot of contact with them any more—except Larry, the gang victim."

"Well, they're growing up essentially wild, so don't be surprised if they show some amount of aggressive behavior."

"Are they going to gang up on me like they did Larry?"

"The weak one? That's natural. If allowed to function, evolution weeds out the unfit."

Carl looked at Fels. His beautiful wife had picked up Larry and was seething, ready to pounce on Rik just as Shemp had done to her little Tod reincarnation.

"Hey!" Carl called. "Let's see if there's any beer in the fridge."

With a last glance around at the now-empty field of logs, the wealthy genetics expert stood up and walked into the cabin.

Fels sat cooing soothingly to her Buddy.

Carl figured he'd saved Rik's life.

ж ж ж

Carl grunted as he rolled the freshly cut log slab. He did his best to steer the two-hundred pound wheel, but like its recalcitrant predecessors, the severed disk wobbled and staggered, fighting him with its own idea of where it should lie. Instead of a pile of log slices ready to be split into firewood, he was creating more of a general zone.

Pausing to wipe the sweat from his eyes, he sniffed. Smoke! Peering off to the east, he saw only blue sky, then reminded himself that the light wind was blowing from the west—the normal afternoon on-shore breeze. He glanced quickly in that direction, but knew he'd find no ominous brown cloud. It was probably a stray waft from the chimney of their closest neighbor a quarter mile away. West winds were generally light, and when they were strong, were wet with ocean moisture. It was the dry east winds—what they called the Santa Anas—gusting along sometimes at hurricane force that stoked the wild fires.

As he reached down to pick up the chainsaw, a raven let loose a raucous protest. The large, black birds were common in the mountains, and he usually ignored their cawing, but something about this one caught his attention. He glanced towards the edge of the clearing and saw a flick of motion, almost too subtle to register. Whatever it was, it had disappeared over the bank. Figuring it was one of the ferrets, he grabbed the saw's pull-cord, but then put the saw back down. He couldn't have explained why his curiosity was peeked, since the ferrets could be seen at any time slinking about around the cabin and felled logs. Maybe it was that the motion had somehow seemed rushed, as though spurred by the unexpected alarm sounded by the raven.

He lay the saw gently back down and walked softly towards the bank, taking care not to step on any twigs. At the clearing's edge he slowed and eased up to the bank's lip. Looking down into the soft, filtered light among the trunks of the pine trees, he saw nothing. Another impulse drew his attention to the right along the bank's bottom. There, almost invisible against the brown needles, was Curly. The ferret didn't see him, and was sitting on his haunches licking his foreleg, like a cat might. In a sudden spirit of devilishness he called out, "Hey you!"

Curly seemed to spring from a catapult, nearly flipping over backwards as his reflexes engaged, and then was betrayed by the same instinct: as his feet hit the ground, the animal scrambled forward, but then, as though brought up short by an invisible rope, jerked to a stop, glanced once at Carl, and ran off to the side, quickly losing himself among the tree trunks.

This was now familiar behavior. The young ferret was trying to hide something, but had given away the location before recovering from Carl's shout. He walked over to where he guessed Curly had suddenly decided to change his direction of flight. There was nothing to be seen, just the thick blanket of pine needles serving as bedding for the remains of long-fallen trees in various stages of decay. Casting his gaze farther, he scanned the forest floor, not sure what he was even looking for. *Something unusual*, he thought. *Something out of place.* And then he saw it. Whereas the needles everywhere else were flat and compact, a patch the size of a small throw rug was jumbled, as though someone had picked up armfuls, dropped them back down, and then walked across them.

Scraping the top layer away, Carl found fresh dirt underneath. For comparison, he pulled away the needles a few feet away and found the dark loam of many decades of decay. Somebody, or something, was hiding a recent dig.

And then he noticed the log. It was as if it too had been hiding and was now suddenly unveiled. Hollow and covered in green moss, its mouth lay at one end of the concealed dirt.

Understanding erupted intact like a stage suddenly bathed in spotlights. Curly, along with probably the rest as well, had dug a tunnel, using the hollow log to hide the entrance. But where was the other end? He looked up the bank and there it was, his mountain of unresolved obligation. Above him, silhouetted against the blue sky, was what in his mind he still considered a pile, but knew was more a hillock, of dead branches.

He now also understood why the coyote had been sniffing around the pile. Its nose told it there were ferret burgers hiding within.

Either that, or Tekumewa was curious about a new type of animal living within his hunting grounds.

Carl climbed the bank and looked into the mass of tree limbs. Under the bright afternoon sun, he could see barely a foot into the mess before the matrix of twigs blocked his view. He wondered how many, if any, of the Hood were in there right now. What about Lilly? Was it her den? And Larry? Did they let their "weak" brother into the stronghold?

The conscientious part of him, the part that stood in for Fels when she was gone, told him to walk away; he had no business disturbing the family. The stronger part of him—the adult extension of the ten year-old who couldn't resist climbing their ash tree to see with his own eyes the Mockingbird's eggs, even as the mother bird screamed and dove repeatedly at him—prodded him to investigate. Inquiring minds need to know.

He pulled out some of the lighter limbs and threw them aside. He stopped, and listened. He thought he heard rustling from deep within. The Fels part shook its finger in admonition, and he felt guilt at what he was doing. From the secret core of the mound, though, the powerful attractive force of curiosity drew him onward. In any case, it was his pile, and besides, they'd never forced the ferret clan to live outside. They had always been welcome to set up house in the cabin.

He removed branches until he'd carved out a small crater. That was probably enough. He then just pushed aside one limb after another, digging a passageway through the gigantic ball of twig cotton. Suddenly, leaning into the mound from a standing position as he burrowed down, his extended hands broke through into an inner cavity. He could tell this by feel only, since the sunlight didn't penetrate this deeply. He moved his head, allowing a stray ray to find an odd angle, and he caught a glint a couple of feet farther down. His eyes slowly adjusted to the dim light, and he began to make out what lay at the bottom of the little cave. Scattered on a flooring of grass and pine needles was an assortment of the food that had been disappearing from their kitchen. There was something else, though, something round and . . . brown. Then he saw a glint from two beady eyes. One of the ferrets—he couldn't tell which—sat hunched, staring up at him.

"Ouch!"

He jerked backwards, pushing himself out of his excavation. A sharp pain had jabbed at his ankle. As he slid off the pile, the sharp points of twigs tearing at his shirt and chest, he could feel something heavy dragging at his pant leg. It was Shemp! The little bitch had bitten him! She now hung on to his jeans with clenched teeth, staring up at him with murderous eyes.

He shook his leg. "Let go, you little hyena!"

His ankle hurt; he could tell she had broken the skin. He had the urge to swing her wide, sending her flying off in an arc, but despite the pain, he really didn't want to hurt her. After all, he had violated their home.

And then he noticed something that made him pause. The young ferret was having a convulsion. At least that's what it looked like. She was still hanging onto his jeans with jaws of death, but her long, sleek body undulated with spasms. And then, just as suddenly as she had attacked, she jumped back and scampered away into the trees.

He watched her, stunned, until she disappeared, and then looked down at his leg. He was bleeding! A patch of dark wetness the size of a hockey puck was spreading from his wound.

Actually, it wasn't really spreading. In fact, it couldn't possibly be from her bite. That much blood soaking his jeans would have meant a massive wound, and her teeth had barely nicked him.

He sat down and pulled his knee up so that he could examine the fluid more closely. A swirling bit of breeze brought him an odor that was recognizable no matter what the source, animal or man. Tiny bits of peanut confirmed the conclusion. Shemp had puked on him.

He pulled up the pant leg, careful not to touch the regurgitated mess. He had been right: his wound consisted of two little scratches barely half an inch long.

He looked around. There were no ferrets to be seen. He was sorry he'd been so damned nosey. He'd had no right to break into their den. Shemp was one brave little ferret. He remembered reading that bravery was facing danger despite fear, while doing the same thing fearlessly was simply stupid.

Well, she'd been plenty afraid. It made her throw up.

"Sorry!" he called out into the quiet afternoon. "I'm a shit! But I promise to leave you alone!"

He'd have to tell Fels about this. He was going to catch hell for sure.

Chapter 13

"I caught hell, that's for sure," Carl said to Defoe. "Man, I thought Fels was going to make me sleep out in the branch pile, and then invite them to use my half of the bed."

His fried eyed the height of the hammock they were hanging, and satisfied, marked the trunk of the tree with the awl. "Curiosity killed the cat but saved mankind from a brutish life of naked survival among the wild animals."

"Kant?"

"No."

"Nietzsche?"

"No. Me."

"So, you're saying that I was justified in taking a peek?"

His friend picked up the old hand-drill he'd brought along and cranked the brace handle, slowly boring a hole in the tree to take the large eyebolt. "I wasn't referring to you."

"But I was the one who ripped a hole in their roof."

"I was talking about me."

The old philosopher pulled the drill out of the hole and looked at him. "I don't trust Rik."

"That's obvious. But I don't understand how that . . ." He recalled Defoe studying the kits' paws. "You're curious too, because you want to know if the Hood are showing human traits."

"I don't know what I'm expecting. I wish you had taken a closer peek, though."

"I would have if a ferret wasn't trying to chew my ankle off while puking on me."

Defoe put the drill back into the hole and cranked a couple of turns, but then stopped. "I'm glad, however, that it was you and not me when it was time to tell Fels—what's the matter?"

A whine had drawn Carl's attention and he saw that the coyote stood at the edge of the trees, watching them intently. It looked back and forth from one to the other of the two men, as though expecting something from them. The animal whined again and hopped up for a moment on its hind legs.

"Did you *see* that?" Defoe hissed.

The coyote continued to stare at them.

"I don't think he's done," Carl whispered back.

Indeed, the hop had been simply an aborted attempt, for with an assured push of its front paws the coyote rose up completely onto its hind legs like Carl had seen several times before. He heard a gasp from Defoe, and spreading its forelegs for balance, the animal turned its back to them with a series of short, unsteady steps.

"Great Zeus!" Defoe blurted, probably louder than he'd intended.

The coyote then did something that Carl would have thought he imagined if not for Defoe's later concurrence. It turned its head to them . . . and smiled.

The image, although forever burned into his memory, lasted only a second. An instant later the coyote dropped to all fours and stood snarling towards the trees.

Carl saw Shemp advancing slowly from within the forest depths, her shiny little eyes fixed on the predator twenty times her weight. He knew that the ferret was committing suicide if in fact it was alone, but . . . yes! There, also approaching from off to the right was Curly, and . . . there! From the other side came Moe, all of them slinking forward on confident paws of deadly intent.

The coyote seemed not to see the flanking Hood members as it growled and snapped at Shemp.

"Tekumewa!" Defoe called out. "Look out!"

The coyote didn't respond, but Moe suddenly turned and ran back. Carl saw that Larry had come to see what all the fuss was about. Like a well-aimed cannonball, Moe bowled his little brother over and grabbed his neck in his jaws.

The motion broke the coyote's fixation on Shemp. It bounded one leap towards Curly, yipping loudly now, then turned and sprang at Shemp.

Deprived of a third of their force, Curly and Shemp took off into the pines.

The coyote turned to the men, and seeming to give them one last reluctant nod, bounded away into the forest.

"That was absolutely—" Defoe started to say, but Carl raced off to rescue Larry, where Moe still had him pinned to the ground by the neck. The Hood brother growled angrily, as if threatening to snap the lithe neck cleanly in two.

"Let him go!" Carl yelled, reaching down to pull off the larger brother. He wrapped his hand around Moe's belly, but the ferret turned and bit him.

"Damn it!" Carl cried, jumping back.

Like his ankle it was just a scratch and he lost interest when he realized that Moe was retching, like a cat bringing up a hairball.

Lilly appeared beside them, sniffing her children. Moe jerked his head up as though suddenly freed from constraint and trotted off. His mother licked her smallest child soothingly where her Hood bully son had clasped him.

Defoe stood with his hands on his hips, gazing off in the direction the coyote had departed. When Carl walked up to him, his friend looked at him and said, "I told you the animal could walk like a man."

"I think I told *you*. Our friend comes around about once a day now to show off."

He sucked at the scratch on his hand. It wasn't deep, but his saliva made it sting.

"He knows what that man has done," Defoe said, nodding at Carl's hand.

"What the hell are you talking about? Who 'he'? And what man?"

His friend tilted his head and shrugged, then picked up the drill to continue hanging the hammock.

"You're talking about Tekumewa, aren't you?" Carl guessed, walking around to face Defoe. "You think a dead Indian has come back to do battle with some pet ferrets. A brave warrior dies protecting his village from Spaniards' guns, and then after a few centuries decides he's bored being dead. Maybe Tekumewa was near-sighted and thinks the ferrets are miniature Conquistadors."

Defoe resumed drilling and said, "Who said Tekumewa had a choice?"

Carl watched the old philosopher a few seconds. "You're talking about that Temesaa ritual you and Toby did back in the summer, aren't you?"

Defoe didn't answer, but instead began whistling a Beatles tune.

"What about the Keruk sacrifice?" Carl challenged, countering his own contention. "I thought that the burned video games were supposed to put Tekumewa at peace so that he'd stay dead."

Defoe pulled out the drill bit and faced Carl. "The Kumeyaay believe that spirits have unique insight into good and evil."

Carl looked into his friend's eyes but found no hint that he was pulling his leg. "You think the ferrets are *evil?* Oh, come on."

In answer, the philosopher nodded at the scratch on his hand.

"Moe was just defending himself," Carl said. "It's instinct. Rik warned us that the kits might be more aggressive since they're growing up practically wild."

Defoe chuckled. "Oh yes. And I suppose you believe the government when they tell us that they're tapping our phones for our own protection."

That wasn't an argument he felt motivated to defend. "Well, what *about* the Keruk sacrifice?"

His friend took a deep breath and held up his palms. "Tekumewa gave us his answer when he dug up his own urn. Did you notice that he was facing in the direction of the memorial when he turned and smiled at us just now?"

Carl felt a hint of a shiver as he remembered the hole dug below the memorial pile. Maybe they shouldn't have covered it back up. Maybe Tekumewa was trying to tell them he wanted out of the dark hole.

"Bah!" he cried, taking the drill from Defoe. "You've completely lost whatever you had left of your twisted old philosophical mind. Now, come on. Let's finish this hammock. You're wearing me out with your superstitions, and now I need to use it."

He drilled away while Defoe went back to whistling. Car recognized the Beatles song: *Fool on the Hill.*

ж ж ж

Carl walked along with Defoe to his cabin and then helped his friend free up some cupboard space by finishing a bottle of Johnny Walker, left over from a previous attempt at pantry house cleaning. The sun had already set behind the peaks to the west when he finally set out for home, and he kept stumbling on stones in the trail as his attention was drawn to the ember-red glow rendering Cuyamaca and Stonewall as stark, black silhouettes. The stunning light of the dusk seemed to draw all that was alive along with it, leaving the mountain path lifeless and lonely.

"Red sky at dusk," he intoned aloud to help ease the feeling of aloneness, "sailor's disgust."

That wasn't how it went. "Red skies tonight, sailor's last fight."

A bird startled him with raucous cawing as it suddenly thrashed off into the dark.

He turned back to the fading light that seemed to evaporate into the dry mountain air. "Wait, wait! Red skies are gone, sailors have spawned. Get it?" he called into the near darkness. "Sailors? Spawning?"

He laughed, but his crassness just made the solemnity of the evening seem reproving. He was glad when he finally stumbled his way into his own clearing to find the cabin lights on. Fels was already home. She wasn't going to be thrilled that he'd been imbibing with Defoe, but unlike the fickle sunset, her rebuke would be followed by a hug, and if he didn't blow it, maybe even a cooked meal.

As he got closer, though, he could see through a window that she was in the Great Hall, and she was . . . dancing. In fact, she was dancing *with* someone! She swayed her youthful hips seductively back and forth, holding her arms out in front of her where she swung someone back and forth. Something didn't look right, though, and he shook his head in a vain attempt to clear the whisky buzz. The "someone" she was swinging in rhythm was standing on the sofa and was only about two feet tall . . . and wearing a fur coat.

He stopped short, nearly falling forward. She was dancing with Larry, and now that the dry twigs weren't crunching under his stumbling feet he could hear her voice singing a familiar tune. Holding Larry's front legs, she swung the ferret back and forth between the sofa and ottoman. Her words were muffled and indistinct, but he had heard them before, and he knew that she was singing a child's song about a tree swaying in the wind, and a bird that had to hang on tight or be blown away.

Two words he did hear clearly. She was calling the ferret her "Little Buddy."

He closed his eyes and took a deep breath. Half drunk, there was no way he could break in on this and not end up in the middle of an argument. He decided that he wasn't willing to forego his hug and hot meal, so he sat down in the sawdust and waited, letting the cold evening air draw away the flush of whisky warmth.

ж ж ж

It was nearly a week later that Carl broke his promise and peeked again into the branch pile. It wasn't truly a broken promise, he told himself, since he had credible reason to believe that he wouldn't find anything. Five days was about all his curiosity could manage, and he had used his binoculars to stake out the log entrance to their tunnel. He'd found that he could see it from the corner of his roof, and he had sat there for two hours without catching any of the ferrets coming or going. That in itself wasn't proof since they might have had a second entrance, but he'd seen two rats exiting the log, and he knew that the Hood would not have endured the interlopers.

Still, he played it safe, and when he investigated the pile itself, he did so by engineering a system that was about as non-destructive as he could imagine short of using some sort of imaging radar. He cut a four-foot length of two-inch PVC pipe that he carefully worked down through the pile to use as a viewing tube. He cut another of equal length, to which he taped a flashlight at the near end and worked the other end down into the pile next to his viewing tube. When he was done he stepped back to admire his handiwork, while a little inner voice remarked dryly that he had way too much time on his hands.

His ferret spy-scope revealed what he had suspected: no ferrets. Instead, when he flipped on the flashlight he was met by multiple sets of beady rat eyes. He had one surprise, though. Not only was the stolen food gone, but there was also no strewn packaging. The Hood had carefully removed the stash as they abandoned their erstwhile home.

They had obviously relocated in response to his earlier intrusion, and Carl felt guilty about that. That hollow log hiding their tunnel was so cool, and the huge pile of dead branches made a perfect haven from coyote predators. It was like burning the shelter that a group of castaways had carefully built from the last remains of their wrecked ship just as winter was setting in.

He decided that there was no need to tell Fels about this quite yet.

Also, the ferrets seemed to be avoiding him now. He only caught rare glimpses, and then it seemed that they kept a wary eye on him—all except Larry. Good old Larry. The smallest brother of the Hood was ready to play with him anytime, as long as Fels wasn't around when the two only had eyes for each other.

If Carl hadn't already resolved to disbelieve it, he would have agreed that Larry was indeed the reincarnation of Tod.

The Hood did help relieve Carl's guilt a bit in one way, though: they continued to steal his food.

ж ж ж

That night Fels stayed with friends in Mission Valley so that she could work late at GeneTrend on a difficult integration. Despite plenty of practice at spending evenings alone in the cabin, Carl was still not good at it. He had shelves of unread books, racks of DVDs, and over a hundred channels of satellite television, but spent most of the evening playing listlessly with Larry and trying to ignore the black windows framing nothing but wilderness beyond. He seriously debated heading off to visit Defoe, but was ultimately stymied by the thought of meeting a coyote on the path—a coyote walking upright and speaking to him in the tongue of the ancient Kumeyaay.

Instead, he went to bed early and woke wide-eyed at 3:15 AM to the bone-chilling cries of a lethal battle raging somewhere beyond the cabin walls. At first he thought it was coyotes tussling with each other, since all he could hear were the yips and growls that he'd come to associate with their fighting cries. After a few seconds, though, he sensed that there was another adversary. After months in the wild, he had learned to discern a distinct, albeit wordless, language in animals fighting. Something sensed in the breathlessly poised pauses and determined modulation of growls painted pictures almost clear enough to see. Lying in bed now in the absolute blackness of the moonless night, he watched in his mind as the coyote struggled against something soundless and obviously determined. About whether it was prey or adversary, the language of fighting was mute.

After perhaps three minutes of demon haunting, the battle suddenly ended when the coyote howled in pain, growled viciously, and then, following five seconds of endless silence, whimpered. Five heartbeats later, the silence of the deep Cuyamaca night returned.

Carl lay among the soft, warm blankets, feeling each surging thump of his heart press against his temples a little less than the one before, as though it was he who had just done battle. He wondered what, if any, casualties had resulted.

In his mind, Fels whispered to him urgently. He jumped out of bed, stumbling on the clothes he'd left lying on the floor. "Larry!" he cried into the darkness as he bumped into the bedroom door casing and ricocheted into the Great Hall. "Larry! Where are you?"

He was terrified for the little ferret. If the larger brothers of the Hood represented those parts of life that were bold and pragmatic, their little brother embodied all that was innocent and joyful. Carl was overcome by a sense of failed responsibility. Allowing Larry to be hurt—or worse—was much more than just letting Fels down; it was turning his back on goodness and light. It was admitting defeat to the tooth and claw of nature. It was abandoning the compassion and altruism that justified the sapient aspect of his species' name.

"Larry!" he called, finding the light switch. "Larry!" he called again, desperate now.

He heard the tap of the ferret door swinging shut and the hurried rattle of claws on the wooden floor. He spun around and bent down to swoop up the animal in his arms. The ferret sniffed his face and peered into his eyes, as though concerned for his big friend's worry. Carl hugged the warm fur to his cheek and sighed.

"Little Buddies have to be careful," he murmured.

He set Larry down and watched the ferret wander around sniffing random objects.

He headed back to bed, but paused. He realized what he'd said.

Chapter 14

The next morning Carl set out to walk the six miles to the market, where a stained glass carafe sat on a hot plate offering up free caffeine to customers. If he was lucky he'd arrive to find a fresh pot just brewed. If not, they sold a caramel candy bar that he found moderated the bitter burn of an aging pot.

These coffee excursions took up the whole morning, and this would be the third in as many weeks. He felt himself drawn out to trudge the long, dusty road when loneliness soured even his music. He hit the road when he grew irritably tired of hanging around the cabin that, hour-by-hour, became just the place where Fels wasn't.

In any case, he told himself, he needed the exercise. His hands and arms had grown strong from wielding the chainsaw, but he imagined his lungs slowly atrophying into little sacks the size and texture of used condoms. Actually, he thought, an atrophied lung was probably one of those old ideas that had morphed into a modern metaphor, like bloodletting and penis envy. Besides, aerobic capacity was mostly determined by the quantity of red blood cells. At least, this was what he remembered . . . which might itself be just another modern myth. He'd have to Google it when he got back.

These and other idle musings occupied him during the two-hour trip, and by the time he arrived, calves tired and cramping, he'd stored away a long list of subjects to look up on Wikipedia. In fact, now he couldn't wait to get back. From twelve thousand footsteps removed, the cabin called to him, a safe and familiar haven where he could explore the wide world through his books and Internet connection.

Sometimes he had to remove himself temporarily from his blessings to see them clearly.

He had imagined that he would engage in pleasant conversation with the elderly lady who owned the store, but a younger woman, perhaps the daughter, manned the register, and she seemed in a dour mood, so he took his bitter coffee and caramel bar outside and sat on the bench against the wall. When he was finished, he got up and scanned across the bulletin board but the collage of notices and ads were the same as the last time he had looked—the ride to El Cajon was still wanting, and Coydog was still missing—a reflection of how slow the universe unwound its spring up here among the pines.

A heavyset man dressed in dirt-smeared jeans came out of the market just as a pickup truck pulled up, and the driver rolled down the window and hailed him, obviously an acquaintance. Starved for any human contact, Carl listened with interest to their conversation while pretending to continue perusing the bulletin board. The heavy man, apparently a construction laborer, told the driver that he was looking for work.

"Big job down near Julian," the driver replied, tilting his head in that direction in case the other man had perhaps forgotten where the little tourist village lay.

"I heard about that rumor—Whispering Pines," the laborer replied, spitting into the dirt. "Somebody's got their head up their ass, though. The developer pulled out after the Banner Fire."

"I know. I heard about that one too. No, this is a private contractor."

"One lousy house. Big deal."

The driver grinned. "It is a big deal. Jack's been down there. He says the foundation looks like a freakin' hotel."

The heavyset man furrowed his brow. "Nah. I'd of heard about a hotel."

The driver shook his head. "Not a hotel. Building permit is for a private residence. The guy owns some company. The job's on a fast track. This guy's throwing money around like there's no tomorrow."

The burly laborer was interested now and leaned his elbow against the truck's doorframe. "They hiring?"

"Yeah. In fact, the contractor's goin' out of his way looking for temp workers."

"Stickin' it to the union?"

"I guess. Get this, though, you won't believe it: the plans call for a moat."

"What are you talking about?"

"A moat. Like around a castle."

"Aw, it's probably a foundation for a high wall. When a wall's higher than about eight feet—"

"No. It's a moat. Pumps and everything."

"Huh. No kidding . . . maybe it's supposed to be a fire-break."

"I dunno. Maybe—"

The driver suddenly pulled out his cell phone, and after grunting a few affirmatives into it, waved farewell, backed out, and drove away. The heavyset man seemed to notice Carl for the first time and gave him a hard look, but then, perhaps realizing the slim man in clean jeans before him was clearly not a potential competitor, gave him an amiable nod and walked off to his own truck.

Carl was annoyed. He'd never set his sights on becoming a construction laborer, and was pretty sure he never would, but that didn't mean he wouldn't mind being mistaken as part of the club.

He decided that next time he'd casually display the palms of his hands. If the light was right you could discern bona-fide calluses.

ж ж ж

Carl may have had workingman calluses on his hands, but he had tenderfoot sore leg muscles by the time he arrived back at the cabin, and so, woke with a start on the sofa when Fels pulled in late that afternoon. She laughed at him as he stood there blinking the sleep away, but he didn't care since she returned his hug with enthusiasm. He marveled at how their bodies fit so perfectly. He breathed deeply the smell of her essence and didn't care if she never stopped laughing at him, as long as she gave him hugs like this.

He cut up fresh vegetables and tossed them into a sauté pan while Fels dished out the curry she'd picked up on the way. In celebration of having Fels home for dinner, he popped two bottles of Karl Strauss beer he'd been saving in the fridge. When they sat down to eat, Larry curled up on Fels's lap, while Lilly roamed the perimeter of the Great Hall securing the borders. The three members of the Hood might as well have been vacationing on the moon. Ever since he'd discovered their den, they seemed to be boycotting the cabin altogether.

"It seems that Rik is moving out to the mountains as well," Fels reported. "Ginny's been taking calls from a building coordinator."

Ginny was the head of GeneTrend's admin department, but served equally as Rik's personal secretary. Fels had befriended her since they were members of the same gym, and they often went together to work out.

Carl sat back in alarm. "I thought we moved up here to get away from your work!"

The thought of Rik's headstrong ego elbowing in on Defoe's companionship struck him as something of a nightmare.

"I don't mean, like, right *here*. He's building up on Volcan Mountain."

That did seem comfortably far removed. Volcan Mountain was part of the next range just north of Cuyamaca, a good twenty miles up Route 79 through . . . "Julian!"

"What?"

"Volcan Mountain is just north of Julian."

She shrugged. "So what."

"I heard about this. The foundation is big enough to be a hotel, and there's a moat all around the perimeter—with water and pumps."

Fels stared at him a moment. "Where did you hear this? Rik has been keeping the whole thing hush-hush. Ginny made me promise not to tell anybody else."

"I overheard a couple of construction guys."

"Where?"

"At the market."

"You went to the market? On foot? You should have sent me an email; I could have stopped on the way home."

"I went for a cup of coffee."

"You walked ten miles for a cup of *coffee*?"

"It's only six miles."

She looked worried.

"I needed the exercise," he added.

She nodded slowly, as though patronizing someone potentially dangerous. "You need more human contact."

"I have Defoe."

"Like I said."

"At least I'm not telling secrets I promised not to tell."

She raised one eyebrow. "You'd rather I don't tell you about them?"

"Uh, I got carried away in my defense against your vicious attack. I retract that and throw myself at the mercy of the court. So, what else did you hear about this private hotel he's building?"

She thought a moment. "Ginny didn't say anything about a moat. Like us, this place will also be self-sufficient, but he's going to have about five times the solar cell area, and at least that much more battery capacity. Plus, he's putting in a sizable generator and a buried two hundred-gallon gas tank."

"Jesus. He obviously doesn't want to give up his luxurious lifestyle. Why didn't he just stay on the grid?"

"He did."

"He did? This is all just for emergency backup?"

"That's what Ginny thinks."

"What kind of emergency would knock out power for more than a couple of days?"

She shrugged. "Earthquake."

"The major faults go up the Imperial Valley. We're only on the very fringe of the quake zone here."

He'd looked into this before they bought the land.

She shrugged again. "Maybe a really big quake in the LA area could knock out the grid for all of southern California."

It seemed paranoid to Carl, but on the other hand, he didn't have Rik's money. If he did, maybe he too would be thinking of all the ways he could spend it.

"Speaking of emergency contingencies, your ferrets continue the ransacking. Last night they took the last of the turkey jerky. Pretty soon there'll be nothing left to take."

"*My* ferrets? You probably forget to close the latch."

He'd installed baby-proof devices on all the food cabinets. This had stymied them for a while.

"Nope. The Hood figured out how to open them. Padlocks are our only chance."

She gave him her look. She didn't believe him.

"Look," he said, "I didn't forget to close the latch. Your beasts are simply evil little geniuses."

"Since when did they become *my* animals?"

When indeed? As much as he felt responsible for Larry, he felt no connection to the Hood. In fact, he realized that he actually didn't like them. More than that, even. "Not liking" is a simply a lack of liking, whereas he felt full-blown animosity.

"Well, if they're not yours," he said, "you won't mind if I put out some traps, then?"

He regretted this even as the words left his lips, but like an email, there was no bringing them back.

Her mouth was a tight, determined line as she put down her fork and picked up Larry off her lap to hug him. "That's a mean, cruel thought." To Larry she murmured, "Don't worry; I won't let him hurt you."

"I wasn't talking about Larry . . . or Lilly."

"Well, they're still his sister and brothers. They may only be ferrets—"

"Unlike Larry."

If his knees could have managed it, he would have kicked himself. He really was an idiot sometimes.

She didn't continue the argument, but finished the meal in a silence that persisted as they cleaned up. Once he'd put away the last plate, though, she must have decided that he'd been punished enough, for she came over and snuggled up with him on the sofa. She even let Larry fare for himself on the floor.

Carl sighed with contentment. For a while there he thought that he'd blown his chances for marital benefits.

In fact, as with every other time she was away for more than a day or two, it was more like a marital exigency.

ж ж ж

The next morning Carl woke early and lay thinking about the Hood and their food raids. Wherever the ferrets were stashing the goods, it was a pretty substantial cache. Where could they hide it all? Ferrets were basically weasels and were fond of holes and tunnels.

He would have smacked his head, except that it might have woken Fels. He eased out of bed and tiptoed out of the bedroom.

He made a quick cup of instant coffee and stepped out the back door into the brisk, pre-dawn air. As he watched, the very tip of Cuyamaca Peak turned amber, catching the rising sun, still invisible behind the hills to the east. He'd promised Fels that he'd leave the ferrets alone, but it couldn't hurt just to take a look without disturbing them. Now that he thought he knew the secret, he was dying to confirm it.

He set off across their cleared lot, into the pines, and down the slope to the north. He'd found the tunnel once when he'd been exploring, just after they'd moved up. The county water resources inspector had explained that it was probably MacFine's Folly. During the last decade of the nineteenth century, San Diego had undergone a period of boom development that included competing efforts to collect and manage water. As this is always a valuable commodity in semi-arid areas, collection and control can be a profitable enterprise, and more than a dozen private companies were formed for the purpose. Only three survived the nine-year drought that ushered in the new century, and over time these were bought by the city and evolved into the present day water distribution system.

Among those that failed was the MacFine Water Company. Abe MacFine was one of three sons of James MacFine, a Scotsman who had immigrated to America in 1839 and subsequently rushed off west at the first word of gold. Unlike the tens of thousands of other dreamers, though, James was lucky enough to make his fortune in the Sierra Nevada Mountains, not far from present day Yosemite Park. But then, unlike most of the other few dozens that also struck it rich, he didn't immediately spend his fortune. Being a good Scotsman, he hid it away and lived a modest life in Mariposa, where he married and raised a family.

When James died, two of his sons invested their inheritance in various businesses in town, and their descendants sprinkle the mountain area to this day. The third, though, named Abraham after the sixteenth president, had more of his mother's Italian blood, and set off to multiply his share by his wits and daring. He found his opportunity in the water development frenzy of San Diego. Unfortunately, although his daring was not lacking, his wits seemed to have taken temporary leave. Whereas everybody else was working out ways to get water to the booming coastal city to the west, Abe decided that the real future lay in the little desert valley to the east called Borrego Springs, so isolated by mountains on three sides that many southern Californians didn't even know it existed. What vision Abe held for the barren land was lost to history. Perhaps he had somehow anticipated the neon lights of a future desert city, where Americans would come from far and wide to gleefully throw away their savings, but had misplaced its location by two hundred miles.

In any event, and for whatever cockamamie reasons, Abe spent all his inheritance, and a good deal of others' ill-guided investments, attempting to turn Borrego Springs into a modern-day Eden. It's doubtful that any amount of money would have succeeded, but MacFine Water Company spent all it had, and then some, before hardly getting started. Apparently Abe's plan was that once a good beginning was underway, other similarly deluded investors would flock to him. His dreams were dashed when the Mountain Water Company won the rights to build Cuyamaca Dam, thus commandeering a large part of the Cuyamaca watershed, and Abe's future revenue.

Abe escaped on a night train, leaving his investors in the lurch, and returned to Mariposa, where, borrowing money from his brothers, he outfitted himself and set out for the wild hills to find more gold. Nobody knows what fate became of him after that, but his brothers never got their money back.

MacFine's Folly was the most prominent part of that ill-conceived San Diego project. Most rain fell on the western slopes of the Cuyamaca Mountains, so in order to get it to the east side without massively expensive pumps—this was the nineteenth century—Abe's plan was to build an aqueduct connecting the west to the east side. Since there were mountains in the way, most of this would have to be tunnels. The original plan called for a total of over two miles of tunnel comprising five segments connected by canals and troughs spanning canyons on wooden trestles. The tunnel next to Carl's lot was the first, the shortest, and the only segment built.

The slope below Carl's lot ended in a dry streambed before rising again up to the next ridge to the north. At the bottom, he turned left and started down the path of odd-sized stones and washed sand. He recalled that the tunnel mouth wasn't far, and walked right by it before realizing he'd missed it. The opening was hidden behind a curtain of vines, and erosion had filled the bottom so that, although the original cut through the mountain had been six feet in height, only four feet of clearance still remained.

He pulled aside the vines, but the inside was invisible in the darkness. "Yo!" he yelled, and jumped in surprise as his voice bellowed back in a ringing rebuke, amplified by the cavity's resonance. *So much for not disturbing them,* he thought.

In the end, though, he decided that they had not taken MacFine's Folly for their new lair for three reasons. First, it was too far for little ferret feet to carry stolen goods; second, the tunnel was probably too big—like a person setting up house in a stadium; and third, the only footprints he found in the soft sand at the doorstep were those of coyotes, and as he knew, The Hood did not like coyotes.

On the way back, Carl noticed an unusual cloud off to the south. It was unusual for being there at all. The last couple of days they'd been enjoying the warm, dry Santa Ana winds from the east, blown in from high pressure in the deserts north-east of them. Under such conditions the arid air cleared the sky of clouds all the way to the coast. Therefore, this wasn't a cloud he saw. The brown color revealed its origin.

Wild fire!

It was south of them, though, and the wind blew from the east. During a wildfire, the wind was everything. It was the wheels, and the driver, and the muscle. If you smelled smoke, you were downwind and you started planning how to get out of the way.

Carl smelled no smoke and knew that the wind could never shift in time to put them in danger.

He'd grown up in southern California, though, and a wildfire wasn't something you just ignored. Throughout the morning he found that he was alternating his time between checking the county fire maps on the web, and stepping outside to see how the plume was progressing. One time he stepped out to find a soaring black smudge drawing lazy circles high overhead. He stepped out later to find two smudges, lower now, weaving slow, intersecting arcs as though performing a silent and stately ballroom dance.

Fels came out and saw him gazing skyward. "Vultures," he explained.

She watched them a moment, head craned back. "Condors?"

"I don't think so. They're too small. Turkey Vultures maybe."

She watched a minute more. "They're circling right overhead."

"Maybe they're waiting for us to go back inside."

She looked at him in alarm. "Something has died!"

His mind raced, trying to remember when he'd last seen the ferrets, while Fels ran inside calling frantically for Larry. He remembered the battle in the dark two nights before. But he was sure that he'd seen Lilly since then . . . yes! She had been in the house during dinner. What about the Hood? Had he seen them all? He couldn't be sure, as they were keeping their distance.

No, that didn't make sense. If the coyote had killed a ferret, it surely would have carried it away to eat. Wouldn't it? Why else would it have attacked them?

He walked over to the pile of branches. He knew they didn't live there anymore, but he still associated it with them. Fels appeared in the doorway, hugging Larry to her neck. He caught a glimpse off to the right. It was Lilly. She stood watching him intently a moment, then ran off up the hill.

Was she trying to tell him something, like Lassie with Timmy's parents? He ran over to where she had been standing, and looked up the hill. She had disappeared. He was about to run up after her when he caught a faint whiff of sewage. His heart sank at the implication. The slight breeze came from behind, in the opposite direction from Lilly's retreat. He turned, but saw only rocks and dry grass. A wayward air brushed him again with the smell of something rotting, almost sour.

It was farther to the left. And then he saw it: brown fur ending in a paw, almost hidden in the tall grass. But . . . the paw was far too large to be a ferret's.

"Over here!" he cried to Fels.

As he took a few steps closer, he saw that the paw was attached to a coyote, lying stiff and very dead. Growing up in Pacific Beach, he'd seen a dead cat or two along the street, but this stopped him cold. Maybe it was because a coyote was larger and therefore in some way more significant than a cat.

Fels appeared next to him and he put his arm out, as if protecting her from this consequence of their new life in the wild.

"It's . . . a dog!" she whispered.

She'd never seen Tekumewa. He shook his head. "A coyote."

"Poor thing. Thank God it's not one of the kits."

Carl wasn't sure he shared her relief. Tekumewa had never bitten him, after all. It had been eerie, intimidating even, to see the coyote stand up and walk like a man, yet now that the living enigma was dead, no more than lifeless meat and bones, the world was a bit less exotic. A promise of magic was gone forever.

"What could have killed it?" Fels asked.

What, indeed. "I think I heard it die".

He told her about the battle that he'd heard waging in the black of night. "Whatever it was that did it in," he concluded, "it made no sound."

She took a tentative step closer. "It doesn't look hurt, just . . ."

"Dead?"

She was right. There was no blood or visible damage. The animal's fur wasn't even ruffled. It could have simply keeled over from a heart attack.

Except for the fact that he'd *heard* the howls and growls. The coyote had not died peacefully.

"Maybe it was a rattlesnake," Fels offered.

"Maybe."

He'd have thought that a coyote would know enough not to tangle with a rattlesnake, but it would explain the lack of visible wounds.

"What do we do with it?" Fels asked. "We can't just leave it here."

He considered his options, and decided he would have to bury the carcass. It wasn't a task he relished. He glanced up. Maybe there was an alternative. "We could let the vultures do their thing."

"Carl Mason! I will not have filthy scavengers feasting on this poor dead animal a hundred feet from my house."

He would have bet they weren't that filthy, but this was not a debate he wanted to initiate.

"Right. I'll get the shovel."

ж ж ж

He never imagined that digging a damn hole could be so difficult. He'd picked a spot downhill another hundred feet among a cluster of manzanita bushes. The ground was smooth, and the first shovel-full, consisting of pine needles and the soft detritus of forest carpet, was like scooping ice cream. All would have been fine if he could have buried the dead coyote three inches down, but below that he found a solid foundation of rocks. He didn't so much dig a hole as pull out a hole's worth of stones. The shovel became a prying tool to loosen and wiggle free each laborious piece from its three-dimensional subterranean jigsaw puzzle.

It took more than an hour of grunts and swearing to wrestle free a cavity three feet wide by that much deep, sweat stinging his eyes and dripping off the tip of his nose to wash clean star-shaped spots on each stone extracted. He'd planned on digging a hole four feet deep, but after taking an ice-tea break, he knew that he was beat and that this would have to do. Any scavenger that was willing to invest the work to get at this carcass was welcome to it, Tekumewa spirit or not.

As he stood over the dead coyote, though, he was tempted to return to tackle the last foot of the hole just to delay this next task. He considered using a plastic sheet to carry the dreadful cargo, but told himself not to be such a wuss. The animal had been dead barely thirty hours; it wasn't like it was full of maggots.

Bad image.

Just do it, he told himself and squatted down in front of the inert burden. His first attempt to pick up the coyote failed, as the thirty pounds was more than he'd expected, and the slippery fur slid out of his hands as he tried to lift it by its haunch and shoulder. He then grabbed pairs of paws, front and rear, in each fist and hefted the carcass like he'd seen rodeo cowboys do with calves. Grunting and trying not to dwell on what flopped heavily against his shins, he staggered down the slope and dumped the fearsome load into the hole, using his feet to push at the head and tail so that the entire creature huddled inside.

Death robbed the coyote its beauty, painting its coat dull gray, and pinching its snout so that it seemed thin and delicate.

It smelled bad as well. Again a whiff of sewer brushed his nose. He unconsciously smelled his hand and recoiled with a cry at the sour stench. It smelled like vomit.

He'd had enough. He grabbed the loose rocks and threw them unceremoniously into the hole, glad for the dirt that smeared across his hand and masked the foul odor. He scraped together enough loose dirt to cover a thin layer over the stones, and then headed for the cabin to wash up with lots of soap.

He had planned to say a few words over Tekumewa's new grave, more in deference to Defoe than the long-fallen brave, but he was tired and disgusted and just wanted to be done with the whole affair.

He understood now what his Sunday School teacher had meant when she intoned that God had a purpose for every creature, no matter how lovely or brutish in appearance. Vultures may be hard to look at, he thought, but they sure serve a useful purpose.

Chapter 15

"It was just a coyote," Carl reiterated for the third time. He lifted Defoe's telescope to his eye, and Stonewall peak floated before him as though he was hovering next to it in a helicopter. "It was a wild animal that had a bizarre habit of walking around on its hind legs. And now it's dead."

"You're rationalizing after the fact," Defoe argued, swatting at a fly on his head. "You believed it was more than that, and now you're hiding from your own disappointment at the loss."

Carl pushed the tube segments of the telescope together to form a single neat cylinder small enough to slip into the pocket of a baggy pair of pants. Defoe had picked it up at the Pine Valley senior high flea market. Carl opened it up again and swung it to look at his friend, but his face was all blurry and out of focus. "It's dead, Defoe. Tekumewa will just have to go back to his clay jar."

In truth, he really did feel badly. He had the sense that the coyote, or the spirit inhabiting it, had been trying to make contact, and now all the fantastic possibilities implied by that were lost. It was the very essence of tragedy, and he did want to go on hiding from it.

"You don't think that it's at all strange," Defoe pressed, "that Tekumewa forsake his borrowed life right outside your door?"

Carl turned slowly, letting the surrounding trees flash by through the circular view as though seen from the window of a speeding train. "From what I heard in my bed, it didn't sound like he had much choice about it—what the . . .?"

"What do you see?"

"It's Shemp . . . no, it's Curly."

In the magnified view of the telescope, he saw the ferret Hood member slinking away from the corner of the cabin. "There's a

146

cellophane bag hanging from his mouth. The bastards! They're not even waiting until night."

"Perhaps they only now discovered that it's a twenty-four hour supermarket."

"I'll give them a market. I'll open a new section in the meat department: fresh ferret steaks. They're worse than rats!"

Curly paused at the edge of the bank and looked back at the cabin, then sideways along each side of the bank before disappearing below. The ferret wouldn't think to look a hundred yards up the hill.

"They're not in the same league as rats," Defoe observed. "In fact, they're not even in the same league as ferrets."

"That's right, oh wise one," Carl teased, watching to see if Curly appeared again below the bank. "Old Indians are walking around in coyote skins, and Rik has mated humans with ferrets."

"I never used the word mated—that, of course, would be ridiculous."

"Excuse me—cloned."

"You know better than that."

He did know better than that. He knew that Defoe was talking about gene splicing, but he liked getting the old goat's goat.

Curly appeared again below the bank, angling away to the right into the pines. From his viewpoint up the hill, Carl saw the ferret pause again and look around once more before proceeding a few feet behind a large boulder. From here, he was hidden from the cabin. The Hood member then trotted off in a direct line away from the cabin for a hundred feet before suddenly disappearing for good.

"Aha!"

"You see a mermaid? If so, I want my spyglass back."

"No mermaid, just a Houdini ferret. Come on," he urged, handing the telescope to Defoe and starting off down the hill.

"Wait!" Defoe yelled.

Carl turned, surprised.

"Are you sure you want to do this? Wasn't there a great deal of trouble the last time you became nosey?"

As usual Defoe had a good point. On the other hand . . . "They're stealing my food."

He turned and trotted off down the hill and over the bank.

From behind the boulder, he walked directly away from the cabin, just as he'd watched Curly do. While he walked, he scanned the ground for a hole, and after he was sure he'd gone well past the point where the ferret had disappeared, he stopped and looked back. What had he missed?

Defoe was following along behind him, pulling thoughtfully at his beard. His friend stopped and looked up at him. "They seem seriously determined to keep their quarters hidden."

"Yeah, well I'm seriously determined to get my food back."

Defoe nodded a cautious agreement. "By your standards that is only fair. By their standards, though, you may be an adversary."

"You're damn right I'm their adversary—"

A ferret was running towards them from the direction of the cabin. He recognized the playful, boisterous gait: Larry was coming to join the fun.

"Here's the only one who's not a thief," Carl observed.

Defoe turned to look. "This must be the one that Fels believes is her nephew's reincarnation."

"Righto. This one's Larry, as in, 'Ow! Hey, Moe! Whad'ya hit me for?' "

The smallest sibling stopped a moment to sniff Defoe's cuff, but became distracted by another smell among the pine needles. He nosed around, back and forth, and then seemed to pick up a solid scent trail leading back the way they'd come. The ferret's olfactory sense guided him confidently to the base of a tree, where he pulled himself up by his front paws to a standing position, as though the trail continued right up the trunk. Larry turned and looked back at Carl.

"The third Stooge seems to have found Houdini's exit," Defoe observed.

Carl was already at the tree gazing up the receding vertical length. And there, plain as day, was Curly's secret. Another tree twenty feet away had fallen, but had gotten caught in this tree's lowest branch a few feet above his head. The fallen tree, rotting away where it leaned, was hollow, and a hole had been chewed into the interior right where it rested on its supporting branch.

Carl pointed it out to his friend. "Curly must have climbed this side of the tree out of view. He's up there in the fallen log somewhere."

"Let it be," Defoe urged. "It's just an animal."

Carl looked at him. "You're the one who thinks they're a whole lot more than just animals."

Defoe only shook his head in disapproval.

Carl glanced around, but there was nothing he could drag over to stand on. He looked at the fallen tree and realized he didn't need anything else. Positioning himself at the unturned roots, he climbed up onto the base of the fallen trunk and worked his way upward along the incline, steadying himself by walking his hands along in front of him. From the ground, the hole Curly had chewed had only been an arm's length above him, but those few feet of vertical height seemed greatly disproportional now that he gazed down from the other end. Defoe's foreshortened form looking up at him appeared part of an Earth he had dangerously abandoned.

Ignoring, or trying to ignore, the disconcerting height, he leaned over and, head upside down, peered into the hole but it was far too dark to see anything. Already he was feeling the pressure of blood collecting in his cheeks and temples, and he lifted himself to think. He patted his pocket and, twisting himself so that he could reach into his pants, pulled out the pocketknife with the little built-in flashlight, the same one he'd used to spy down Tekumewa's hole. Leaning over once again, he pointed the tiny light inside. Like before, it was too dim to show much detail, but he saw a myriad stars flickered in the depths below the hole as the feeble beam glittered off cellophane packages of food. Among such a host of twinkles, two glinting eyes would be lost.

He heard Defoe say, "Uh-oh!" followed by the sound of scrabbling little toenails. Before he could lift himself from his precarious inverted perch, something brushed past him from above, and he caught the unmistakable scent of ferret. Curly must have been hiding farther up the log.

"Oh, no you don't!" Defoe warned.

Carl lifted himself, and his vision fuzzed momentarily as blood adjusted to the new load. Below him, Defoe had trapped Curly against the base of a rock with his foot, and was holding him down, while Larry looked on, seemingly confused by events.

"The bugger was going after our little informant," Defoe explained.

Curly squirmed, trying to bite his captor, but was foiled by the sturdy hiking boots.

Carl started backing down the log the same way he'd gone up.

"Damn it!" Defoe cried. "Where'd *you* come from!"

Carl looked down. Defoe still held Curly under one foot and was now also reaching out with a stick to keep Moe from getting at Larry.

Carl realized that the game had escalated; Larry's brothers were after blood. It would take too long to crawl down, so he jumped. He tried to slow his fall, but the dead bark peeled off in his hand, and he hit the ground with a surprising impact. The bottoms of his feet stung with a wash of pinpricks, and he staggered sideways, trying to regain his balance.

Moe, snarling at Defoe and clawing at the end of the stick, worked his way around just beyond its reach, towards Larry, who cowered, clearly terrified now.

Carl leapt between the little brother and Moe, and the ferret spun to face him, fangs bared. The animal's long, smooth midsection rippled, as though harboring a storm-tossed ocean within, and as Carl watched, saliva the color and constancy of motor oil dripped from its jaws.

This was not the cute little kit that Lilly had proudly brought to show them months before. Carl had a sudden urge to stomp on the murderous little beast and quell the alien undulations. Instead, he grabbed a stick, thinking that he might use it to keep Moe occupied until he could pick up Larry. The barbarous ferret, though, still snarling, crouched low, and then, as though daring Carl to follow through with his urges, rolled over on its back, exposing a white, fine-furred belly.

Carl stood transfixed. He wanted to do it. An inner voice screamed to jump on the beast, to kill it *now!* He couldn't though. What had they really ever done to him? Stolen some food? He felt ashamed at his dark thoughts.

Carl was pulled from his confused anguish by a pitiful squeal from behind. He twisted around to find Larry on his back, his little eyes wide in pain, pushing his forepaws against Shemp, who had buried her teeth into his hind leg. Carl jumped to the rescue, but before he could intervene, Larry's sister shuddered with one last convulsion and ran off, followed by Moe and Curly.

He gently picked up the trembling, wounded ferret as Defoe joined them.

"Judas Priest!" the old philosopher exclaimed. "The devils have gone mad!" He glanced at Carl. "Is the little fellow okay?"

"I think so," Carl replied, studying Larry's hindquarters. "Shemp only bit him in the leg."

He thought at first that the bite had drawn a profusion of blood, but he saw that it was just Shemp's molasses-thick saliva. He couldn't even see the tooth marks under the fine fur. There was that acrid smell, though, a repelling stench that was becoming all too familiar.

Defoe peered closely at the shivering ferret, face tight with concern. "I don't like this. There's something fundamentally evil in those little antagonists."

For once Carl had no desire to contradict his friend's bizarre theories.

"That was a coordinated attack," his friend declared. "Two of them kept the two of us occupied, while the third went in for the kill."

"If Shemp had wanted to kill Larry, I think she would have gone for his throat."

Defoe was right about the first part though; Moe had laid himself out as clear bait.

"It's just an expression. It's clear, though, that they wanted to at least deliver pain to the little fellow as punishment for revealing their den. Revenge requires a higher order of reverse cause-effect associations, and is almost exclusively limited to primates, of which we humans are most proficient."

Carl barely heard his friend's musings. The little ferret's shivering had intensified so that the whole furry package seemed to vibrate in his hands. "Let's get Larry inside and cleaned up."

Ahead, between them and the cabin, Lilly sat watching. He had the sense that the ferret mother was waiting.

"The poor fellow seems to be in shock," Defoe said. "Perhaps a nice hot bath is in order."

Larry's eyes stared, unseeing, and the shivering suddenly exploded into violent convulsions so that Carl could barely hang on to him.

"Good God!" Defoe cried.

Carl hugged the little ferret to his chest, trying both to contain the wild spasms and provide some degree of warmth. His mind spun, searching for what else he could do for Fels's special little friend.

Then, with one last jerk, the animal went limp in his arms. Carl closed his eyes tight, refusing to face what had just happened.

"Oh Lord!" Defoe whispered beside him.

The dead ferret lay in Carl's hands like a bag of sand. The reek of Shemp's vomit seemed the smell of death itself.

Carl opened his eyes and Lilly was still there watching them. She pushed herself to her feet and walked slowly away.

Chapter 16

"She hasn't gotten out of bed all morning," Carl reported. "She tossed and turned the whole night."

They spoke quietly so she wouldn't hear them. Defoe, uncharacteristically somber, just nodded. His friend had walked all the way from his cabin to see how she was doing, and Carl realized yet again what a good friend indeed he was.

"I was afraid of something like this," Carl added.

Defoe stared into his cup of tea. "We can't tailor our beliefs according to our fears."

"But the whole thing was—" Carl lowered his voice still more "—nutty. I saw what she went through when Tod died—"

"The first time?"

"Come on. You don't really believe that Tod was reincarnated in Larry."

"It doesn't matter what I believe. What Fels believes is true to her. In her world, her nephew has been killed all over again."

As usual, Defoe's point was hard to argue. "But if I could just get her to see the truth—"

"Your truth."

"Okay, my truth. Still, Larry was just a ferret. It was terrible, and he didn't deserve to die that way, but he was just an animal."

Defoe placed his hand on Carl's shoulder. "You, my friend, are also just an animal."

He nodded and sighed. "I definitely felt like some kind of animal when I told her. I thought she was going to hate me forever."

"She blames you?"

"She thinks that I could have done more to prevent it."

Defoe was silent.

"I told her that you warned me not to climb up to look."

His friend was silent a moment longer, then said, "That is admirable. It causes immediate pain, but this is a wound that will heal, whereas keeping the truth from her would have been a malignant tumor growing over time."

Defoe took a sip of tea and went on. "It was inevitable, you know."

Carl looked at him. "That they would kill him?"

"He was different."

"Boy, was he; like night and day. It was almost as if they didn't come from the same womb."

Defoe just looked at him with one eyebrow raised.

"Oh, come on! Lilly gave birth to them all. There's no way—"

"Of course not. There are two parents, though."

Carl took a deep breath. He didn't want to get into Defoe's wild monster theory about Rik crossing humans with ferrets. Instead, he said, "If the Hood really wanted to kill him, why didn't Shemp go for his neck?"

"Maybe the bastard didn't mean to kill the little one. After all, the wound shouldn't have been lethal. Not nearly. In fact, I don't understand why the little fellow expired in the first place."

Carl had wondered that himself. "Maybe he had a heart attack."

"To die of fright. What a horrible way to go."

"Ferrets seem to scare easily, that's for sure."

He was recalling when Shemp had become so frightened that she had thrown up on his leg . . .

And then, as though a light had been flicked on, it all came together.

"Puke!"

"Excuse me?" Defoe asked.

"Shemp puked on Larry."

"I noticed that. It seemed odd. The little bastard attacked so ferociously, yet it must have been quite frightened itself to—"

"Shemp wasn't frightened. She puked on me when she tried to bite me. The Hood puked on Tekumewa. The sons-of-bitches puke on all their victims."

"You believe the ferrets killed Tekumewa?"

Carl didn't answer. He was recalling his own incident with Shemp. When she had bitten him after he'd uncovered the den in the branch pile, she'd clung determinedly until she had regurgitated, at which point she immediately let go and ran away. Her monstrous convulsions weren't nervous spasms, but something she forced upon victims. The rippling of her belly as she had clamped her jaws onto Larry's thigh seemed alien and malevolent, as though the belly had a life of its own. He shuddered at the memory.

Defoe's question finally registered. "Yes," he answered, "I think the Hood killed the coyote."

He recalled that Lilly had seemed to try to draw him away from the dead carcass, like a mother protecting her delinquent children.

"How? It seems infeasible."

He had an idea, but his belief that they caused the coyote's demise was based more on his growing conviction of their innate evilness and the magnitude of destruction that such malice could incur than on the viability of his theory.

"Their vomit is poisonous."

Defoe stared at him incredulously.

"That would explain everything," he went on, "why Larry died from just a bite on his leg, and how little ferrets could bring down a full-grown coyote."

His friend continued to think a moment, then said, "You indicated that Shemp had bitten you and then puked, yet you experienced no ill effects."

That was true. He replayed the scene in his mind. "She only nicked my skin. Then she puked on my pant leg, and I changed before it touched the open skin. Maybe she was just learning how to do it; maybe she hadn't figured out yet that she had to vomit *before* biting down."

Defoe sat back and sighed. "It sounds preposterous, but that may only be an indication of my own limited imagination." He nodded, and then shrugged. "Do we still have samples of the vomit? Perhaps we could have it analyzed. I could contact my colleagues in the chemistry department at the University."

The bedroom door opened and they turned to find Fels standing there, looking as though she'd been run over on her way back from a refugee camp. "Who's tasting vomit?" she mumbled, rubbing her eyes as she shuffled to the stove to put more water on for tea.

Carl glanced quickly at Defoe. He'd wanted to avoid talking to her about the ferrets for a while. "Not tasting—analyzing. Defoe has this crazy idea that the ferrets may be venomous."

His friend shot him a surprised look at this bald lie. She had her back to them, and Carl shrugged his shoulders and held out his palms, hoping Defoe would understand that it would be more trouble if she knew he was denigrating the ferrets.

"I wouldn't be surprised," she said, turning to face them. Her face was lifeless, as though shot through with Novocaine. "The little fiends," she added, slumping into a chair to wait for the water to boil.

Carl was relieved to hear her turn her anger on the Hood instead of him. "It would explain how they were able to kill Tekumewa—the coyote."

And by extension, he hoped that she would see, Larry.

"I don't understand how Satan incarnate could have come from Lilly," she added.

Silence hovered above the table.

She looked up at them. "It's an expression. Don't worry; I don't really think that the Hood is Satan." She thought a moment. "Maybe I'll reserve my judgment on that."

She had never referred to Larry's siblings by the Hood moniker before. He was happy to have her on his side.

"Do you think they all have it?" she asked. "The poisonous vomit?"

"Hmm, good question. I've only seen Shemp use it. She bit my ankle and killed Larry. But I remember that both Curly and Moe had this saliva that was thick like molasses dripping from their mouths when they went after Larry."

He shivered thinking about it.

Defoe looked at his watch and announced that he'd better be going. Toby was arriving again for another visit.

Fels's water was boiling. She got up and poured it over two tea-bags she'd dropped into her carry-cup with the dolphins on the side, then put on her jacket.

"Where are you going?" Carl asked.

"I think a check came. I forgot to pick it up on the way in last night."

She meant that it was probably sitting in the mailbox a half-mile away at the county road turnoff. "I'll walk with Defoe a ways and pick it up," he offered. "With the shape you're in, you might not find your way back."

The ferrets, both the Hood and Lilly, were nowhere to be seen, and that was fine with Carl. He would have been happy if he never saw another one for the rest of his life.

Defoe's turnoff was halfway to the mailbox, but he was only just beginning to get warmed up with an argument positing that language structures our thoughts, and consequently that the tonal nature of Chinese makes it easier for them to handle multi-variable problems, and so the old philosopher decided to continue on and take the long way home. When they arrived at the bank of mailboxes that they shared with half a dozen of their neighbors, Carl found that the check had not arrived, but that there was a hand-addressed letter to Fels with no return address. The sender had transposed two digits of their house number, and one of their neighbors had corrected it and added, *wrong address*. The postmark was a week old.

He looked at Defoe.

"It doesn't matter what I say," his friend predicted. "You're going to open it anyway."

"She won't mind," he replied tearing it open and thinking, *depending on what's inside.*

There was a single sheet written in precise and fluid script. He glanced down to the bottom at the signature. "It's from Weinermach!"

The letter read:

> *I apologize for corresponding via the post, but I didn't want to talk to you at GeneTrend, and I am afraid that our email might be monitored. Please call me at home. The matter is urgent. In the meantime, it is very important that you stay away from the ferrets. Most importantly, you should not provoke them.*

Weinermach ended with a cordial sign-off and his home telephone number. Carl handed the letter to Defoe.

Stay away from the ferrets. It couldn't be a coincidence. Weinermach must know something about the animals' nasty predilection to regurgitate on their victims.

When his friend had finished reading, he looked at Carl with a furrowed brow. "Do you remember when I erroneously indicated that Weinermach had won a Nobel Prize for research on stomach bacteria, and Rik had quickly corrected me? Well, I was curious, and I looked him up. His Nobel Prize was indeed for brain research, but I was n't completely wrong. He had done his doctoral thesis on stomach bacteria, and he had used genetically modified strains to study immune responses to infections in the brain."

"Do you think there's a connection?"

"I think that Fels should contact him immediately as he suggests." Defoe glanced at his watch. "Oh dear! I must run or Toby will be sitting on my doorstep in the hot sun."

"You lock your door?"

"No, but the boy is probably too polite to just walk in."

Carl re-read Weinermach's letter several times on the way home, trying to glean something more from the sparse communication. One thing was for sure: they were going to take his advice very literally.

The Hood had other ideas, however. A hundred yards before the cabin, the dirt road cut through a small ridge, forming banks on both sides. As the bases of pine trees rose to eye level, Moe came skittering down the bank ahead, turning in the middle of the road to face him. Even from fifty feet, Carl could see molasses dripping from the ferret's jaws. He heard a scrabbling sound from behind and turned to find Curly, who growled at him. The beady little eyes locked on him like targeting radar.

He'd gotten Weinermach's warning too late. He had already provoked them by searching out their new lair.

He calculated whether he might outrun them. They had short, stubby legs, but could run surprisingly fast for short distances. If he could get past them, he was sure that he could outdistance them. It was the getting past part that made him pause. His running shoes and shorts provided almost no protection, leaving his bare legs as easy targets. He doubted that he could get by either of them without risking a bite, and as far as he knew, a mere nick might be fatal.

He glanced up at the lowest bank. He could easily climb it before his attackers were upon him. Shemp hadn't shown herself, though. She could be waiting at the top. If only he knew where she was . . . but the Hood leader was obviously too smart to show her hand.

He could feel the sweat, sticky on his palms. Maybe he could kick them. They were no bigger than a cat. The ferrets were extremely agile, though. He imagined them leaping as he kicked and wrapping their slim bodies around his leg. He could almost feel the claws grabbing his skin, and the sharp little teeth coated with lethal goo sinking into his calf.

The two Hood members provided precious little time to formulate a plan, and immediately started for him at a trot. It felt like his heart had expanded tenfold and was choking him. He desperately searched the ground. Maybe he could throw rocks. Even as the thought formed, he realized that this would be stupid against such small targets. Instead, he picked up a stick barely two feet long.

Moe and Curly were already upon him, and he twisted around, swinging his little sword in an arc along the dirt. The two ferrets paused, snarling, just beyond reach. Vomit wet the fur under their chins, creating little goatees and imparting the appearance of miniature devils.

Each time he fended off one, the other would advance so that he was forced slowly backwards, step by step until he felt the bank rising behind him. His back was literally against the wall.

He reached down, grabbed a handful of dirt, and tossed it at Moe. The ferret flinched, but then immediately sprang forward as though proving they couldn't be intimidated, forcing Carl to concentrate his stick in that direction. Grabbing the opportunity, Curly also sprang, and Carl reflexively kicked, catching a lucky blow with his toe under his assailant's chin so that the ferret spun away, raising a small cloud of dust.

With this bit of fortune Carl saw a glimmer of hope. He gauged whether he might also kick Moe while Curly was recovering from the blow. As though aware that he might be next, Moe took a step back and crouched down.

A waft of acrid vomit reached Carl's nose and he suddenly became aware of a growling, gurgling sound behind his head. He turned, and there, not two feet away, Shemp was staring at him from the edge of the bank. The she-Hood opened her mouth wide revealing needle-sharp teeth swimming in vile brown goo.

She crouched back, preparing to spring, and he instinctively lifted his arm across his face, even though this merely afforded a larger target of bare skin. Instead of jumping, however, she spun to the side, hissing menacingly. A flash of brown fur bowled her over, and she tumbled away. The interloper then leaped from the bank onto the road. There, miraculously, stood Tekumewa, strong and tall, studying the remaining two Hood.

Moe and Curly spun to face this new foe, while Shemp appeared again at the bank's edge spitting brown gravy in anger. The coyote circled slowly to the other side of the road, positioning all three ferrets to his front. He raised his noble snout and let go a piercing howl that echoed among the surrounding peaks. The ferrets hunkered and glanced around, as though nervous that reinforcements might be arriving.

Tekumewa sprang forward, nipping repeatedly at Curly and Moe, and then dancing away again. The ferrets cowered before the ferocious onslaught, as though they'd forgotten that they harbored a lethal bite, or perhaps not willing to risk a broken neck in order to land one.

Carl saw that he could escape and he turned to run, but his conscience laid a restraining hand. Despite the teasing he gave Defoe, he had come to think of the coyote as embodying Tekumewa. He turned back just in time to see the warrior's fighting dance take him close to the bank. Finding the opportunity she'd been waiting for, Shemp leaped onto the coyote's back. Tekumewa whirled and twisted, desperate to dislodge the beast, but the ferret dug her claws into its back and hung on. Shemp tried to sink her teeth, and only the coyote's frantic bucking prevented her from immediately finding contact.

No time to contemplate. Carl leaped forward, swinging his stick, but found only air as Tekumewa suddenly jerked sideways.

Carl followed and swiped backhand with the stick, and this time he felt a satisfying concussion as Shemp flew off and rolled in the dirt. The ferret found her feet and spun to face Tekumewa, growling. The two foes stared at each other for a moment until Shemp finally backed slowly away, brandishing dripping needle teeth. She then turned and ran off into the pines, and Moe and Curly followed close after.

Tekumewa started after them, but Carl called out. He was surprised at himself for expecting a wild coyote to listen, but more surprised when the animal did stop and turn to him expectantly.

"Good boy!" he called.

Adrenaline urged him to hoot and holler and maybe dance a jig with the coyote.

"I hope I'm not being disrespectful," he added, gleefully. "Allow me to offer my deepest thanks, Chief Tekumewa," he said, bowing dramatically.

The coyote wagged its tail curiously a couple of times, but then turned its attention to its backside. It twisted its snout around and sniffed the regurgitated mess that Shemp had left behind, then looked at Carl and whined. The animal sat back on its haunches and tried to reach its back, but the contorted stretch was difficult.

Carl had thought that Shemp failed to accomplish her lethal chomp, but what if she hadn't? Larry had died within minutes, and the ferrets had managed to bring the other coyote down. As if fate was listening to his very thoughts, Tekumewa suddenly whined and crouched, prostrated flat against the dirt road. The sleek body shuddered, and the tail lay lifeless in the dust.

"Tekumewa!" Carl cried.

The coyote looked at him, and the stark blue eyes seemed sad. The head trembled as though aged with palsy, and the animal laid its chin onto the dirt between its front paws and closed its eyes.

"Shit!" Carl whispered, approaching the prostrate Tekumewa slowly. He thought the coyote had died, but another involuntary shudder wracked the poor beast, and he realized that it was unconscious.

He squatted next to the fallen warrior and nearly recoiled at the acrid stench. This close, he could see that the animal trembled continuously, only occasionally erupting into violent shakes. He'd never been this close to a coyote, and he wondered at how much like a dog it looked. This could have been Bart, his mongrel companion when he was a child. Only the long, bushy tail and large ears gave away its true heritage. He saw, though, the differences between Tekumewa and the coyote that the ferrets had killed. That one's snout had been slimmer, and the ears more pointed. Tekumewa's coat was also yellowish, almost blond.

He couldn't leave Tekumewa to die here all alone. The damnable ferrets might come back to harass the poor creature. He reached out and carefully slid his hands under Tekumewa's underside. At his touch, the coyote jerked once involuntarily. As he lifted the inert body, it seemed to come alive, kicking frantically so that he had to let it fall back onto the road. He waited and tried again, and this time there was no reaction. He would have preferred a good, strong kick.

Carried carefully in two outstretched arms, thirty pounds was a heavy load, and Carl was grunting and sweating when he pushed the cabin door open with his foot. Inside, Fels was staring at the computer monitor and she glanced at him once, frowning at his inert burden, but turned immediately back to the glowing screen.

"Weinermach is dead," she reported, turning again to him. "He committed suicide yesterday. We were wondering why he didn't show up for work."

She looked worse than when she'd emerged from the bedroom. Her face had been lifeless, but now it harbored confusion and fear.

She seemed to finally understand that he was standing there holding a lifeless coyote. "Did you dig that poor thing back up?" she cried, nearly in tears.

"No," he said. "That one was a wild animal, this is Tekumewa."

His explanation sounded odd, yet satisfying.

She wrinkled her nose. "I smell . . . it was the Hood, wasn't it?"

He nodded. "They caught me just down the road. He saved my life—"

He turned at a noise behind him. It was Defoe, huffing and puffing, stumbling up to the door. Toby trotted along easily just behind him. "I remembered. . ." the old philosopher started, but had to stop to catch his breath. He leaned over and braced his hands on his knees a moment, then stood back up. "I remembered where I had previously heard the name . . ." He took a breath. ". . . Lilake, from which Lilly was derived." He sucked in another deep, wheezing breath, and coughing, motioned to Toby to take over.

"Lilake was another name for Lilith," the boy explained.

Carl shrugged, and Defoe spun his hand in a circle, urging Toby to continue.

"She's described in the Talmud—an ancient Jewish book. She was the first wife of Adam, before Eve. Their children were demons."

PART IV

FIRE

Chapter 17

"**D**emons!" Carl cried. He tried to hold all the events of the last few minutes together in his mind, and failed. "Defoe, I can't deal with this nonsense right now. I've got a poisoned reincarnated Indian warrior, and Fels just found out that Weinermach has committed suicide."

His friend's eyes went wide. "This is Tekumewa!" he exclaimed peering closely at the limp animal in Carl's arms. He looked up, alarmed. "You dug him up?"

"No, I didn't dig up the damn coyote carcass! That wasn't Tekumewa."

Defoe sniffed and recoiled. "Did the ferrets bite him?"

"I guess so. They attacked me, and he came to my rescue."

"Is he dead?"

"I don't *know!* But if I don't put him down I'm going to pass out from the stench."

Defoe reached out and gently took the fallen warrior from him. He carried the precious burden into the Great Hall and laid it on a small throw rug in the middle of the room.

"How do we take the pulse of a coyote?" Carl asked, squatting down next to the unconscious casualty.

"That is, unfortunately, one question I never had reason to contemplate," Defoe replied. "In the movies they use a small mirror to check for breathing."

Carl ran off to find Fels's purse. He dug out her compact and when he held the little mirror in front of the coyote's nose, sure enough, a faint fog spread and rapidly disappeared every half dozen seconds.

"So, what do we do?" he asked.

"Since mouth-to-snout resuscitation is not necessary, perhaps all we *can* do is keep the animal warm."

Carl grabbed the blanket off the back of the sofa but hesitated. It had been a wedding present from Fels's aunt. Fels was still engrossed with her email, so he tossed it back and ran off to the closet for an older one. When he returned, Defoe had wiped his fingers across some of the vomit that had gotten on his shirt when carrying Tekumewa, and was holding it out for Toby to smell.

The boy looked alarmed and stepped back. "I thought it was poisonous! Aren't you scared?"

"It won't hurt you. The ferrets must pierce your skin to inject it into your bloodstream."

Toby shook his head distrustfully. "I'm not taking any chances."

Carl doubled the blanket and laid it across Tekumewa, pulling the edge back from the animal's head.

"You can't let your fears make you a prisoner, my boy," Defoe said, reverting to his professor tone. "Logic must always rule. Now watch."

Carl glanced up to see his friend dab his tongue against his forefinger.

"Ew!" Toby cried. "You're crazy!"

"Not at all! Logic, my boy. Logic. Think about it. The ferrets live constantly with this substance in their stomachs, and occasionally, when they are feeling particularly aggressive, in their mouths as well. Clearly it is not dangerous unless injected by a bite."

Toby shook his head. Logic or no, he was having nothing to do with ferret puke.

"They don't know his method," Fels reported, turning to face them.

Carl looked from his friend, who was tasting vomit to prove a point, to his wife, who looked like she probably needed to vomit. "Who?"

"Dr. Weinermach!" she cried, upset. "What's the matter with you? He just *killed* himself!"

Unlike her, he had never seen or even talked to the man. Weinermach was just a name. "Right. So, uh, they don't know how he did it? How do they know it was even suicide?"

"He left a note," she replied, turning back to read some more. "On his computer."

"He left a suicide note on his *computer*? Boy, that's a scientist for you. What if the power had gone off before they found him? On the other hand, he probably didn't care—"

Fels threw him a "watch-it-buster" look and went back to reading.

"Oh my!" he heard Defoe say.

The daredevil philosopher was leaning over and supporting himself with the back of a chair. His normally ruddy face had gone pale. He stumbled forward and flopped onto the sofa. "Perhaps that was a mistake."

"What's the matter?" Carl asked, going to him.

"I don't feel well. Not well at all."

"I wouldn't either if I just ate vomit," Carl joked, but he was afraid for his friend.

"Toby!" Defoe called, lying down on his back. "Never trust logic. It has no soul."

Carl watched in horror as the old man's hands began to tremble.

"What's wrong with him?" Fels asked, suddenly by his side.

"He ate some ferret puke. We have to call 911 . . . shit!"

After nearly a year, he still forgot the consequences of having no wired phone service.

"Maybe we can use the Internet phone," she said, running to the computer and putting on the headset.

Carl went to the kitchen and got a glass of water. He didn't know what else to do. Defoe lay with his eyes closed and just shook his head when Carl offered the glass to him. Toby stood a few feet back looking lost and scared.

Fels was using Google to find the nearest hospital. He watched over her shoulder and thought how odd it was that they hadn't done this immediately after moving up here. The closest she could find was all the way down in El Cajon, nearly an hour away, and that wasn't even a hospital, just an urgent care clinic. She used the keyboard to dial the number shown on the website, but was tripped up by the satellite delay; the clinic's operator hung up after a few seconds of "Hello—hello!" with no response. Fels dialed again, and this time began talking immediately, trying to get across to the woman the situation. The operator seemed annoyed, and explaining that they were very busy hung up again.

"How can a hospital just hang up on you?" Carl exclaimed. "That seems, like, illegal or something."

"They're not a hospital," Fels reminded him distractedly as she searched out another number. "They're probably not supposed to handle real life-and-death emergencies anyway."

The next clinic in El Cajon she contacted was more cooperative, and the operator patiently explained through the long satellite delay pauses that they did not have an ambulance service, and in any case—just as Fels had guessed—weren't equipped to accept life-threatening poison emergencies. This person was kind enough, though, to give Fels the number of an El Cajon ambulance service. They too almost hung up, but Fels provided compelling motivation with some language that, coming from a lady, must have surprised the operator. That person initially declared that such a remote location was outside their contract service area and suggested that they call their local rescue squad, but Fels ratcheted up the profanity and the dispatcher agreed to send a crew. Fels was prepared to provide detailed directions, but all they needed were GPS coordinates.

After nearly ten minutes of frustrating shouting and maddening satellite delays, Fels finally sat back and tore off the headset. "They're leaving immediately, but it's going to be about forty minutes 'till they get here. How's Defoe?"

"Still conscious, but clearly not happy. He drank some water and I put a blanket over him. Listen, I think we need to call the police as well."

She looked at him through exhausted eyes. "We don't really know what's going on. How do you know the ferrets' vomit is poisonous?"

He related all the details of the Hood's attack on Larry that he'd held back, and then described the attack on him. "I'm telling you," he reiterated, "Tekumewa was in perfect health until Shemp bit him on the back. He was out cold just minutes later. Defoe had a similar reaction after tasting the vomit. Shemp only bit Larry on the leg. There's no way he should have died from that, otherwise. The coyote that they killed a few days ago—they only bit him on the leg as well."

He dug Weinermach's letter out of his back pocket and handed it to her. "But this is why I really think we should call the police."

As she read the letter, he checked on Tekumewa. The mirror showed that the coyote was still alive. Defoe watched him dully, while Toby sat in a chair clasping his hands, as though not sure what to do.

Defoe had taken just one little taste. The stuff must be potent. It was surprising that Tekumewa wasn't already dead. Unless . . . what if Shemp hadn't managed to bite the coyote? He'd watched Tekumewa twisting around to investigate Shemp's damage. Coyote's were probably like dogs: they would smell and then lick anything, given half a chance.

"You think Weinermach knew about the ferrets' poisonous vomit?" Fels asked, putting the letter down.

"What else? Why didn't he want to talk to you at GeneTrend, or email you? Who was he afraid of?" He caught his breath, just now registering what Fels had seen on the Internet news. "Suicide is awfully convenient sometimes."

Fels wrinkled her brow, and then shook her head. "You're thinking that maybe . . . that's ridiculous! That kind of stuff doesn't happen in real life."

"Ferrets with poisonous puke isn't my idea of real life either."

She shook her head more adamantly. "No way! There is just no way that GeneTrend would somehow arrange to kill—"

"I didn't say it was GeneTrend."

She squinted at him. "You think it was Rik? Oh, come on."

On impulse, he went to the computer and put on the headset. "What's Rik's number?"

"You're jumping to wild conclusions. You can't just accuse somebody of—"

"I'm not going accuse him of anything. I just want some answers."

He went to Fels's GeneTrend folder and found an Excel file titled "contacts." The entries were in alphabetical order, and seconds later he was dialing the number. After four rings, he heard Rik say hello.

"This is Carl. I'm talking over the satellite connection and you're going to hear this a few seconds from now," he explained. "I'll probably be talking over top of you soon, but I'm going to keep going, and I want you to just listen." He heard Rik's voice, but continued as promised. "We have one hell of a mess up here, and I want some answers from you about these goddamn ferrets you've stuck us with. We're about ten seconds away from calling the police, so don't screw with me."

After an interminable number of heartbeats Rik said, "I assume it's now my turn now. I wouldn't even consider screwing you, Carl. You're not my type. If can hold off bothering the police needlessly, I will be there soon to explain everything."

"You're coming up?"

Silence, and then, "I'm about three miles away. In fact, I think I'm losing the cell. Just sit tight and—"

The connection broke.

"He's going to come up?" Fels asked.

Carl shook his head. He wasn't sure what to make of this news. "He's already up. He'll be here in a few minutes."

Just then, a distant explosion rattled the cabin. The reverberating echoes made the location difficult to pinpoint, but it seemed to be from the east, in the general direction of the road. Minutes later, they heard the rumble of the Hummer, and the dusty black behemoth wallowed into view. As it turned to park next to their pickup, Carl saw that the rear window was shattered. Rik stepped out and stood looking at them as though dazed. His hair was rumpled and half of his shirttail hung out.

"What the hell was *that*?" Carl asked.

Rik blinked and looked at him. "What?"

"What do you mean, 'what'? That explosion!"

The disheveled executive glanced back, as though trying to remember. "Oh, that. I passed a road construction crew along the way. They must be doing work."

"What happened here?" Carl asked, pointing to the broken window.

Rik looked at it. "Teenage delinquents. They smashed it last night."

Carl noticed a red gash along Rik's hairline under the mussed hair. "The hooligans attacked you as well?" he asked, pointing to his own forehead to illustrate the location.

Rik reached up and touched the wound, and then studied the blood on his fingertips. "I ran into a big pothole. I must have hit my head."

The genetics engineer seemed to regain his composure. He looked at Carl and grinned. "Any other questions?"

Carl had several, like why a road construction crew would allow the public to pass so close to powerful explosions. He had more pressing matters, though. "What have you done to these ferrets?"

Rik pretended to be concerned at the obviously irrational question. "What do you mean?"

"You know perfectly well what I mean. Defoe is inside dying because of them."

Rik's cocky demeanor slipped and he frowned. "What did he do to them?"

"What did *he* do to *them*? He's the one who's dying!"

"I mean, what did he do to provoke them? Did he threaten them?"

"Christ! Are you insane? No! He didn't threaten them. He just licked some of their vomit."

After a moment Rik grinned. "Since we are in the mode of challenging basic sanity, I'd say that eating vomit isn't a very sane thing to do. Perhaps our friend has other problems."

"Look, you arrogant bastard, Defoe is saner than . . . no, no. You're not going to change the subject. What the hell did you do to these ferrets?"

"Me?" Rik defended with exaggerated surprise. "How could I do anything? They've been with you the whole time. I might ask the same: what have you done to my Lilly?"

"Lilake, you mean."

He'd forgotten completely about Defoe's revelation in the last mad twenty minutes of turmoil.

Rik looked at him through cold, hard eyes.

"Or should I say, Lilith?" Carl offered. "I understand that Her children were demons."

"What in God's name are you talking about?" Rik asked, feigning ignorance.

"You know damn well. Fels saw it on your desk."

Rik glared at her accusingly. "Well, so much for non-disclosure agreements."

Carl realized that he'd blabbed. Fels, though, seemed not to care. She returned her client's stare with equal resolve. They were past caring about her career status.

Rik shrugged. "It's a name. I happened to like it."

They obviously weren't going to get any more out of him on that subject. Carl wished that Defoe wasn't laid up; his friend would have known how to tease more from Rik.

He caught a whiff that set off alarm bells. "You smell that?"

Rik sniffed and shook his head. "What?"

"Smoke. Wood smoke."

The visitor shrugged. "It's probably coming from the road construction."

Carl took a deep breath through his nose. He didn't smell it anymore. "So why are you here?" he asked.

It had been bad manners not to ask Rik inside for tea, but he sensed that this wasn't a social visit anyway.

"I haven't been up in a while. I thought it would be good to see how the ferrets are doing."

Carl just looked at him. He knew it was a lie, and his silence communicated the fact.

"I also wanted to make sure Fels got the news about poor Weinermach," Rik added.

That's more like it, Carl thought.

"We saw it on the Internet," Fels joined in. "It's terrible. In fact—"

"We saw it just before you came," Carl blurted, cutting her off.

He guessed what she was going to say, and he didn't want to give that away just yet.

Rik looked from him to Fels, searching for some clue. "Have you heard from him lately?"

Bingo! "No," Carl replied quickly before Fels could respond. "Why do you ask?"

Fels glanced at him, surprised, but looked back to Rik nonchalantly.

Rik stared at him, as though seeking to penetrate his shields. He shrugged. "Just trying to understand what would make a man end a life with so much promise."

"What's your working theory?"

Rik clasped his hands like a minister might when finally getting to the meat of the sermon. "Weinermach was unstable and delusional. He seemed depressed lately. It was probably genetic. I understand his mother tried to commit suicide a couple of times."

"Delusional, eh? About what?"

The engineer gazed at him a moment and said, "He was paranoid. He thought people at work were conspiring to get him." He glanced quickly at Fels but she just watched him.

"Paranoia," Carl confirmed, nodding sagely. "Terrible thing. No specific delusions? Like, for example, that he was developing poisons in the ferrets?"

He was taking a wild shot, remembering what Defoe had said about Weinermach's early work on stomach bacteria, but Rik fell into the trap. His eyes went round, and then squinted in anger. "What did he tell you?"

It was Carl's turn to grin. "I lied when I said that we hadn't heard from him. But with you that's no crime. Weinermach sent us a letter. He spelled out in detail the whole situation."

One good lie deserves another.

"Let me see it."

"Sure, and maybe I should sign over the deed to our cabin while I'm at it?"

Rik stared at him impassively a few seconds, and then nodded slowly. "I see. Well, I guess that's that," he said, turning and walking to the Hummer.

Carl looked at Fels to see how she was taking her husband's bravado. She blinked and smiled. He felt okay. He could be a hard-ass if needed. Fels looked past him, and her face suddenly swelled with alarm.

He turned to find Rik standing next to the Hummer holding a pistol.

Chapter 18

R ik made a point to examine the compact little semi-automatic gun, glancing up to make sure they'd seen it before slipping it into his pocket.

Carl caught another whiff of wood smoke. He would expect a road construction crew to throw up a lot of dust, but not smoke from burning wood. He would have bet that dynamite wouldn't even leave any smoke at all.

"I'd really like to see Weinermach's letter," Rik said in a reasonable tone, walking back to them.

Carl knew that Rik was only playing along with this feigned cordiality, but it was a lot easier to take than staring at a brandished weapon. "He warned us not to provoke the ferrets," Carl explained, using up all the meat of his bluff.

Rik nodded with a patronizing grin. "That was good advice. I'm glad you followed it."

"We might have if we'd gotten it in time."

Rik peered at him suspiciously, probably wondering what game he was playing now. "You said you hadn't provoked them."

"I said that Defoe hadn't. It was me."

"I," Fels corrected wearily.

He looked at her. She returned his gaze impassively, as though it had been someone else who had spoken. Why was she trying to protect him? "Um, it was me that found the second den—"

"No," she interrupted. "I mean, you should say, 'I,' not 'me.' "

"What did I say? 'It was me.' Isn't 'me' the object?"

"A word isn't always the object just because it comes after the verb. Would you say, 'Me found the den'?"

"Nobody says 'It was I.' That may be correct, but—"

"Shut up!" Rik shouted.

They looked at him. He glared at them, his hand clutching the gun in his pocket. "Did you provoke the ferrets?" he asked.

Carl glanced at the outline of the gun through the fabric of the pants. "Not intentionally."

He related the collaboration with Larry in their discovery of the den in the hollow log, and the little ferret's subsequent demise. With each sentence Rik's eyes grew larger. "Jesus Christ!" he exclaimed when Carl had finished. "Are you an idiot?"

The thought of Rik's gun inhibited the obscene answer that came to mind. "You could have told us that your monsters were poisonous," he shot back instead. "The damn things are lethal!"

Rik peered around the perimeter of the clearing, ignoring him. In any case, the not-so-subtle threat of death by handgun tempered the effectiveness of indignation at poisonous ferrets.

"Come on," Rik ordered, shooing them along with his hands like they were children, "let's get inside."

Carl hesitated. The ambulance crew would arrive in twenty minutes. Maybe he could stall Rik until they arrived. He wasn't sure what they could do to help, but surely their presence would provide some inhibition to whatever Rik had in store.

And then he smelled it again—smoke. He looked at the T-shirts he'd hung on the line. They were already dry, and they waved and flapped in the direction of the ocean—the wind was from the east, and dry as a bone.

A Santa Ana! He looked up, and there, looming above the cabin roof was a billowing brown plume, as though an atom bomb had been detonated on Laguna Mountain. "Look!" he cried, pointing.

Rik glanced up once, and continued herding them into the cabin.

The smell of smoke was unmistakable now; not the welcoming promise of warmth on a snowy winter's evening, but obliteration by scorching heat.

When they came through the door, Defoe opened his eyes, but closed them again without saying anything. Toby looked up from the computer, apprehensive about being caught there. "I, uh, smelled smoke," the boy explained. "I'm looking at the San Diego County website. There's a wildfire near Cottonwood Canyon."

"Who's this?" Rik asked, clearly not happy about the unexpected visitor.

"A friend of Defoe," Carl answered.

"And what the hell's *that?*" he asked, pointing to Tekumewa lying on the carpet.

"A coyote. He also licked the vomit."

Rik shook his head and muttered, "It's a goddamn pagan vomit ritual." He looked around, studying the Great Hall. "Can the ferrets get in?" he asked.

Carl pointed to the little swinging door he'd made.

"Christ!" Rik cried, going to it. "You just let them come in anytime they want?" he rebuked. Glancing around, he slid a heavy trunk in front of the door. The metal corners probably scratched the floor.

"It wasn't so long ago that you were upset that we let Lilly go outside," Carl retorted.

"Things have changed. You've activated them with your stupid nosiness."

"Activated?" Carl questioned. "What is that supposed to mean? It sounds like they're robots or something."

Rik ignored him. He was studying the unconscious coyote.

"Wait a second," Carl defended. "The ferrets were poisonous, or at least three of Lilly's kits were, before I found their second den."

Their quasi-captor looked at him, annoyed. "What the hell are you talking about?"

"They killed a wild coyote by biting it on the leg."

Rik looked at Tekumewa and back at Carl, perplexed.

"Not this one. The one they killed was wild."

"They killed a coyote?" Rik repeated, seeming to welcome the news. He appeared to come to a decision. "Here, help me carry this," he directed, bending down and grasping one end of the carpet under Tekumewa.

"Where are we taking him?"

"Outside."

"Why?"

Rik just glanced at him and nodded towards the other end of the carpet.

"You're going to use Tekumewa as some kind of sacrifice?" Carl exclaimed. His voice went squeaky at the last word.

"Come on," Rik ordered, ignoring the question. "Lift the other end."

"No!" Fels cried, running over. "You are *not* taking that coyote outside where those demons can get at him."

"I think that's the whole idea," Carl guessed. He could tell by Rik's quick glance that he was right. "He wants to use Tekumewa as bait."

She turned her furious eyes on her boss. "Is that it?"

He just looked at her, his face a stone mask.

"You *shit!*" she cried. "Well, you can just forget it. This coyote is not going anywhere."

She stood with her hands on her hips, her chin jutting out, daring the man to take a poke at her.

Rik straightened up slowly and slid his hand into the pocket with the gun. He returned her stare calmly. The message was clear.

"What are you going to do?" she taunted. "Shoot me?"

Rik didn't reply. His eyes bore into her with a confidence that only a gun can bestow.

"Yes!" Carl whispered. Neither of them seemed to hear him. "Yes!" he said louder.

That caught Fels's attention and she looked at him.

"He might shoot you," he affirmed.

She turned back to Rik, discounting his warning.

"He killed Weinermach," Carl blurted.

At this, she turned to him in surprise. Rik's eyes squinted their anger.

"Weinermach was trying to warn us," Carl went on. "He had a change of heart about what was going on at GeneTrend."

Rik lifted his head high and said, "And, what do you think that would be?"

You didn't deny it, you son-of-a-bitch! Carl thought. "Making poison vomit."

After a moment, the stone face relaxed into a smile. "I'm steering a billion-dollar company towards a goal of developing vomit that is poisonous?" he challenged. He shook his head in mock sympathy. "I don't think the Board would go for that. I would be fired."

Connections clicked into place for Carl. The idea of being fired from GeneTrend was familiar: Kaj had been afraid they would fire him for snooping around about Lilly. But, instead he had . . .

"You killed Kaj too!" he cried as though the news had suddenly scrolled across Rik's forehead. "He found out about Lilly. He tried to warn us but we . . ." He choked thinking about his friend. "We didn't listen."

Carl had blamed himself for introducing Kaj to Jimsonweed. But now he remembered that Rik had been surprised and alarmed at the funeral to hear that Carl had just told his friend about the plant. Rik had obviously overheard Kaj talking about the drug at work, and assuming that the drummer was already a dabbler, didn't think anyone would be surprised at an overdose. Rik hadn't realized that Carl was the Jimsonweed connection.

He looked at Rik. "You then killed Weinermach when he tried to warn us."

Rik stared at him a moment and then sighed. Carl had never imagined that a sigh could be so threatening. "Let's have it," Rik demanded, holding out his hand. "The letter."

Carl nodded to Fels and she picked it up off the desk and handed it to him. Rik read it quickly and then folded it and jammed it into his pocket. "Let's go," he said to Carl, pointing at the other end of the carpet.

Carl looked at Fels, and her face pleaded for him to do something.

Time to play the card. "The authorities will be arriving any minute," he announced.

Rik studied him a moment. "I doubt that," he said, pointing again to the carpet and bending over to pick up his own end.

"We called them just before you arrived. An ambulance crew from El Cajon."

"And the police," Fels added, glancing quickly at Carl.

Rik stood up, looked at them, and sighed again. "I'm afraid not."

Blaine C. Readler

"You want proof? Well, here you go," Carl said, walking over to the computer where Toby was reading something on the screen. The boy had pulled up the San Diego Sheriff website, but on top was an email he was reading. He looked up, and his face spoke of bad news. The message had been sent by the ambulance service just minutes before. Their crew reported the road blocked by a landslide. They recommended contacting the county Office of Emergency Services.

A Landslide? There had been no rain in months. It must have been the explosion from the road construction. The crew must have . . .

He remembered. Rik had arrived disheveled and shaken. It had been him! The blast must have been stronger than he was expecting and caught him by surprise—

Rik interrupted Carl's revelations by shoving him aside, and with one solid push of his foot, he rolled the chair with Toby still in it across the floor. He pulled the desktop computer off the shelf, yanking at it a couple of times to tear loose the attached cords, then lifted it high above his head and smashed it to the floor. He walked back to the carpet and barked, "Now, pick it up."

Carl's heart had seemed to stop, and now pumped double time to make up. As much as the shock of the rash violence, he was stunned by the implications of this new reality. Rik had blocked both their escape route and outside help. And, now accusations of his murders of Kaj and Weinermach had been unveiled. Rik must have arrived with the idea that he might be the only one leaving. The threat of the gun in his pocket was no longer abstract.

Carl finally grabbed his end of the carpet, and Rik led the way as they carried it out the front door. Tekumewa swung back and forth in the makeshift sling, oblivious to his fate. Outside, Carl found that the force of the wind had doubled, setting the pine trees swishing and swaying nervously, as though alarmed to discover that they were anchored in place by their roots. The rest of the world, though, had gone silent, as though the smoke, which was now strong enough to sting his eyes, had driven all the birds and insects into hiding. *If you smell smoke, you're in the fire's path.*

"Here," Rik ordered, and they stopped twenty feet from the cabin and set the carpet down on the dirt.

Rik started for the cabin, but Carl hesitated, standing over the enigmatic animal. He looked up at the sky. The sun was brown and indistinct from the fire's haze, but despite the wind, its heat seemed amplified by the smoke.

"Maybe we should move him into the shade," Carl suggested.

"It won't matter soon," Rik replied without looking back. At the cabin door, he paused and looked at Carl. "You can stay out here if you like; you've both provoked the ferrets. But if you think you're going to save the coyote, you're more of a fool than I guessed."

Carl looked at Tekumewa, the coyote that walked like a man. He couldn't just abandon him here. He'd seen the power of the ferret's poison and it terrified him, but friends looked out for each other. It was the basis of morality. He found a limb the size of a baseball bat and gave it a few practice swings while scanning the clearing's perimeter for signs of the Hood.

"Put it down and get in here," Rik commanded.

He had taken the compact little gun from his pocket and was pointing it at him. The captor had apparently decided that he wasn't willing to risk harm to his ferrets.

Carl hesitated, considering for the briefest moment calling Rik's bluff, but found that facing down the barrel of a loaded gun was far too intimidating. With a last look at the fallen coyote, he tossed aside his unused club and preceded Rik and the gun into the cabin.

Fels stood just inside, and as Rik came through the door, she slapped him across the face. "*You're* the monster," she hissed. "And, I quit."

Carl's heart stopped again as Rik swung the gun's tip to touch the spoon-shaped hollow at the base of her throat. Her boss's temples bulged, and Carl held his breath, waiting for the explosive report. After an interminable few seconds, the muscles of Rik's face relaxed, and he lowered the weapon. "Working at GeneTrend will soon be irrelevant."

Brandishing the gun openly now, Rik made them sit at the kitchen table while he watched through the windows and waited. At one point Defoe mumbled something, and Carl went to him without bothering to raise his hand for permission. His friend seemed conscious, and Carl lied and told him to hang in there; help was on the way. The stricken man whispered for water, and Carl brought him a glass and helped him sit up to drink. The effort seemed to take whatever energy the old philosopher had left, and he slumped back down and fell asleep.

Carl wished he could take some water to Tekumewa as well.

Fels talked quietly to Toby, making casual conversation about his school and friends, a way of reassuring him that things were under control and would be okay. Whether the shy boy believed it or not was hard to tell since cautious watchfulness was his normal demeanor anyway.

"There!" Rik suddenly whispered hoarsely.

The utterance seemed to be directed at nobody in particular. Rik leaned forward, and Carl caught a glimpse of movement through the window, out near the clearing's edge. After a minute, Rik relaxed, settling back into waiting mode. On impulse he reached into his jacket pocket, took out a small vial, and placed it on the windowsill at ready.

Carl remembered a similar small bottle from the visit two months before. "Time for the monsters vitamins?" he asked.

Rik glanced over, but immediately returned his attention to the window.

"You could have just asked, you know," Carl prodded. "We would have given it to them. It wasn't necessary to blow up our road."

Rik glanced over again, and turning back to the window replied, "They're not vitamins."

It came to Carl that he had been duped. "The other bottle wasn't vitamins either, was it?"

Rik ignored him, but seconds later he pointed out the window excitedly. "Look at them! They slink along like perfect little predators."

For a moment, Carl thought he was referring to ferrets in general. "Why wouldn't they? They *are* ferrets . . . aren't they?"

Their captor was grinning like a child who just found out that school would be closed for the day. "In the same sense that we are apes," he said without turning around. "You're looking at the most dangerous predator on Earth."

Carl could only see Rik since the Hood members were out of his view through the window now, but he knew what the man meant. "That was poison in the bottle you gave me," he proclaimed, taking a probing shot.

Rik shook his head and snorted at such a naive idea. "How long would that have lasted?"

He was right. Even if the Hood were immune to the poison's effects, it would have passed through their system in a day or two. "What was it?"

He really didn't expect an answer, and so was surprised when Rik said, "A bacteria culture."

Carl glanced at Fels, but she just gave him a worried look and returned to her mollifying conversation with Toby.

And then it came to him: Weinermach's early work. "The bacteria live in their stomachs and create toxins, like botulism!"

The ferret Fuehrer snorted again. "Next to these babies, botulin is a mild caustic. The Earth has never seen a bacterium like this before."

The man was a genetics expert, after all. "You genetically engineered them! You . . . made them!"

Rik shook his head, never taking his eyes off the invisible progress outside. "That was Weinermach's department. Child's play, but I didn't have time to do everything myself."

"So this bottle must be a recharge. Maybe the bacteria die in their stomachs after a while?"

He was just guessing, but he wanted to keep the momentum going.

"Of course not. That would be quite a deficient design, now wouldn't it? No, this is a new strain—phase two, if you will."

Design—as though he was developing a new cell phone.

"Why doesn't it kill the ferrets?"

"Ah," Rik said with pride, "that's the mental gulf between you and me."

Carl bit his tongue. Rik had the gun. "You genetically altered the ferrets to be immune to the toxin."

"A simplistic view, but as close as you're going to understand."

He pressed on. "You said that we'd activated them. That was when the bacteria started making the toxin?"

Rik glanced around at him and scoffed again in derision. "You have no clue what's going on here."

Carl indeed felt like a child asking stupid questions, and he struggled along anyway. "You're right, I don't have a clue. So, humor me. What is the activation?"

Rik turned in the chair and faced him with a look like one might give just before pushing an adversary off a cliff. "A dramatic and permanent behavioral response, manifesting as exaggerated and persistent causal reciprocal aggression implemented by embedded cognitive triggers."

The genetics genius continued to stare at him just long enough to make the point that he didn't expect him to understand what was said before turning back to the window.

Carl blinked. "You mean you've modified the genes of the ferrets so that they get really pissed off and forever try to bite anybody who screws with them."

He'd formed this response more from the context of the last couple of days than Rik's intentionally obtuse answer, but was gratified when the genius glanced back for a second, surprised.

"I'll be right back," Fels suddenly announced, getting up and walking to the bedroom.

Rik turned and watched her close the door, then resumed his Hood watch.

Carl guessed that their kidnapper thought she was going to the bathroom, forgetting that they didn't have one.

So then, Carl wondered, what was she doing?

"Yes!" Rik hissed in triumph. "Look at that belly!"

Carl took Rik's renewed enthusiasm as an opportunity to casually stand and walk over to look over the man's shoulder. "Where?" he asked nonchalantly.

In his excitement, Rik seemed to not only have forgotten that there was no bathroom beyond the bedroom door, but that Carl was even a prisoner. "There," he said, pointing out the window. "The female."

Carl saw all three Hood weaving cautiously among the field of logs, advancing slowly on Tekumewa. "That's Shemp," he said. As usual, she was in the lead. Sure enough, her midsection bulged perceptively, just like Lilly's had.

"She's pregnant!" he exclaimed.

"Damn right!" Rik crowed, as though he himself was the proud father.

In a way, Carl thought, he was.

And then another thought struck him, an unease that had been hovering just under the surface. He saw suddenly that it was quite bad news that Rik was so forthcoming with explanations. Enemies don't reveal secrets unless they are confident their audience will never have an opportunity to recount. A sinking feeling settled in that his probing was going to backfire—as in a gun's report.

"What the hell!" Rik cried in anger, jumping out of his chair.

Peering past his shoulder, Carl saw Fels running from around the corner of the cabin. She clutched a shoe in her hand, and was sprinting for Tekumewa.

The members of the Hood had advanced to within ten feet of the helpless coyote, and now raised themselves, teeth bared in defiance, to meet the human interloper.

From their little jaws dripped lethally toxic molasses.

Chapter 19

"God damn it!" Rik cried. "What the hell is she doing?"

To Carl, it was obvious. She was going to get herself killed defending Tekumewa. She hadn't watched Larry die. She didn't fear the ferrets with the dread they were due.

"I'll get her back," Carl offered, going for the front entrance.

"Stay close to the door!" Rik called.

He was surprised that Rik was concerned for him. He looked back to find the black cavity of the gun barrel staring at him. Maybe not.

"You'll scare them away," Rik warned.

Carl wished he knew that trick as he stepped outside. The air burned his eyes, and his lungs cried out to cough. The smoke was choking, hardly bearable. Fels must have crawled out a bedroom window. The shoe she carried was a hiking boot from the closet. Shemp, belly bulging with second generation Hood, faced off with her, while the two brothers circled around to the sides.

"Fels!" he called. "Come back!"

She ignored him. He saw that it was too late in any case; Moe and Curly had closed the circle, cutting off retreat. Even from this distance, he saw the rippling of their abdomens as they primed their jaws with vomit poison. Fels's bare ankles were peeled bananas ready for chomping.

"Get back inside," Rik said to him from the doorway, still brandishing the gun.

"But she'll . . ."

The look in Rik's eyes gave him the answer. Now that it was clear to him that Fels wasn't going to drive them off, that they weren't afraid of her, there was no need to intervene.

"You can go to hell," Carl muttered, picking up the broom handle that he used to knock off the wasps' mud nests from under the eaves.

"Hold it!" Rik called. "I will shoot you."

With each step possibly his last, Carl held his breath, waiting for the bullet to slam into his back. He focused on saving Fels. Shemp had waited until her brothers had closed the circle tight, but now attacked, snarling and snapping. Fels held the boot out, keeping the ferret at bay while kicking sideways at Curly and Moe.

"Hey! Get away!" Carl cried springing forward, trying to get the Hoods' attention. The broom handle was unwieldy, too long and thin for such small targets. He needed a baseball bat or, better yet, a tennis racket.

He heard Rik yelling, but it seemed to be to somebody else, and the shouts faded, disappearing back into the cabin.

When he reached the battle, he swung the broom handle at Moe who was closest, but the makeshift club's long reach made for difficult aim, and he only managed to slap the ferret's tail. This was enough, though, to cause the beast to spin around, teeth gleaming with saliva and vomit. Instantly Moe sprang for him, and Carl danced sideways in panic from the deadly tiny jaws. He shortened his grip on the handle and struggled to keep the tip between him and his attacker. On his left, he saw Curly lunging for Fels, who was completely occupied with Shemp. He used the only weapon available. Kicking sideways as far as he could reach, he caught Curly just as the monster-ferret sprang for Fels's exposed skin. The animal's head bumped hard against his ankle, and as he turned his attention back to Moe, he felt a weight dragging against his leg. One of Curly's teeth had caught in the sock, and the ferret thrashed desperately as Carl dragged it along through the sawdust.

Now he had a real problem. As soon as Curly had slack, the ferret would surely bite him. But he only had one stick between Moe and Curly. He swung his leg around to the front, ferret in tow, towards Moe so that he might deal with both enemies together. He took a chance and swung the stick at Curly, catching the animal in its midsection. The broom handle had no weight, though, and the blow was barely more than a tap, which merely infuriated Curly into even more frantic flailing. Moe seized this chance and sprang in for his other ankle, and would have certainly killed him if the world didn't at that moment explode.

It was a gunshot from inside the cabin, and the blast seemed like a physical concussion to Carl. The ferrets were startled as well. Moe froze, inches from his leg, and Curly jerked forward, finally breaking free. Carl jumped back, this time taking a swing at Moe and missing, but the Hood apparently had had enough for now, and scampered away, Shemp in the lead as usual.

Fels knelt on the ground, head buried in the crook of her arm.

"Honey!" he shouted, "Are you okay?"

He dreaded to look closely, afraid that he might find a small red knick on her leg portending death within minutes.

She lifted her head and nodded. "I hate the little bastards," she said almost in resignation. She was clearly exhausted.

"What in Christ's name have you done to my ferrets!" Rik screamed from the doorway. He marched out, holding the pistol like it was a rock that he was going to beat them with.

"Your monsters are fine," Carl replied. "Aren't you going to ask how we are?"

"I don't give two turds about you."

Carl knew he was sincere. He noticed blood on Rik's sleeve. "What happened to you?" he asked, pointing.

Rik glanced down and said dismissively, "That's the boy's blood."

Time stopped, and then rushed forward as though catching up. Carl took off for the cabin at a sprint. Inside, he was relieved to find Toby at the kitchen sink, washing his hand. The water bloomed bright red as it swirled down the drain.

"What happened!" Carl cried.

"I tried to stop him," Toby replied, inspecting his wounded left hand. The ring finger seemed to hang at an odd angle. "He was going to shoot you."

It looked like the bullet had broken the bone below the first joint. Toby was lucky it hadn't taken the whole finger off. Fels arrived and took over the cleaning and bandaging. Carl was amazed. Other than a flinch or two, the boy didn't register what must have been excruciating pain, but just watched in fascination.

Rik stood in the doorway looking outward, watching for some sign of his prototypes.

Carl walked over to him. "We have to get him to a hospital," he said quietly so Toby wouldn't hear. "Your Hummer is the only hope."

The engineer didn't even look at him. "No."

"He'll lose the finger," Carl whispered.

"It won't matter."

Carl stared at the rigid profile, so confident, so cold. "What in God's name are you?"

Rik finally looked at him. His eyes betrayed no hint of insanity. "Mankind's salvation."

Carl just stood, looking at the enigmatic genius. He understood the words, but they didn't have any meaning in the context of the violent events at hand. It was as if their captor had just declared that he was actually a mouse.

Outside, he could see Tekumewa lying like a corpse in the hot, diffused, unbearably intense sunshine. The coyote might already be dead. He went to the bedroom and pulled out a white sheet from the closet, then filled a jug of water and carried them both out the front door. Rik stopped him. "What are you doing?"

"Your ferret bait is only good as long as it's alive."

After a moment Rik nodded and let him pass.

Outside, it was almost impossible to breathe. His throat was raw from coughing. He tried to get the animal to drink some water, but settled for dousing him instead. He then spread the white sheet to reflect the heat.

When he came back to the cabin Rik objected, "You've hidden it from view."

"Your monsters aren't smart enough to know where they left him?"

Rick let it go.

He checked to see how Fels was doing with Toby, noting ruefully to himself that the boy would never play blues guitar, and then went to Defoe. His old friend opened his eyes. "I heard a gunshot."

"Our chaperone became boisterous. Toby got a nick on his finger, but he's fine."

No use worrying him.

The old philosopher closed his eyes, but opened them again and looked at Carl. "Lilith," he whispered.

Carl knelt down next to his friend. "We know—you already told us."

Defoe seemed to concentrate. "Night demon, in the Talmud," he said as though recalling something he hadn't thought about for decades. He looked up at Carl. "Storm demon for the Sumerians."

"Okay," Carl said, nodding affirmatively. "Thanks. Now rest, you old goat."

Defoe closed his eyes and Carl stood up. Through the window, the sunlight was muted by the smoke, and glowered with an orange hue. White flecks of ash blew by in the strengthening wind. It reminded him of the snowstorm he'd seen as a teenager skiing at Big Bear Lake with his friends. What was the last thing Defoe said? Lilith was a Sumerian storm demon.

He looked down at his feet. His sock was stretched and sagging from Curley's wild ride, and the ferret's saliva and vomit had stained the white cloth and leather shoe like a splash of mauve paint. He felt sweat on his brow. The pungent reek murmured evil power. Defoe lay incapacitated from merely taking a lick. Contact with just a scratch could kill him.

He carefully removed the shoe and sock, and tied them tightly in a plastic garbage bag, then scrubbed his hands thoroughly. Twice.

ж ж ж

The smoke and ash thickened as the afternoon sank into an early and sullen dusk, which lingered, Sartre-like, with no inclination to pass on into night. Defoe finally sat up and asked for a glass of juice. The old man seemed dazed, but managed a brief smile when Carl asked if he'd like some soy and bio-engineered barf-blended latte on the side.

If the ferrets were nearby, they remained undetected, despite Rik's continuous vigilance. Like the decaying light of the day, Rik's mood thickened and became heavy with brooding threat. His gaze occasionally swung inside with vindictive accusation, clearly resentful of their intervention.

Defoe continued to improve, and the three of them—he, Fels and Toby—played cards, an attempt, Carl knew, to distract the boy from his wound and their dire predicament. Carl, though, was far too restless to play a game. He paced and peered out one of the windows every few minutes, trying to gauge whether the smoke and ash were letting up. The wind had increased until it whistled and whooshed as though angry that it couldn't get in. Ash flakes, along with twigs and torn leaves, rushed sideways past the window. The batteries in their portable radio had died long ago, but he argued with Rik until he let him try the radio in Fels's truck. Surrounded by peaks, their retreat had always suffered with poor reception, and he beat back and forth across the dial among the prickly brush of static and ephemeral pop songs for forty minutes before snaring significant news.

Rik still stood vigilant watch, and listened dispassionately when Carl related quietly that the Cottonwood Fire had split into two separate fronts, which were now called the Cuyamaca and Laguna Fires. "The county authorities have declared mandatory evacuation for everybody north of Route 8 all the way to Julian," he concluded.

Their captor turned back to the window without comment.

"We have to get out!" Carl whispered urgently.

Rik ignored him.

"You're going to get us all killed."

"It's your own fault," Rik finally said, still without looking at him. "You chose to scare away the ferrets."

"What good is it if you manage to give the new bacteria to them, but we all burn up in the process?"

Rik finally looked at him and said, "If I don't introduce the new strain, it won't matter anyway."

"What's that supposed to mean?"

But Rik had already turned back to his vigil, and Carl knew that the door to the man's attention had once again been shut.

Ten minutes later Carl was pulled from his pacing when he heard Rik mutter, "Shit!" He followed his abductor's gaze out the window to where the white sheet he had spread flicked and jerked with motion from below.

Without even glancing at Rik, Carl rushed out and pulled the sheet out from under the stones he'd placed to hold it down against the gale. Underneath, Tekumewa lay awake and struggling to get to his feet. Carl knelt and laid a hand on the coyote's neck, saying, "There, boy. It's alright."

At the touch, the animal seemed to relax, content that somebody was nearby.

He carried Tekumewa inside and laid him gently on the floor, while Fels poured a bowl of water. They lifted him so that he could drink, and drink he did. Fels had to refill the bowl. Once quenched, the coyote relaxed again and seemed to sleep.

"It's just an animal," Rik observed.

Now that his bait was gone, he turned his attention inside the cabin, not to Carl's great joy.

"So are your ferrets," Carl countered.

Rik grinned for the first time in hours. "Not quite."

"You're right. They're not just animals, they're genetic perversions."

The genius's smirk didn't waver.

Carl smelled vomit, and it set alarm bells ringing. They hadn't washed Tekumewa, and the puke had dried, matting the animal's fur. They laid towels and garbage bags under him, and then washed him with soapy water that Fels heated on the stove, and finally covered him with the blanket. The coyote was awake and watched them, but seemed content to be cared for, and promptly fell asleep again once they were done.

The smell of vomit persisted on Carl's shirt, and he took it off and tossed it outside into the darkening storm of smoke and ash, then washed thoroughly at the kitchen sink before putting on new clothes. As he scrubbed his arms, he recalled his remark about genetic perversions. Rik had clearly performed some kind of genetic manipulation on Lilly and her offspring, but he wondered to what extent. Lilly had always been wily, extraordinarily intelligent even for Rik's ninety-seven percentile. He decided to ask Rik, even though he didn't expect to get anything.

Their captor didn't give him the chance.

"Come here," Rik ordered, standing over the trunk they had dragged in front of the kitchen door. "Help me move this."

"Why?" Carl asked, drying his arms.

Rik nodded for him to push the other end while he pulled. "Because I said so."

Carl looked at him, and then glanced at the other three who were watching them. He stepped closer, saying quietly, "You want the demons to come in, don't you?"

Rik just raised one eyebrow. It was a self-evident question.

"You're crazy!" he whispered moving closer so that he was inches from his enemy's face.

"Regardless," Rik replied, "you're going to help me move this."

He felt something poke his stomach, and looked down to see the barrel of Rik's gun.

"So much for rational discussion," Carl muttered, and together they slid the trunk away. He looked down at the little swinging door he'd made and he imagined that he knew what the Titanic's captain had felt as he looked at the hole ripped by the iceberg.

Carl stepped outside to relieve himself, and found that the darkness had finally deepened into night. It was a disorienting darkness, as the smoke obscured the stars. He became acutely aware of his bare ankles, and fought an urgent inner call to run back inside. His bladder was near bursting, though, and he decided that he would just pee on them if they came near. Normally he used the portable latrine or walked a hundred feet to the north-side bank, but now he peed against the cabin's foundation, telling himself he'd hose off the spot in the morning.

When he was done, he stepped to the corner of the cabin so that he could look to the east. The indistinct horizon seemed to glow with a faint orange frill, but it might have been just his imagination. The wind, although still blasting in strength so that his eyes itched and burned with blown ash, had moved into the southeast. He wasn't sure if this was good news or not. If Rik hadn't destroyed the computer, he could have pulled up the burn maps on the county website to find the location of fire-lines.

Something bumped his ankle, and he yelped, jumping and kicking blindly at the darkness. He realized it must have been just a twig blown by the wind, but he hurried inside, closing the door quickly behind him.

Rik had pulled a chair up next to the back door, from where he could watch the ferret portal, his little glass vial ready on his knee.

Fels, Defoe and Toby had set aside their cards when the light faded, and were talking quietly in the dark with just the dim camp lantern on the table to illuminate their faces in a ghostly séance circle.

Carl realized that he was hungry and figured everybody else must be as well, so he went to the kitchen and flipped on the light above the stove.

"Turn it off," Rik commanded from his watch post next to the back door.

"In a minute," he replied.

Minor acts of defiance helped him get used to the constant threat of the gun.

On the other hand, a gun was a gun, and he hurried, making short order of dinner preparations. He sliced four apples and a whole slab of cheese onto a plate, and poured crackers and almonds into a bowl, all of which he carried to the table. He then walked back and turned off the kitchen light before joining the séance, leaving Rik sitting alone in darkness.

After a few minutes he heard Rik's chair scrape on the floor, and then the light from the refrigerator flooded the kitchen as their captor scrounged for his own dinner.

When they were done eating, Defoe announced that he was pooped from his near-death encounter and figured that he had better be heading home. Carl knew the old fart was just pulling their captor's chain, but Rik didn't catch this and barked that nobody was going anywhere. In fact, he didn't even trust them to use the bedroom, and they dragged the mattress and all the blankets out to the Great Hall. Carl was both disappointed and relieved by this, as he had indeed intended to climb out the window and head off for help, and the thought of making his way through Hood territory in the dark terrified him.

They gave Toby the sofa, but Defoe insisted that Carl and Fels sleep on the mattress, so they spread cushions from the kitchen chairs on the floor for him, and all settled in for the night. Tekumewa lay quietly, stirring now and then, but remaining on his carpet, apparently content to sleep off his near-death brush with ferret poison. In the faint light cast by the digital clock above the sink, Carl could see the vague shape of Rik manning his post, attentive as a mother penguin who has just heard the first tap from inside her only egg.

Fels, exhausted to the point of catatonia, was asleep within minutes, and Toby began snoring softly soon afterwards. An hour later, though, Carl was no closer to sleep, and he gently pulled himself off the mattress and stretched. Rik sat in exactly the same spot, as though he too had fallen asleep, but the watchman stirred and changed position, still vigilant.

Carl knew that he wouldn't sleep now that the little portal to hell was unlocked, and demons, dripping death from their jaws, could rush through at any second. He quietly picked up a chair and sat down in the kitchen, facing Rik across the ferret door. At least from here he could sound a warning when the horde broke through. He expected to be told to leave, but Rik said nothing, as though beyond knowing or caring about other people.

After a minute, Carl got up and softly gathered, by feel, kitchen paraphernalia—a spatula, barbeque fork, and serving spoon—which he piled on the counter next to his chair. This was his weapons cache. After a minute he got up again and found a pan lid. This would serve as his shield.

Killing wasn't something that came naturally or easily for him. Other than mosquitoes and the big ugly spiders that built massive webs at face level, he avoided killing animals. This didn't spring from a religious or even a philosophical position, but from a built-in bias that it was simply wrong. He wouldn't kill a bird or a mouse any more than he would needlessly cause pain to a fellow human. He'd often wondered if he would have survived before civilization isolated people from the slaughter part of meat eating.

He was ready to kill now, though. The Hood had crossed a line when they'd gone after Fels. He probably could have killed one of them if needed while defending Tekumewa, but he wouldn't wait to act in defense now that they'd threatened Fels. This was a duel to the death.

During their quiet dinner in the dark, Defoe had suggested that, regardless of their "activation" and subsequent mission to wreak revenge, the ferrets might try to enter the cabin anyway seeking refuge from the fire. They might view the cabin as a cave, he'd explained, and their instincts would tell them that caves are fireproof.

Well, too bad. They should have thought of that before attacking his wife. He picked up the serving spoon and waved it a bit, gauging the balance, then put it down and picked up the barbecue fork.

In any case, Defoe had added after a moment of contemplation that, even if they entered the cabin solely for refuge, the invaders would probably want to clean it of human vermin first.

Rik hadn't tried to stop his weapons gathering. Perhaps he couldn't see what he'd been doing in the dark. Or, more ominously, maybe their captor

A glow seemed to fill the cabin. At first Carl thought that his eyes had adjusted so that the clock display just seemed brighter, but the LEDs were green, whereas the diffused glow was orange.

His heart tripped on itself.

Fire!

Chapter 20

Carl jumped up, startling Rik and causing the watchman to reflexively raise his gun.

"Take it easy!" Carl whispered, looking out the east-facing window. He was relieved to see just the indistinct outline of the trees at the edge of their clearing. To the north, though, the sky did seem to pulse with reddish blood, most of it hidden by the cabin on his left. The best view would be from the bedroom, but rather than tussling with Rik and possibly waking the others, he went to the front door, where the cabin slanted in that direction. His breath caught in his throat. On the far hill, not more than a half mile away, the forest was burning in a blazing orgy of all-consuming combustion. Tongues of flame danced in a snaking line in slow motion, a testament at this distance to their enormity. The nuclear-core light from the fire illuminated an even vaster plume of roiling smoke that rushed off into the black night above.

"Christ!" he whispered, opening the door a crack.

Above the howling wind he could hear the distant crackle and roar. It sounded like how he imagined an erupting volcano would—except that this volcano didn't stop erupting.

"He's come back?" Defoe whispered from behind him.

Carl jerked around in surprise. "I'm glad to see you've recovered enough to become a plague on humanity again."

He stepped back so that his friend could see.

"Judas Priest! Armageddon is upon us!"

"Shh! You'll wake the others."

"Isn't that the point? Shouldn't we be fleeing for our lives?"

Carl opened the door a bit more and peered over his friend's shoulder. "We got lucky. It missed us. The wind has swung to the southeast. It's blowing it off to the north."

Defoe peered around the door into the darkness. "So it has. Providence has decided to spare me another day to mull its misguided motives." He looked around in the opposite direction to the south where the sky was black with no trace of sullen glow. "It appears as though my humble abode has survived the maelstrom as well."

The old professor took a tentative sniff, then a deep breath and smiled.

Carl sniffed as well. "No smoke!"

It worked both ways: if you don't smell smoke, then you're not in the fire's path.

Rik called to them to shut the door, and Carl silently cursed the kidnapper for talking so loudly. Both he and Defoe lay back down, but after a half-hour of tossing and turning, imagining he was hearing the ferret door popping open, he got back up and positioned spare cushions, piles of books, and boxes in a semi-circle around his sleeping wife and friends. When he was done, he contemplated his handiwork in the red glow washing through the windows from the receding fire. "A towel to hold off a tidal wave," he muttered to himself. The ferrets would scamper over his wall like ants over dental floss.

He didn't bother to lie back down, knowing that sleep waited far beyond the invisible lurking Hood. Instead, he wearily resumed his post across from Rik.

"The fire's moving off to the north of us," he whispered, partly to probe his captor's mood, but also hungry for human contact, even one evil and possibly insane.

Rik said nothing. Carl would have thought he had fallen asleep, but he knew the genetics engineer would stop breathing before falling asleep when his precious creations might slip in at any second.

"Why are you doing this?" he asked on impulse. "Why have you made poisonous ferrets?"

Rik finally spoke. "Shut up," he said.

Carl waited. The wind whistled and moaned outside the kitchen window, and every time a blown twig tapped against the door, he jumped and clutched his spatula sword. He felt dizzy with fatigue and closed his eyes, thinking he might sleep right there in the chair.

Dreams seemed to hover, ready to fill his mind with blissful repose, but the fear of the Hood held them at bay.

"Don't move," Rik whispered so softly that his words were almost lost among the rush of the wind outside.

Carl opened his eyes, and saw that Rik had risen, and stood before him expectantly with the open vial held delicately between thumb and forefinger. A faint sound, like eyelashes blinking, urged him to turn his head. There, not six inches away, hovered two beady eyes on the counter. He recognized the fine, almost sensuous, lines of Shemp's face.

"Hold still," Rik quietly urged. "It won't hurt you as long as I am here."

Terror screamed for him to fly away, but simultaneously held him frozen in place.

"Creator has come to fulfill your destiny," Rik coaxed softly.

Carl realized her creator was now talking to Shemp who opened her jaws to show needle teeth glistening with venomous intent.

Suddenly a low and ominous gurgling sound arose from behind Rik. The genetics genius turned and faced Moe who had climbed up on his vacated chair.

"Ah!" Rik exclaimed joyfully, "they're gathering for the indoctrination."

In response, Moe opened his jaws wide, revealing a tiny pink tongue, and hissed in challenge.

"No!" the Creator objected, confused. "It's me!"

Both Shemp and Moe, as if working from the same cue, pulled back in preparation to spring.

At that moment, though, a growl, deep and throaty, erupted from the darkness of the kitchen and exploded into a howling cry as something heavy and violent slammed into Carl's shoulder. Crying out, he tried to jump away, but tripped and fell heavily to the kitchen floor. The struggle moved towards the sink, and he perceived that the interloper was Tekumewa. The coyote had drawn Shemp away.

He scrambled to his feet, but was instantly blinded by a flash from the center of the Great Hall. Red afterimage mixed with a frantic sweeping beam that flashed about like the strobing interior of a discotheque. He realized that it was from a flashlight. Defoe's concerned calls bellowed out from behind the beam.

Through the mayhem, one sound caught his attention like targeting radar: somewhere in the dark spaces of the Great Hall among the probing beams of light, Fels cried out in desperation.

Carl still clutched the spatula, and he reached out and grabbed a second weapon from his kitchen stash as he rushed to her aid. Whatever it was that he had snatched was soft, but he didn't stop to investigate.

"Fels!" he shouted.

"Here!" he heard her cry. The fear in her voice galvanized him to an equal level of desperation.

He wished he had turned on a light, but it was too late now. Maybe Defoe was heading for the switch. The flashlight flicked and arced somewhere near the kitchen door, and in the fleeting splashes of illumination he saw that Fels was huddled up against the sofa holding Curly off with her pillow. The ferret clawed and bit at the fabric, which was shredding under the onslaught so that feathers danced in a cloud about them.

Using the spatula, he tried to knock Curly aside, but the lithe, supple body seemed to just glide around the kitchen tool as though he was trying to swat away water.

In the reflected light of the dancing beam, he saw what he had picked up in his other hand. It was an oven mitt, apparently knocked off its hook by Tekumewa's assault. As though rehearsed through many dry runs, he instantly pulled it on and used his padded hand to bat the Hood member away. This was more effective than the spatula; so much so that Curly was forced turn his attention, and the ferret wrapped itself around the mitt and sunk its teeth into the material.

In a panic now, Carl raised his arm high, but the ferret hung tight, chewing at the cotton-filled matting, searching for flesh. He still held the spatula in the other hand and used it to swat the tenacious beast, but his left hand was clumsy and the weapon too light, so that Curly hardly felt the ineffectual blows.

Suddenly Carl felt a painful prick on his wrist, and imagining poison-tipped teeth piercing him, cried out in despair and swung his arm in a wide arc onto the floor.

This was finally effective, and the stunned ferret thrashed about trying to gain footing on the smooth wood floor before scrambling away into the darkness.

At the kitchen door, caught in the harsh white light of Defoe's beam, Rik was on his knees holding off Moe, who gnashed and gnawed at the handle of a ladle the Creator held like a Kung Fu pole. Defoe hesitated a bare moment, then kicked with his foot, knocking the ferret aside. The old philosopher then danced frantically backwards in order to prevent the demon beast from twisting around to attack his bare ankles.

The sound of scuttling and scraping echoed through the dark expanse of the Great Hall, and then there was only silence. Defoe swung the flashlight beam back and forth, along the wall and under the table, but the Hood had apparently retreated for now.

Carl squatted next to Fels to see how she was doing, and she pulled him in, hugging him and breathing heavily into his neck as though she'd just finished a race. Defoe found the light switch in the kitchen and the resulting illumination manifested familiar walls and a sense of safe containment. Toby sat on the floor blinking dazedly, still waking up from a deep sleep. The whole battle had lasted no more than two minutes.

Carl gently pulled away from Fels to examine at his wrist. A red line an inch long was beading with tiny droplets of blood where Curly had caught him. But, had it been the monster's tooth, or one of its nails? He saw that the oven mitt was covered with puke, and he tore it off and threw it in the sink. He sniffed his wrist. There was a faint smell of acrid vomit, but he couldn't tell how much. He washed his hands and wrist under the faucet and closed his eyes, checking his mental pulse, probing how he felt. He felt like collapsing, but that could have been fatigue and exhausted adrenaline. Based on the reactions of the previous victims—Larry, Defoe, and Tekumewa—he guessed that he would know one way or the other in the next few minutes.

Tekumewa! Did he survive the fray? He spun around, but the coyote was gone. "Where did—" and then he saw that their new friend was with Fels. She was rubbing his head in both her hands as though he was a dog, and he seemed to enjoy it like one as well.

Carl didn't bother to see if Shemp had bitten Tekumewa—like he himself, the coyote was going to be either dead or alive soon.

He did check Fels over closely, though, and had a moment of renewed panic when he smelled vomit, but saw that it was just what he had smeared on her back when hugging her. He helped her off with the shirt and threw it in the sink along with the mitt, then soaked a washrag and cleaned her back. Toby still seemed half asleep, and sat staring and blinking slowly. Carl realized that Fels was wearing only a bra, so he handed her a blanket. No use tormenting the boy.

Defoe sat melted into a chair looking spent, and Rik had returned to his post next to the back door. Their captor's brow was furrowed in thought—Dr. Frankenstein, puzzling why his creation had turned on him.

Carl washed out the rag and searched for stray droppings of poisonous puke to clean up, and soon Defoe got up to help him.

"They didn't come through the ferret-door, did they?" Defoe whispered so that Fels and Toby wouldn't hear.

Carl shook his head in agreement.

"Do we know how they get in?"

He shook his head again and shrugged. He had plugged up the chimney months ago, but both Lilly and the Hood continued to come and go as though they could walk right through the walls.

Carl urged Fels and Toby to try to get some sleep. Defoe had lain back down, and his breathing was already slow and rhythmic.

"Don't worry," Carl assured them. "I'll keep watch."

He waited until they were both settled back into their blankets before finally returning to Rik and the back door.

"Can we block the portal to hell now?" he asked quietly.

The genetics engineer looked up as though just aware that somebody had arrived, and then shook his head irritably.

"After what just happened, I'd think—"

Rik didn't say anything, he didn't even look up at Carl. He just waved the gun in answer.

With a sigh, Carl picked up his chair where it had toppled and sat on it. He left the kitchen light on. He wasn't sure he could keep his sanity sitting in the darkness now. Rik didn't protest; he didn't even seem to notice.

The minutes ticked by, and Carl jumped, heart racing, with every tap and bump from the wind. After perhaps an hour, though, his heart slowed and the adrenaline dissolved, leaving him feeling as spent as he'd ever remembered. It occurred to him that sitting next to the ferret door was probably the least strategic position; if the Hood returned, they surely wouldn't come ambling in through it. Better to be next those he was protecting, since he didn't know from which direction the ferrets would arrive. He sat on the floor next to Fels, and after a while found this uncomfortable, and so lay down on his back to stare at the rough beams of the Great Hall ceiling. He closed his eyes, and it felt like exactly the right thing to do. He'd promised that he'd keep watch, so he mustn't fall asleep. He told himself he'd open them in just a minute.

ж ж ж

Carl's eyes snapped wide to the welcoming blush of pre-dawn light. Defoe was talking angrily, arguing.

Damn it! He'd fallen asleep after all.

He scrambled to his feet to find his friend gesturing wildly while Rik worked at something at the kitchen table, seemingly oblivious to his harasser. Fels sat cross-legged on the mattress, rubbing her eyes, obviously also just awakened. Toby sprawled with his blanket wrapped around his head, hiding from the world for a last bit of sleep, while Tekumewa lay near them with his chin on his paws, watching all the activity.

"What's going on?" Carl asked, getting up.

Defoe looked at him, exasperated. He glanced at Fels, and then gestured for Carl to come closer.

"Gene-man wants to use Tekumewa *and* Fels for ferret bait," he whispered.

Chapter 21

Carl looked down at Rik, who was sitting uncoiling a bundle of clothesline as he cut it into smaller pieces. Next to him on the table was a packet of tie-wraps. Despite a night without sleep, their captor was smiling and seemed happy at his task.

"You're insane!" Carl exclaimed loudly.

Rik glanced up. "Possibly. Sanity is relative, though."

Carl was suddenly overwhelmed with the man's utter lack of compassion, his total absence of basic morality. He reached down and grabbed the bundle of rope, and the next instant he was staring into the barrel of the pistol, which had been lying on Rik's lap.

He dropped the rope, but Rik continued to hold the gun in his face. He seemed to be contemplating whether to shoot, as though deciding if it was worth the mess it would make.

Rik finally grinned and lowered the gun. "Why not make a party of it? There should be enough rope," he said, proceeding with his preparations.

"That's for me, isn't it?" Fels asked, suddenly beside them, pointing at the severed pieces of rope. "I was the last one to provoke them, so now I'm the most likely to attract them back."

"No!" Carl cried.

Defoe looked at him skeptically. What use was it trying to lie to her?

"No," he repeated simply.

A sudden gust shook the cabin, and he noticed that the dawn light that was building outside smoldered a deep, dirty red, as though he had slept through the entire day and awoke just in time to catch a blazing crimson sunset. More disturbing was the smoke and ash, which streamed past thicker than ever. Where the hell was *that* coming from? Last night the air had been clear as the fire passed north of them.

He turned his attention back to the more immediate threat. "After last night," he said, to Rik, "I figured you'd give up on your monsters."

Their jailer glanced up. "Why? Because they attacked me as well?"

"For starters."

"Quite the opposite. It demonstrates their superb degree of aggression. It's better than I'd expected."

"Better than you . . . they tried to *kill* you! They would have if Defoe hadn't saved your butt. They're out of control! They've never *been* under your control!"

Rik put down the pocketknife and looked at him. "You really don't get it, do you?"

"You mean, beyond the fact that you're a raving lunatic? I guess not."

His captor went back to his task and talked as he worked. "That is exactly the point: the ferrets are completely beyond our control—at least, once I introduce this next strain."

"But, why, for God's sake?"

Rik glanced up and smiled. "Why would the ferrets steal pasta from you?"

"To piss me off?"

Rik nodded as he cut open the pack of tie-wraps. "That's part of it. It was Helmut's first assignment, to introduce a gene that produces an enzyme to break down complex carbohydrates into simpler forms that the ferrets could absorb."

"Helmut?" Carl asked.

"That's Weinermach," Fels explained.

"Of course," Rik continued, "digestion is of no use without the inclination to eat the food source in the first place . . . and to steal it. The gene manipulations required for this required subtle brain manipulations, and was a thousand-fold more complex than merely producing one new digestion enzyme." He glanced up, as if to make sure they were paying attention to his lecture. "So, naturally, that was done by me."

"Naturally," Carl agreed.

Fels poked him with her elbow.

Rik ignored the dig. "I don't mean to belittle Helmut's contributions. He developed the toxin-producing bacteria that could survive indefinitely in the ferret's stomach and be passed down through succeeding generations by mother-to-kit mouth contact. Helmut saved me months of time with his work."

"Why don't the bacteria kill the ferrets?" Carl asked. He'd wondered about this all along.

Rik smiled, as though relishing the thoughts this evoked. "Like the competing organic structures inherent in all fabrics of the evolved natural environment, the toxin production involves a delicate balance. On one hand, the ferret's stomach acid is continually breaking down the toxin produced by the bacteria. On the other, the copious oxygen of the air is required to fully develop the toxin's potency."

"I get it," Carl said. "The poison isn't turned on until the little bastards puke it up, and whatever they accidentally swallow is then destroyed . . . but, Defoe was nearly killed by eating it."

Rik shrugged. "Some of the toxin was probably absorbed through his lips and mouth. Also," he added almost as an afterthought, "the ferrets develop immunity."

"Why the second strain now?"

"A final tweak. Their acquired immunity to this new toxin is tailored specifically to their system."

Carl had the sense that there was more to this second strain than Rik was letting on. He was, after all, resorting to awfully extreme measures to deliver it.

"It is Helmut's final contribution, and we salute him," Rik went on. "Unfortunately, the sensitive German didn't have the stomach for the larger picture. The project had reached the point where it was no longer possible to keep him compartmentalized, and he was beginning to understand the grand plan."

Rik was effectively confessing, and Carl found this disturbing. "The larger picture being, of course, mankind's very salvation."

Carl was making fun of Rik's earlier reference, but his response was simply, "Of course."

Their captor collected the pieces of rope together and stood up.

"Wait a second," Carl pressed, realizing that Rik wasn't going to amplify. "How the hell are poisonous ferrets going to save mankind . . . and what are we being saved *from?*"

Rik lay the rope back down and checked the gun's safety before looking at him. "From ourselves. From the artificial environment that we've created with our technologies, which incubates and promulgates every inherited weakness until our species has degenerated into a spreading mass of maladjusted deficiencies."

Carl recalled a similar conversation months ago with Defoe. "That's a lot of depressing adjectives."

"Appropriate for a deeply depressing state of human evolution."

"I still don't get it," Carl confessed.

"Weeding," Defoe offered from where he stood watching them.

Rik tilted his head towards the philosopher in acknowledgment.

Carl turned to his friend.

"The ferrets are supposed to kill off the weak among us," Defoe explained.

Like an encouraging teacher, Rik nodded for him to go on.

"Gene-man thinks that because we no longer have any natural predators, the evolution of the human species has been stalled."

Rik's eyes flashed. "It goes far beyond that! We not only protect our weak from dangers, we go out of our way to practically ensure the propagation of inferior genes. Congenitally blind people are coddled and nurtured. Diabetes, cystic fibrosis, muscular dystrophy, and near-sightedness are passed from generation to generation, spreading throughout the gene pool. The mentally retarded are guaranteed the right to pro-create—by *law*, for God's sake!"

Mankind's self-proclaimed savior paused and straightened his shirt, as though regretting that he'd lost his composure. He told Fels to bring him a bowl, a glass of water, and a small brush.

"It's ludicrous," Carl declared.

Rik had lost his light, breezy air after his outburst, and scowled without looking up.

"It's comical, in fact," Carl goaded.

"I didn't see you laughing last night."

"I'd be scared shitless if I suddenly found a rattlesnake next to me too, but nobody thinks that they're a peril to mankind."

Rik now looked up at him curiously, as though realizing that the man standing next to him was wearing his hat on upside-down. "You really are an idiot, aren't you? You think that all I've done is developed a venomous mammal."

"That's all I see."

" 'There are none so blind as those who will not see.' I introduced an enzyme so that the ferrets can digest carbohydrates, but why would they instinctively steal and hoard a type of food for which they have no evolved use? Once provoked, why would they doggedly pursue the provoker until they'd killed him? How would they know that they are poisonous, and that once they had delivered a single bite, they could retreat before being themselves harmed? Why, finally, are they so intelligent? Or haven't you noticed even this?"

Carl's mind swirled so that he had trouble standing, and he slumped into a chair at the table. The extent of the genetic manipulations secretly developed at GeneTrend suddenly coalesced into a single, clear picture.

He had thought that Kaj's warnings were mere drug-induced hallucinations, but now . . . "Kaj said that you were trying to combine ferrets and men, that their genes were going to collide together." *What else had his friend said?* "This was going to create a new master race that would rule the whole galaxy."

Rik stared at him a moment, and then laughed. "The nitwit must have looked at my notebook." He thought a moment, then his grin broadened, and he reached into his jacket pocket, pulled out a small leather-bound logbook, and flipped through the pages. When he found what he was looking for, he handed it over.

Written in compact, neat script, Carl read:

> *Ferret and human genetic destinies will collide, and no compromises will be made—one species, strengthened and purified, will emerge, the confirmed master race, whose galaxy-wide rule will be a testament to the contribution conferred by the little mammal's genetic manipulation.*

Carl handed the book back.

"I can sometimes wax poetically prophetic," Rik explained unapologetically.

Carl shivered, chilled as much by this man's utter lack of human compassion as by the specter of spreading hordes of poison-dripping ferrets. He understood now why Rik was happy that the Hood was so aggressive that they had attacked even him, their creator, the previous night. He also understood now why Rik was building a veritable fortress near Julian. The moat, filled with a noxious substance rather than water, could keep at bay the poisonous ferrets that would spread inexorably and with geometrically increasing speed across the countryside. Eventually they would stow away on cargo ships and infest other continents.

"You used us," Carl declared, feeling finally defeated. "We were your incubation farm."

Pieces fell into place, one after the other. Rik had come up to the cabin immediately after learning about Fels's fleeting obsession that Lilly was an angel. Carl now saw that Rik had probably been worried that Fels would blow the whole thing if she got out of control with her delusions and attracted attention. He had to tread carefully, convincing Fels that Lilly's unique qualities were due to her exceptional intelligence, but stopping short of hinting at the possibility of genetic manipulation.

And now the incubation was complete.

"Shemp is barely three months old, and already pregnant," Carl noted.

"Nice touch, that one, if I do say so," Rik replied. "Accelerated fertility. If you want to populate the Earth, a reduced generation span is useful."

"What about Lilly?"

They hadn't seen the mother ferret for many days. Although exceptionally intelligent, she had never displayed the extreme aggressive behavior of her Hood brood.

"The genetic manipulations were done through the father. Lilake is a normal ferret—she was selected for her intelligence. Her stomach chemistry isn't able to support the toxin bacteria."

That explained why the father had been destroyed—eliminate the evidence.

"We haven't seen her in a while."

Rik shrugged. "Her offspring may have eliminated her."

Carl closed his eyes in resignation. Was there no end to the horror wrought by this madman? A thought came to him that made him almost gasp. "Why are you telling us all this?" he asked.

"Because you asked."

Rik's smile portended a finality that Carl found difficult to contemplate.

"Enough mental masturbation," Rik announced brusquely, getting back to business. "Let's wrap this up."

As directed, Fels brought a bowl, a glass of water, and her mascara brush to the table. Rik poured out all but perhaps a half-cup of the water, and added the contents of his vial. He then told Carl to use the brush to spread the resulting liquid across the others' ankles, hands, and wrists.

It took a moment for him to understand what this was all about, but when he realized, he nearly choked on the idea. "You want us to deliver the new strain!"

Rik just waved the gun at him to get on with the task.

Although neither said anything, it was obvious that Fels and Toby were horrified at what was developing. Defoe, although clearly not happy, joked that this could be marketed as a new killer cologne.

When he was done painting the others with the bacteria solution, Carl brushed it on his own skin as directed, using one hand and then the other, while pleading with Rik that what he was about to do to them wasn't necessary, that they would promise not to talk, that he'd never get away with it, and did he really want to become a murderer?

After the last, he shut up, remembering that their kidnapper had effectively confessed to two murders already. There was no way he was going to let them live.

Rik had Carl secure the other three's hands behind their backs using the small tie wraps, attaching four together, tip-to-tail, to get enough length for each. Finally Rik instructed him to tie a length of the rope he'd already cut up around each of their necks, including Carl's own.

Once Carl had accomplished everything he could as a free man, Rik made him turn around, and he could feel Rik binding his wrists. Holding the gun in his mouth, their captor tied the ends of their neck ropes into one big knot, bundling them all together like so many sheep being herded to market. As their tormentor pushed them towards the door, the ropes yanked against their necks so that they stumbled and choked. Toby tripped and nearly strangled before they were able to squat down all together and position themselves to give him slack. Rik had to help them back up, as they were nearly helpless with their hands bound behind them.

Carl pleaded that he lengthen the ropes, but Rik just grunted and told them that it would all be over soon anyway.

The coyote followed them to the door, seemingly confused by their odd predicament, but Rik kicked the animal back, forcing him to stay inside.

As soon as they opened the back door, Carl saw that their world was layered with a whole new dimension of threat. Smoke rushed past so thick that visibility was less than fifty feet, and more ominously, it was *hot!* As he watched, bright, glowing embers flew past like jet propelled fireflies. Grit from the ash crunched between his teeth.

Far more frightening than the smoke and embers was the fire's roar, which seemed to emanate from the very ground. Explosive thuds like cosmic popcorn peppered the near-distance as entire tree trunks burst under the pressure of sap boiled by the unimaginable heat.

A fluke twist of wind cleared the smoke for a moment, providing a fleeting glimpse of the closest hill a quarter-mile to the east. Flames, forming a wall a hundred feet high, undulated their seductively evil belly dance down the slope. The sight, although lasting a bare few seconds, was hypnotizing in its malevolence, promising absolute obliteration.

Carl's mind was paralyzed by the illogic of the titanic threat. The fire had already passed them in the night, missing them to the north. It was as though God had decided to play some gigantic sadistic joke.

But then he remembered that before Rik smashed the computer Toby had reported that the fire had split in two. During the night the wind had shifted to the southeast, carrying the original fire line north of them, but the same wind had now steered its southern brother northward as well—right on top their heads.

Rik was visibly shaken by the sight. He appeared uncertain,

pausing just outside the door, transfixed along with the rest of them. But then his head shot to the side. There, snaking among the jumbled puzzle of logs, was the stealthy form of one of the ferrets. Rik seemed to forget the fire. He shouted for them to move forward.

Progress was nearly impossible, however, as the continual gut-wrenching coughing disrupted the cooperation that was required by their leashes. Embers planted themselves in their clothes and hair so that they were in continual danger of bursting into flames, unable to use their hands to pat out the incendiary seeds.

After little more than twenty feet, Rik commanded a halt, and again seemed at a loss. He cradled the gun in both hands and looked at them, one after another. Carl shuddered to think what the man was contemplating: the best way to keep a collection of ferret bait in place was to shoot one of them . . . but which one?

As Carl shivered despite the blasting heat, almost unable to bear the tension, he saw the ferret door pop open behind Rik, and Tekumewa's head appeared in the opening. The snout wiggled back and forth and slid slowly forward as the coyote pushed with its hind legs from behind. It seemed impossible that the animal's body could squeeze through the opening, but like a butterfly emerging from its cocoon, it slithered forward. Once the front legs were free he quickly pulled through the rest of the way.

Rik didn't hear Tekumewa's struggle behind him above the fire's roar. Instead, his attention was fixed on something off to the side of the hapless group. Carl followed his gaze and saw that Moe had approached, baring dripping teeth. He reflexively looked to the other side, and there, demonic fate inescapable, was Curly. Carl knew that Shemp would be attacking up the middle.

Eminent death poised on all sides, by bullet or by poison. There seemed no escape.

When all other options failed, there was nothing to be lost in turning to powers beyond this Earth.

"Tekumewa!" Carl beseeched above the firestorm. "Save us!"

Fels glanced quickly at him, then called out, "Help us!"

Defoe and Toby joined in, and together they all begged for his aid.

Rik finally understood that something was going on behind

him, and he turned just as the coyote lifted itself up onto his hind legs and started forward on unsteady legs, front paws spread wide as though welcoming Rik into his embrace.

The genetics genius, man of science, cried out in alarm and staggered backwards at the sight of a coyote walking like a man.

Turning to the power that he trusted, Rik raised the gun and fired.

Chapter 22

The coyote's slim body and clumsy, weaving gate saved his life, for despite being barely ten feet from Rik, the bullet missed him. Tekumewa collapsed to all fours at the sound, and crouched down in defense.

Rik aimed the gun for a second shot, and this time it was the ferrets that saved the coyote's life, for Tekumewa finally saw them and lunged forward as though propelled by a powerful spring. Rik swung the gun as Tekumewa charged past him, but a stray glowing ember ended its wild ride by planting itself in his eye. He howled in pain and clapped his hands to his face, nearly knocking himself out as the gun slammed his forehead.

Moe and Curly were gone, fleeing from their mortal enemy who yipped and barked somewhere among the sea of logs, lost in the impenetrable roiling smoke.

"Come on!" Carl shouted above the screaming wind and fire's roar, which seemed almost on top of them now. He started away, but the leash pulled tight, choking him.

"Hold it!" Defoe called.

His stout old friend stood erect, straining as though being electrocuted. His face turned red and the veins along his temples bulged. Suddenly his arms swung away to each side and the broken tie-wraps flew away into the smoke, his wrists bright red where the restraints had dug deeply during his struggle.

Defoe pulled the group together to provide slack, and then attacked the mass of knots where Rik had tied their leashes together.

Carl glanced over at Rik. He was bent over, one hand on his knee still holding the gun, the other holding his eye, clearly in great pain.

"Hurry!" Fels cried.

One line came free, and Defoe shoved Toby out of the group, instructing him to run and hide.

As he waited for Defoe to undo another one, Carl tried to break his own tie-wraps. He pulled with all his strength but was hampered by the awkward position of his arms bent backwards. The pain was intense as the strips of plastic dug into his skin, but the ties held firm.

"Shit!" the old philosopher said, looking towards Rik.

The wounded savior of mankind had stood up and was squinting towards them. His face was wet with streaming tears.

"Come on," Defoe urged, leading them away into the driving smoke. He had managed to untie his own leash, and he pulled Carl and Fels along like two circus animals in tow.

The field of logs was a giant maze through which Defoe led them, stumbling and choking as their leashes yanked at them. With the smoke reducing visibility to little more than a few dozen feet, the jumble of tree trunks was a surrealistic expanse of endless geometric complexity, and Carl was soon lost on his own property.

Defoe halted the troop and they sat on the ground while he worked at freeing the rest of the neck restraints. When the rope fell away from Carl's neck, Defoe told him to lie on his stomach. Hesitating just one small part of a second, Carl lay back and rolled to the side so that his chin dug into the sawdust. A moment later, he felt something soft brush his wrists. He realized this was Defoe's lips when a wetness of saliva and the rough brush of his beard followed. His friend was chewing off the tie-wraps.

When Carl's hands finally came free, it felt as though his arms had been removed and now re-attached. He sat up clumsily, as his new arms learned to work again. They had gotten away from Rik, but as far as Carl knew, the madman might just thirty feet away about to shoot them. Fels lay prone, and Defoe was working at the tie-wrap around her wrists.

"I can do it," Carl whispered.

Defoe shook his head without looking up. "Split up. We have to get the gun off of Rik."

He knew his friend was right, but it was almost impossible to leave Fels. He bent down and kissed her temple, and she turned her head and smiled. He kissed the side of her mouth and took off at a loping sprint.

After zigzagging around a half-dozen logs, he realized that he had no idea where he was. The wind roared, blasting him with ash and embers, and he had to brace himself to stay upright. Looking down, he saw a piece of two-by-four the length of his forearm, and it was like finding his wallet lying in front of him on a city sidewalk. He knew this piece of lumber. He had used it to prop up the ends of smaller logs while he sliced them with the chainsaw. With the southeast wind orienting his direction, he could now place himself in his mind's map of their property. He picked up the beam, the only weapon available, and headed off towards the cabin, peering through the driving smoke through watering eyes for some sign of Rik and the gun.

Something lay on the ground ahead. As he got closer he saw with despair that it was Tekumewa. Next to the fallen coyote lay the lifeless body of Curly. His newfound friend had saved his life more than once, and his eyes welled with new tears to join those drawn by the smoke. The brave warrior had at least taken one of the bastard demons with him. True grief would have to wait, though. He pressed on.

Suddenly the cabin loomed in front of him. Where was Rik?

Above the scream of the wind and the crackling roar of the approaching forest fire, he heard his enemy call out. He couldn't make out the words, and he took a few steps in that direction. Rik yelled again, and this time Carl understood: he had Fels, and he would shoot her if Carl didn't give himself up. The son-of-a-bitch must have indeed been very close when Defoe had freed Carl.

Carl ran towards the hated voice, leaping and crawling over the rough bark of the fallen pine trunks. Rik called out yet again, and now he seemed close, almost next to Carl.

And then he saw him. Rik was not more than twenty feet away, standing in profile as streams of smoke and ash whirled past, arm wrapped around Fels's neck, gun to her head. Rik wiped his wounded eye with his forearm, and tears continued to stream down his cheeks. Defoe stood a few feet away, fists clenched, helpless.

Carl quickly jumped to the side, moving behind Rik so that he wouldn't see him. The tip of the gun pressed against Fels's temple.

Rik's finger strained, tense, against the trigger, ready to propel a bullet of death through her brain. Closing his eyes a moment to prepare himself and whisper a last prayer of love, Carl crept forward.

Movement caught his eye and he saw a ferret slinking towards them out of the smoke. It was just Lilly, though, so he pressed on. When he was just a few feet behind Rik, he stopped and pulled back the two-by-four as though preparing to receive a pitched baseball. Defoe suddenly saw him, and his eyes opened wide in reflexive surprise. Rik picked up the unintended warning and spun around just as Carl swung with all his might. Fels was pulled around with her abductor, and the club caught her first, and she slumped away, out of his grasp. Rik staggered backwards a step, obviously catching some of the blow, but recovered and held the gun up at Carl. The stunned man's face was smeared with soot and tears, but the grimace of anger and hate proclaimed with no doubt that the genetics genius and self-acclaimed savior of mankind was indeed going to shoot him.

Rik clasped the gun with both hands and looked Carl in the eyes as he pulled the trigger. Carl's mind was paralyzed by the terror, but his body reacted instinctively—his hands lifted the two-by-four as though blocking the swipe of a clawed paw. The next instant an explosion seemed to blow apart his brains, and thoughts were replaced by blackness.

He was lying on the ground on his side, and his eyes struggled to focus. He saw the sleek, dark form of Lilly before him, and Rik's shoes and legs.

He was alive. The beam must have caught the bullet, the momentum then smashing it back against his forehead.

He rolled onto his back to find Rik's puzzled face hovering above him, obviously surprised by his victim's miraculous escape. He raised the gun for a second shot, but suddenly his eyes went wide and he jumped back with a shout, reaching down to his ankle. Lilly stood watching him. She had bitten him.

Rik's face was contorted in terror, and Carl realized that Rik didn't recognize Lilly. The man who had brought Lilly to them thought that he'd just been bitten by one of the Hood, a certain death sentence. He howled in anguish and, mad with terror, fired the gun without aiming and the bullet thudded into the sawdust next to Carl.

From behind Rik, Defoe appeared. His friend shouted, "Catch!" and tossed something black and writhing, which attached itself to Rik's shirt. Cursing, Rik tore the object away before realizing that it was Moe. He watched in horror as the animal planted its venom-soaked teeth into his arm before he threw it away high and wide with a pitiful scream. Moaning, he fell to his knees. He'd dropped the gun, and held his face in his hands as he sobbed.

Carl heard a hiss. He turned his head to find glistening teeth inches from his face. Shemp had finally tracked down her provoker. Her beady eyes had found their target.

A hand swooped down, and the ferret disappeared as though carried off by a cannonball. Defoe flung the she-demon into the air, and the twisting, evil form disappeared into the smoke.

Head still swimming, Carl crawled on his hands and knees to Fels. She lay where she'd fallen, but her eyes were open, and she blinked as though waking from sleep. Her cheek was wet with blood where he'd struck her. When she saw him, she smiled. "Next time I'll duck."

He helped her to her feet, but had to hold her, since she was still too unsteady to stand on her own. Rik lay on the ground twitching and squirming. Foam bubbled from the corners of his mouth. The engineer had developed one of the most potent venoms the world had ever seen and designed a delivery system so fantastic in its apparent innocence as to be undoubtedly the product of supreme genius. His intention was that his creation would kill millions of people, testing the species and strengthening it in its adversity. Perhaps it was fitting that he would have the honor to be the first to fall for the good of all.

"Defoe!" Fels cried, breaking away and stumbling to their friend who was sitting on the ground with his legs outstretched. The old man looked up blearily and let his head flop back down on his chest. When Carl knelt down next to him, he saw tiny red puncture marks on his friend's hands and arms where Moe and Shemp had bitten him.

Carl's neighbor and patient teacher looked at him, seeming to struggle to focus his eyes. "Toby," he uttered, the word slurring slightly.

Carl nodded. He was also having trouble focusing through his tears.

"Take care of him," Defoe urged, and his head flopped down again, senseless now.

Carl kissed his friend on the forehead and laid him gently on the ground.

"Oh no!" Fels wailed. She buried her head in Carl's chest and he hugged her.

Blasts of heat burned his face, and the embers flying past were now like bats drenched in kerosene and set ablaze. The haze of smoke flying by above them from the east glowed with the fire of Satan.

They had escaped poison only to be burned in a hell-fire.

Chapter 23

"Come on!" Carl cried, pulling Fels along towards what he guessed was the direction of the cabin.

She tugged at him, resisting. "We can't just leave him here!"

"We have to! There's no time. The fire's already here!"

She looked to the east, shrinking at the looming threat. "Where can we *go*?"

That was the question. How do you escape a wall of fire, one that was consuming a whole forest as though it was kindling? All the preparations he'd made—clearing the safety zone, constructing the sprinkler system—it was too late, and all for nothing now in the face of a monster too vast to even contemplate.

Carl almost ran headlong into the side of the cabin. He ran along to the back door, and inside they found Toby huddled in a corner in the kitchen. "I heard shots," he said.

"It's okay," Carl replied. "Rik is dead, but we have to get out of here before the fire arrives."

Toby looked back and forth between Carl and Fels. "Where's Defoe?"

"Come on," Carl directed gruffly, waving the boy up. "He can take care of himself."

He didn't want to lie to the boy, but they had no time for explanations or grief. They had to go!

But where?

For one brief second, he considered staying with the cabin, but he knew it would never withstand the heat and flying embers once the fire reached the pines at the clearing's edge.

Maybe try to flee ahead of it? With this wind, it would be racing along as fast as they could run, and how long could they keep it up?

He remembered stories of firefighters during past wildfires who found themselves caught by freak changes of wind. They survived by making their way to areas already burned.

That was it.

"Come on!" he cried, running for the front door. He stopped, thinking that maybe there were things they should take along. Passports? Money? Pictures?

To hell with it. He ran out the door into the solid wall of hot smoke and waited for Fels and Toby. When they were together in front of the cabin, he told them to follow him as closely as they could. If they couldn't keep up, they should call out. He considered tying them together with rope like rappelling mountain climbers, but it was all lying in pieces somewhere among the sea of logs.

"Where are we going?" Fels called above the roar.

"North! Where the fire already came through last night! Now, let's *go!*"

He kept the wind on his right and within minutes was stumbling along among trees as unfamiliar in the blinding smoke as if he had been dropped in the middle of the vast Siberian forest. He wouldn't be able to find the cabin again now even if he'd wanted to.

The ground sloped down in a long incline, and he guessed that this was the cut that lay between them and the slope to the north, just beyond which he and Defoe had seen the fire during the night. He was relieved when they came to the dry streambed at the bottom, for this confirmed his reckoning.

"Oh shit!" Fels cried next to him, and grabbed his arm, pointing up the hill ahead. As the vicious wind gusted and swirled, tearing apart the wall of smoke in places, Carl caught glimpses of towering flames along the top of the hill. *Damn, oh damn!* The wind would be strongest along the top of the ridge, and the fire would move fastest there, reaching ahead of the main line, which couldn't be very far now to their right.

"Run!" he called to Fels and Toby, as he took off up the hill. "Run for your lives!"

Their only hope was to try to race ahead of the advancing flames along the top of the ridge. Safety lay just beyond.

They almost made it. The hill turned steeper as they climbed, and their advance slowed to barely a walk as they wheezed and coughed, struggling to grab oxygen from the hot air. As they approached the top, the trees burst into flames before their eyes, practically exploding before the onslaught of unmitigated combustion. The scorching heat burned his cheeks so that he had to turn his head away, afraid that he too would burst into flames.

They were done. There was nowhere else to hide.

It had all been one huge mistake—the whole move to the mountain wilderness. In trying to escape Fels's past, they had found only their demise. The entire idea that they could survive outside the support of civilization was pure hubris. They were children of technology and should have remained within its secure cradle.

The whole thing was foolish. It was folly.

Folly.

He remembered. He realized that they might have one last chance. It seemed ridiculous, but when death came stalking, the ridiculous became sublime.

"Follow me!" he called, running back down the slope, but now angling eastward, into the wind and the approaching main line of the fire.

"Where are you *going*?" Fels screamed. "Are you crazy?"

"Folly!" he called out, waving them forward. "MacFine's Folly!"

When he saw the dry rocks of the streambed he turned directly east. How far ahead was it? He had no idea. How far had they come from the cabin? Five minutes? Ten? The fire along the top of the ridge to their left was working down the hill, trying to cut them off. On and on they ran along the bottom of the cut. Closer and closer the fire line moved down the hill towards them. They had to find the tunnel now—it was too late to turn and run back.

What if they had already missed it? It seemed that they'd already come twice as far as they should have. He stopped, and Fels and Toby nearly bowled him over. Was it behind them? Should he turn back? If it wasn't, it would mean their death.

Tree trunks a hundred feet up the hill were exploding like a barrage of cannon fire, and he could feel the concussions. The heat on his exposed skin burned as though he was already on fire. The very air was almost too hot to draw into his lungs, and he thought he was melting from the inside out.

But suddenly, like a splash of cold water on a blistering August day, a rush of cool air washed over him. It was gone as suddenly as it had appeared, but then he felt it again. He looked around, and there, no more than fifty feet still ahead of them, nearly invisible under the tangle of vines, was the opening of the tunnel. The boiling hot air rose away above them, pulling out the cool air from the old aqueduct as a chimney pulls air from a house.

He scrambled forward, but stopped halfway when Fels cried out behind him. He turned to find Toby on fire! An ember must have ignited his black shirt, which was probably already nearly hot enough to self-combust. The boy hopped around in terror and pain, but Fels grabbed him and pulled him close, batting the flames with her hands until only smoke rose from the tattered cloth.

Directly above them, forming a ceiling of red hell, fire roared like an enraged grizzly, sweeping across the tops of the trees—a crown fire, so hot and catapulted by the hurricane force wind that the flames leapt along from treetop to treetop, leaving the ground fire to follow behind.

Doom had arrived.

He grabbed Fels and dragged her to the tunnel. The dry leaves of the vines burst into tiny little flames as he tore them aside and pushed her through. Toby was right behind her, and he shoved the boy in. Burning limbs fell like lava rain about him as he dove inside, landing on Toby who had tripped in the darkness.

It was as though he had stepped through a magic curtain. The chimney effect drew a steady flow of cool, wonderful air from the other side of the ridge. Just five feet away, he could hear the fire-beast's roar, and feel the radiant heat of burning chaparral almost within arm's reach, but the steady wash of blessed clean air was like a sparkling mountain stream flowing past.

"Honey!" Fels called from the darkness farther in. "Are you okay?"

Her voice rang in the stone chamber, as though produced by a spring instead of a human vocal cord.

"I'm fine!" he called back.

In fact, he'd never felt better. It was great to be alive. There was nothing to compare.

Toby had already moved on and Carl followed. It wasn't easy going. There wasn't enough room to stand upright, and the floor of the tunnel was littered with debris washed in over the last century. His eyes adjusted to the darkness and the firestorm receding behind him lit the inside with a pulsing glow.

He thought he heard something, and he paused. It seemed as though someone called to him—perhaps Defoe, or Tekumewa. He turned and the tunnel opening was a bright orange circle. He saw movement, a low black silhouette nearly merging with the floor debris. The motion was smooth and slinky. Next to it was another—two smallish, lithe animals.

The Hood.

Shemp and Moe must have followed them, or perhaps had figured out for themselves the only escape.

An anger boiled in Carl such as he'd never before felt. He'd had enough. The monsters had had their way for too long. They'd killed his two friends and had tried to do the same to both him and his wife. As Rik had so confidently explained, given half a chance they would overrun the Earth and do their best to exterminate humans.

Enough was enough.

He found a stick and charged for the opening, screaming like the wild man he had become. He came upon Moe first, and the animal crouched with venomous teeth bared. He swung the stick, but the ferret ducked, so he kicked with all his might and the animal flew towards the entrance like a football, caroming off the tunnel wall.

Shemp hissed at him and the she-devil's eyes seemed to reflect the orange fire, as though her very brain was a portal into Satan's lair. He picked up a rock and threw it, but she dodged and it missed, bouncing away and setting the tunnel ringing.

She charged. He jumped to the side, but her reflexes were quick, and she followed his feet. She sprang for his ankle, and he jerked his foot up so that the needle-sharp teeth found his shoe instead. He kicked, and she somersaulted. Twisting like a cat, she landed on her feet.

Moe had returned, and now both ferrets faced him, waiting for some cue to spring forward together.

For two hundred thousand years, Carl's ancestors had hunted prey using cunning, the specie's supreme weapon. For millions upon millions of years before that, however, instinct had ruled, and it still lay ready to leap into battle. Cunning now gave way to a deluge of rage. Bellowing like a wounded bull, Carl sprang at the little monsters, arms flailing, and feet kicking madly. He swung the stick wildly, mostly feeling the hard recoil of stone, but twice the soft give of skin and bone. The toes of his running shoes found fur and flesh as well, and this delivered most of the damage. He had a strong urge to stomp on the beasts, but a deeper reflex warned that, once pinned, they would bite his ankle. And so he continued to thrash and kick and scream and flail, until he suddenly realized that there was no longer anything to flail at. The Hood had retreated.

He walked towards the tunnel entrance, beyond which the forest consumed itself completely now in blinding fury. But the genetically perfected killers had disappeared, apparently believing their chances better among the flames of the forest rather than the fire of his wrath.

But then he gasped. What if they hadn't gone for the entrance? In his mindless rage, what if they'd gotten by him and gone *inward*?

Crying with frustration and fearing the worst, he ran as fast as he could into the darkness, stumbling and falling over and over in his haste. When he finally came to Fels and Toby lying on the ground, he nearly ran over them.

"Fels!" he cried, squatting down next to her. "Are you okay?"

After a moment, she laid a hand on his cheek. "Honey," she said concerned, "I think the question is, are *you* okay? What in God's name were you doing down there? It sounded like you'd gone insane."

He flopped down between her and Toby and took a long, deep breath. "I think I did," he replied, and lay back on the hard, wonderfully cool rocks and sand. "It was the only thing the little bastards weren't designed to handle."

Far down the tunnel, the world burned as though hell itself had manifested on Earth. He closed his eyes and felt the blissful fresh air on his face and reached out to clasp the hand of the woman he loved.

Chapter 24

"It's still hot!" Fels announced, holding her hand out experimentally through the charred remnants of vine.

"It was a big fire," Carl replied. "I expect that it has advanced global warming along by a few years."

She knew enough not to respond to his nonsense.

Toby leaned out to have a look, and Carl burst out laughing. In the daylight, the boy looked like a Hindenburg survivor. His T-shirt was shredded, and his face and hands were nearly black with soot. Carl looked at Fels and then down at his own hands. They all looked like the last survivors off the ill-fated air ship.

Carl stepped out from their haven. They were in no hurry to discover what the fire had left behind. It had been two hours since the maelstrom had moved on . . . and it still felt like he was standing in a huge oven. Tree trunks, arrayed like an army of soldiers suddenly snapped to attention, smoldered and smoked, their bowels glowing with every gust of wind, as though each were actually a coal stove whose door had been torn off.

Even the ground beneath his feet was hot so that he kept shifting around, unconsciously trying to find a cooler spot. Other than the smoldering tree trunks, no sign remained that the mountain had once hosted a living forest. Branches, fallen logs, ground cover, pine needles, even the loam dirt were all gone, turned to ash and blown away under the inferno. Only blackened rocks remained, guarded by charred remnants of once-glorious pines. He glanced around, looking for slender black cinders shaped vaguely like ferrets, but they too had been reduced to ash in the vast all-consuming crematorium.

Most odd was the blue sky and clear air. Once the fire was past, the wind carried the belching exhaust with it, inundating those still in the path to the west. Only telltale whiffs of smoldering trunks caught his attention, and this was almost pleasant.

Fels and Toby stepped tentatively out and gazed around in amazement. It really did look as though, like Rip Van Winkle, they had slept for twenty years while the world had transformed completely around them. They had talked about trying to transit the tunnel and come out the north side, but Carl was afraid they'd get lost finding their way from there. He had no great desire to return to whatever was left of their beloved cabin, but it was the only way he knew to get them back to civilization. Even here, barely five minutes from their home, he felt lost in the alien landscape. Only by reconstructing the topology of the former forest in his mind could be begin to navigate.

From the barely recognizable streambed, he led them up the south slope, being careful to watch for smoldering logs. He had been silently steeling himself for the task of dealing with the bodies of Defoe, Rik, and Tekumewa. His secret prayer was that, like the Hood, they would have disappeared as windblown ash. As they neared the crest, he held his breath, preparing for the pitiful and tragic sight of a crumbled and smoking cabin foundation, and so stopped dead in his tracks when a complete and beautifully intact home hove into view.

For a moment he thought that he had gotten them turned around and had come upon someone else's cabin, but he recognized the bench against the west wall under the laundry room window, and the solar panels on the roof, and most telling, the sea of logs surrounding it all. Off to the side, however, a blackened hulk squatted on bare metal wheels, barely recognizable as Fels's truck. Rik's Hummer, despite pretending to be war-worthy, had fared no better.

"Oh . . . my . . . God!" Fels whispered, and shot off. "It's a miracle!" she shouted.

Carl hesitated only a second before taking off after her.

Suddenly, though, Fels stopped short. A second later Carl saw it as well. A coyote sat next to the cabin, watching them. It got up, took a few steps, and then with one push from its front paws, lifted up on its hind legs.

"Tekumewa?" Carl offered skeptically, his mind reeling at the implication.

From around the corner, a man stepped out and stood looking at them, fists on hips. He lifted his hand and waved.

It . . . it looked like . . .

"Defoe!" Fels shouted, taking off again at a youthful sprint.

Carl followed and when he reached them, his friend had both arms wrapped around Fels and opened one to take in him as well. Toby appeared a moment later and stood shyly off to the side until Carl pulled him in to join the group hug. Tekumewa sat watching them calmly.

"How in God's name are you alive, you old goat?" Carl asked. "You should have been dead two times over!"

"In His name we are all alive, and this time it was both providence and good luck. My vomit tasting experiment saved my life—Tekumewa's as well."

It took Carl only a moment to understand. "Immunity!"

"I thought I was indeed dying after the final great Battle of the Ferrets. I was paralyzed, but could still hear and feel—that was a tender touch, by the way, kissing me on the forehead like that. I recovered quickly, but you were already gone. I knew I was in no shape to outrun a forest fire, and it was far too late anyway, so I hunkered in and made good use of your excellent emergency preparations."

Carl was still absorbing the idea of acquired immunity to the ferrets' poison. Rik had mentioned something about the second strain of bacteria having ferret-specific immunity. The bastard obviously knew that there was a flaw in his monsters and that once the word got out the government could easily administer raw poison as a vaccine. The second strain was intended to address that.

Defoe's words finally sunk in. "Preparations?" he asked distractedly.

"Your sprinkler system," Defoe explained. "It worked perfectly."

"Huh? You saved the cabin?"

Defoe chuckled. "It was hardly a heroic effort, and I didn't have very many alternatives. I simply flipped the switch that turned on the pump."

Carl stared at him, and then looked up at the cabin. It was bone-dry. But of course it would be. Although there was enough water to keep the roof and walls from burning, there had certainly also been enough heat to evaporate every last drop.

"It got a good bit toasty inside, though, and for a while I wasn't sure I would survive, even if the cabin did. If it weren't for the buffer provided by your cleared zone, I would be dead for sure."

Carl glanced around the log sea. The grass and twigs were gone, incinerated in the heat, but the logs themselves were intact and relatively unburnt. Without limbs and needles to provide kindling, and lying against the ground where the oxygen couldn't surround them, they would be difficult fuel to ignite and sustain combustion.

The fire also failed to reduce to ash the one object that Carl would have been glad to sacrifice: Defoe had thoughtfully spread bath towels to cover what remained of Rik's body.

Carl wondered why the genius hadn't immunized himself with the first batch of ferret poison. Had it been arrogance, or lack of confidence in the process? Defoe had, after all, been quite ill from his own inadvertent inoculation. Maybe it was simply that whatever genius a man might wield in one field, the range of human experience was just too broad to expect exemplary intelligence in all areas.

In the end perhaps Rik, the self-proclaimed genius of genetic science, just screwed up. He forgot that people need people, and no man is an island.

"I found where the ferrets were getting in," Defoe said, breaking up the group hug and walking inside.

Carl's mind was still reeling and he felt almost dizzy. The air in the cabin seemed stale and smoky. It would take a while to clear it all out. They had insulated their home well to conserve heat, but the smoke and ash had found its way in as they had opened the doors coming and going under the command of Rik's gun.

Defoe took them to the desk where the computer had been and pointed at the floor underneath it. A spray of black soot shaped like a fan extended across the polished hardwood from the wall. At the apex, where the fan's handle would be, the satellite dish cables came through the wall. Perhaps to ease his task, the installation person had drilled an oversized hole in the wall, and then covered it with a small piece of paneling, which the ferrets had just pushed out of the way. Boxes had hidden the entry point, and he'd never noticed the shoddy job.

After a lunch of dried apricots, cookies, and tea, they decided that they should probably see what was up with the rest of the world and also get word to all those who might be worried about them. Carl packed water and apples in his knapsack, and they took off up the dirt road that was now somewhat superfluous with all trace of ground cover burned away. It did serve for navigation, though, which was necessary, as the denuded landscape was as foreign as any random moonscape.

Tekumewa followed along, sniffing everything he had time to get to as they strolled along through the wasteland, sobered by the vast scale of destruction. At least the wind had finally died, leaving their eyes free from blown ash.

They came to the turnoff for Defoe's cabin, and after a moment's hesitation, their friend nodded and they followed his road over a ridge, down a cut, and across a small cement bridge spanning a seasonal stream. When they topped the second ridge, their friend stopped and stared. Ahead, like a crushed black fedora, the charred remains of his cabin hunkered on a small hillock.

Defoe stood silently for a few minutes, and then, without another word, turned and walked back the way they'd come. Carl glanced at Fels and Toby, and they set off after him.

An hour later they came to the edge of the burnt zone and it was like waking from the dead. The four of them stood gazing in awe at green foliage, dancing butterflies, and singing birds. After that their spirits rose and Defoe even joked about being happy to be freed from the burden of earthly possessions, but Carl knew that his friend was hurting. The old professor's pension was barely enough to buy food and pay taxes.

When they finally came to the market, they found that it was closed and the whole place deserted, as though Rod Serling would appear from offstage to explain that there are many worlds and this hapless group of humans had inadvertently stepped into one where the ferrets had prevailed.

"Evacuated," Defoe declared, trying the door to the market

anyway, but finding it locked.

Just then they heard the whine of an engine, and soon a black SUV with the San Diego Sheriff's Department emblem on the door pulled up. A uniformed man stepped out and looked at them in surprise. "Where in God's name did you come from?" he asked incredulously.

Carl glanced at the rest of his group. They were absolutely grimy with soot, torn clothes, and blood. "A forest fire."

It was a long story, and there was no way to summarize it in a couple of sentences.

The Sheriff's deputy noticed Tekumewa and raised one eyebrow. "Where did he come from?"

"He's been hanging around for a while," Carl replied. "He's sort of adopted us—very friendly for a coyote."

"Coyote, eh?"

The deputy got down on one knee and whistled, holding his hand out to Tekumewa who immediately trotted over. The man rubbed the animal's head affectionately and then gazed into its eyes. He smiled and got to his feet. "This fellow isn't exactly a coyote."

Carl glanced at Defoe and Fels. "What do you mean?"

"He's a coydog. Look at his eyes, they're blue."

Carl had noticed Tekumewa's bright blue eyes, but hadn't thought about it before. "A coydog?"

Where had he heard that before? He remembered: he hadn't heard it—he'd read it. He ran to the bulletin board, scanned down and found it—the ad for the lost pet.

He turned to the deputy. "You're saying this coyote's name is Coydog?"

The man laughed. "A coydog is half coyote and half dog. Sometimes a male coyote will mate with a female dog. Coyotes' eyes are always brown. This fellow's mother had blue eyes."

Carl looked at Tekumewa, and as though seeing him in full light for the first time, saw that indeed his snout was wider and his tail somewhat shorter and not as bushy as the wild coyotes he'd seen around the cabin.

"I think I know the owner," the deputy went on.

"Owner?" Carl said.

"A young couple rented a cabin for a month in the summer and their coydog pet took off the first day they were here. They got pretty mad when I explained that I'd keep my eye out, but that the Sheriff's Department couldn't send a search party through the mountains after it."

Carl looked at Defoe, and his friend was grinning. It would explain why Tekumewa was happy to make friends with them. And also . . .

"Uh, did these people happen to teach their pet to stand up on its hind legs—as a trick, maybe?"

The deputy shrugged. "Don't know, and too late to find out. The owners are long gone. You might try calling that number," he said, indicating the bulletin board ad. "You folks need a ride to an evacuation center?"

They looked at each other. "Um, actually," Carl explained, "we just came out to let our families know that we're okay. We could use a ride back to our cabin, though."

"Where's that?"

Carl pointed.

"That's where the fire came through."

"Right. It came right past our cabin."

The deputy stared at him. "You're kidding," he finally said.

"No."

The man stared at him some more, as though trying to decide if he was lying. He finally shook his head. "I'm sorry, but this whole area is still under a mandatory evacuation order."

Carl sighed. They'd have to deal with this sooner or later. "There's a dead man back at our cabin."

The deputy's eyes went hard. "Get in," he said, opening all the doors of the SUV.

ж ж ж

Authorities get excited over dead bodies. Finding one is sort of the pinnacle of their careers, Carl decided. The Sheriff arrived an hour later and took their statements. Carl was first, and when he started to explain how Rik had genetically modified the ferrets to have poisonous vomit in order to destroy the human race, the Sheriff turned off the recorder and warned him of the consequences of impeding the investigation. They started again, and again the recorder was turned off. The Sheriff gave up and took Defoe into the bedroom, only to reemerge minutes later looking flustered.

He pointed his pen at Fels, "You going to tell me about poisonous ferrets?"

She nodded, and he pointed the pen at Toby who did the same.

The Sheriff told the deputy to keep them all there until he could get the coroner out, and then took off. The wildfire was seventy percent contained, but he still had three other fire-related deaths to check out.

The coroner declared that, other improbable possibilities notwithstanding, the body lying among the logs was indeed dead, and had it hauled away after many dozens of pictures were taken. At Carl's urging, the official also took along the mauled corpse of Curly.

The report came back three days later. Officially, the dead man was indeed Rik, and he had died of heart failure due to an undetermined nerve poison. The most likely cause was a rattlesnake, as evidenced by puncture marks on the man's arms. The snake's venom had probably decomposed under the intense heat of the subsequent fire, rendering it unidentifiable.

As far as the dead ferret, its cause of death was massive internal trauma, probably caused by a natural predator. As an incidental note, the coroner had added that the ferret had apparently eaten some of the same snake poison. The good doctor's duties did not, probably most gratefully for him, include proposing an explanation for how *that* would have happened.

Thus, no murder charges were filed, but the Sheriff warned the group that he'd be keeping his eye on them, as though they were wacko mountain survivalists. When Carl replied that they would have tea ready any time he wanted to visit, the official pointed his finger threateningly at him and drove away.

Ж Ж Ж

Defoe and Toby moved in, or rather, since every last bit of their possessions had burnt, simply remained with Carl and Fels. Defoe slept on the sofa and Toby was content to take the floor. Tekumewa settled in as the fifth member of the group, sleeping on an old blanket in the corner and keeping watch in case any other ferrets got ideas about bothering his new masters.

They called the number from the bulletin board, but to their relief, the exchange had been disconnected, and satisfied that they'd done their duty, threw the card away and thought nothing more about the previous owners.

Fels, to her surprise, continued to work at GeneTrend. The company CEO delivered a solemn and inspiring eulogy to the gathered employees, and then reminded them that they still had projects and deadlines, so snap to it. Four small groups, previously under the direct supervision of the deceased president and none having any clue what the others were up to, were dissolved and the personnel assigned to understaffed positions on projects that might actually generate revenue.

With trepidation, but also irresistible curiosity, Fels sent out feelers, casually asking people who had worked with Rik what they had been up to. To her surprise she found that they didn't really know. At least not the big picture. Working directly for Rik, it was all they could do to keep up with him day to day. He truly had been a genius when it came to genetics. They had a vague idea that Rik was working on some cancer therapy research involving organic toxins, but due to the revolutionary nature it was total hush-hush. Apparently only Weinermach had gleaned something closer to the truth, and he had died because of it.

A week after the great Cuyamaca fire had become another touchstone of local history, Defoe asked Carl if he'd like to take a walk. Carl followed his new roommate up and down ridges of mute, black trunks until they came to one conical hill whose green cap stood out from the surrounding barrenness as a tropical island might appear over the horizon to a shipwrecked sailor. Long, graceful tufts of grass waved peacefully in the afternoon breeze, untouched by the firestorm perhaps because of a lack of ready fuel, or maybe a result of some fluke counter-mixing of winds in the confused maelstrom. Near the top stood an unnatural pile of stones, and Carl suddenly realized where his friend had brought him in this land that was now so unfamiliar.

Defoe knelt at the memorial pile and dug out some dirt before holding up a handful for Carl to smell.

He shrugged—it smelled like dirt.

"Don't you smell the cologne?"

He sniffed again, and he could, or at least he imagined he could. It had been months, after all, since Toby had deposited the Brut as part of their sacrificial ceremony.

"I'd bet money that Tekumewa's previous owner was a Brut man," Defoe declared, continuing to dig under the stone pile.

Carl thought about that a moment, and then he smiled. "That's why Tekumewa was digging around in here!"

Defoe sat back, pulling a small wooden box out from the hole. He stood up, and without another word started back towards home.

"What is it?" Carl called, running after his homeless companion.

Defoe stopped and undid a latch after cleaning away some of the dirt. He lifted the lid and held it out to Carl. Inside was jewelry and a wad of fancy bank notes—certificates of deposit.

The old philosopher closed the box and continued on.

"You made your own sacrifice to the old Indian warrior!" Carl exclaimed. It was something he could imagine Defoe doing.

"I'd rather not talk about it," his friend said.

"You did! You made a sacrifice! That's pretty nuts, you know. That looks like a lot of moolah."

Defoe stopped and turned to him. "It wasn't as though the spirit of Tekumewa was going to spend it."

His homeless, but no longer destitute, friend continued down the hill, and after a last look at the serene, seemingly timeless beauty of the hilltop, Carl ran to catch up.

Ж Ж Ж

Under the soaking rains of winter the blackened landscape seemed to explode in low-lying growth so that by April the burnt hills of the Cuyamaca Mountains glowed under the bright sun with a florescent green that hurt Carl's eyes if he gazed too long. The endless standing army of burnt tree trunks stood at eternal attention while a sea of returning life flowed about them, soothing their scorched toes and ankles. It was both alien and exhilarating to live among such a rush of sprouting growth. Sometimes Carl felt that he could just go and lay down among it, and be carried away like a raft floating along on the ocean's swell.

One spring morning, as Toby rushed around getting ready so that Fels could drop him at the school bus stop on her way to GeneTrend, she reminded Carl that it was really way past time to get back to clearing the logs out of the lot. After she and Toby left, he and Defoe finished their third cup of tea while listening to NPR on the new radio they'd bought. Carl stood up and stretched. "Well, I guess we'd better get to it."

The retired, but never inactive, professor eyed him a moment. "Have you ever tried to find out if MacFine's Folly still provides passage to the other side of the ridge?"

Carl looked out the window at the platoon of logs that had been patiently waiting their turn for over a year now. "Do you think we could be back in time to get a good start?" he asked.

"Most certainly. I have the highest confidence."

They grabbed their hats off the rack, which was the cue for Tekumewa to dash to the door lest he be left behind.

"Have you ever considered," Defoe asked as he stepped across the doorstep, "that a voter qualification test might vastly improve any democracy?"

Carl's answer was cut off as he closed the door.

The cozy cabin was filled again with silence as it waited, a schooner bobbing among a sea of green, for its occupants to return.

About the Author

Blaine C. Readler is an electronics engineer, inventor, and writer (although, that's rather redundant considering the context). He lives in San Diego, from where he ventures forth in spring and autumn when the rest of the country is habitable. He comes to you courtesy of his wife Monica, who keeps him alive and healthy against the adversities of his cantankerous protests.

He encourages you to visit him at his web of wonders:
http://www.readler.com/

If you enjoyed this book, or even if you didn't, please beg everyone you know, and even those you don't, to buy it.